PRAISE FOR
JUDGEMENT NIGHT

"Great!"
—*DRAGON® Magazine*

"Very funny."
—*Locus*

"High adventure, highly reccommended."
—*Science Fiction Chronicle*

"A wonderful read. Extremely humorous."
—*Moscow Times*

"This is the X-Files meets the Marx Brothers!"
Raymond's Reviews

WILDSIDE PRESS NOVELS BY NICK POLLOTTA

Judgment Night

FORTHCOMING

Bureau 13: Doomsday Exam
Bureau 13: Full Moonster
Bureau 13: Damned Nation

OTHER NOVELS BY NICK POLLOTTA

Satellite Night News (as Jack Hopkins)
Satellite Night Special (as Jack Hopkins)
Satellite Night Fever (as Jack Hopkins)
Illegal Aliens (with Phil Foglio)
American Knights
Shadowboxer
The 24 Hour War
Free-for-All*
The Guardians of Cascade*

Forthcoming:

The Bureau 13 Omnibus, Drofa Press, Moskow
Hunter/Killer
Red Dagger

JUDGEMENT NIGHT

Nick Pollotta

Wildside Press
New Jersey • California • Ohio • New York

BUREAU 13: JUDGMENT NIGHT

A publication of
Wildside Press
P.O. Box 45
Gillette, NJ 07933-0045
www.wildsidepress.com

Copyright © 1990, 2001 by Nick Pollotta.
Introduction copyright © 2001 by Nick Pollotta
All rights reserved.
Printing history: 1990, Ace Books, New York.
1995 Armada Press, Moscow
2001 Wildside Press, New Jersey

Bureau 13 is based upon the RPG "Stalking the Night Fantastic"
copyright © TriTac Games 1982.
www.TriTacGames.com

Join the "Bureau 13" fan club!
www.Bureau-13.com

Cover illustration by Larry Dixon.

This edition has been revised and expanded from the first edition.

No portion of this book may be reproduced by any means, electronic or otherwise, without first obtaining the written consent of the author. For more information, contact Wildside Press or email info@wildsidepress.com.

Wildside Press edition: January 2001.

watching him, my mind already spinning along the lines of a novel about a supernatural investigation team. Yeah, I'd call it "The Wolf Pack." Good title.

Once I got back home, I started amassing notes and soon roughed out a plot and the main characters. The hero would be Richard "Wolf" Anderson, a self-made wizard grimly determined to battle with the forces of evil and thus learn more magic.

His muscle would be, hmm, Mindy Jennings, a petite, but deadly, martial artist who was bored with contests and tournaments. She wanted to actually test her skills, and fighting demons sounded just fine to her. The team would need financial aid for equipment, silver bullets and such, so their backer for this endeavor was, George d'Renault, a bored millionaire who flipped a coin and decided to back a paranormal research team or buy the Dallas Cowboys. George became their gunbunny, a rank amateur now carrying a M60 machine gun.

But months slipped by and I just could not seem to get the background for the characters to gel. Something was missing, something basic, yet very important. But what could it be?

To rest my beleaguered brain, I went over a friend's house for some war gaming and was introduced to the RPG (role-playing game for those who don't know) *Bureau 13* from TriTac Games. (although at the time it was called "Stalking the Night Fantastic.") As I read the box, all of the little pieces fell into place. Hey, the Wolf Pack could be team of FBI agents! Nobody has ever done that before! (remember, this was almost a decade before *The X-Files*) And this covert branch of the FBI fought supernatural criminals, but not all supernaturals. Case in point, it is not illegal to be a vampire. So if a vampire owned a herd of cows and only drank their blood, then no laws had

JUDGMENT NIGHT

been broken and the Bureau will have to defend the vampire against a mob of angry villagers.

Hot damn, now you're talking! This is exactly what the Wolf Pack was supposed to be. Now I knew that with enough effort I could get the novel there, but I liked the tone of this. It resonated in my head and I made a decision.

Swiftly, I started creating an FBI investigation team: the dashingly handsome Ed Alvarez, a private detective from Chicago. Ed looks a lot like me, and talks like me, and eats at my favorite restaurants, but then this was only my second novel.

Then came, Jessica Taylor, the sexy telepath that Ed was secretly in love with. She knew (of course), but he didn't know that she knew. Now I could have fun with that. Ah, love!

Okay, Mindy was perfect so she would stay as Mindy, but I'd give her a special weapon. Nice. Richard stayed the same, except I combed his wild mane of hair and removed his nickname since it was too distracting. As the team was FBI, they had ample monetary support from the government and thus no need of a financial backer, so George gained fifty pounds and became a war veteran from Viet Nam, an overweight warrior, still hard as steel in spite of the passing years. Pausing for a moment, I gazed thoughtfully at my alligator shoes, and out of the blue came Amigo, their pet lizard with a very big secret. As a military historian, it was obvious that having only one wizard was poor tactics, insufficient firepower, so I added Raul Horta (as strange a character as I have ever penned), and then rounded them off with a big, beefy, redheaded Irish Catholic priest, Father Michael Xavier Donaher. After all, somebody had to do the exorcisms. (Remember the movie that started this?)

While my friends gamed, I furiously wrote in the corner, cackling in delight, knowing I had a winner here. That is, if I could get the book rights.

A month later I finally tracked down Richard Tucholka, the creator of Bureau 13, introduced myself to him in the middle of the dealer's room at a SF convention and passed over the first chapter of a novel.[1]

Knowing of me from the hit SF/humor novel *Illegal Aliens*, Richard decided to read a page or two of the sample chapter right there. When he lowered the last page with tears of laughter in his eyes, he extended his hand and said let's a make a deal. Shazam, I had the complete rights to writing Bureau 13 novels.

Over time, I gave him back the short story rights as other great writers wanted in on the fun; Lawrence Watt-Evans, Mercedes Lackeys, and such. But the novels were mine alone and I ran with the ball.

After the convention I got hard at work and two months later, I sent the first book, originally titled simply *Bureau 13* (now called *Bureau 13 #1: Judgement Night*) to Ace Books in New York. They called back in record time and offered a three book contract. Three? Sure! Then they delivered Dorian Vallejo, the son of the genius Boris Vallejo, as my cover artist. Superb stuff. If the paintings are ever on display at a SF convention, go see the original oils. The printed covers can not do them justice.

The novels hit the bookstores, and suddenly fan clubs started appearing across the country, Baltimore, Pittsburgh, New Orleans, Seattle, then there was a Bureau 13 convention! My books were a hit with the cast of hard-boiled, wise cracking heroes who faced down any danger and fought hard to deliver justice, often at the end of a gun or magic wand. Suddenly, I was the Mickey Spillane of the supernatural.

---

1   Included in this volume—'Initiation.'

JUDGMENT NIGHT

Then a Moscow publisher contacted me about translating the trilogy into Russian. Smiling broadly, I signed, and the books went ballistic in the Ukraine. Selling over half a million copies, just in time for Soviet Communism to fall apart and democracy to return to Russia. I take some small measure of pride in thinking that maybe my books helped bring down the Red Menace. Okay, they didn't, but it makes a hell of a story for me to tell over beer and pizza.

Now this cult-classic trilogy has been rewritten, the real-world technology updated, and the books expanded, with a brand new fourth novel, *Damned Nation* written just for this re-release for Wildside Press in New Jersey, and Drofa Press in Moscow. Plus, additional deals are in progress with Germany, Australia, France, Italy, and Great Britain.

An amusing anecdote for my English speaking readers, the Russian translators changed a few things, mostly that Mindy became a six foot tall Norwegian blonde, and a certain group of villains became ex-KGB agents now using necromancy to try and topple the god-fearing democracy of Russia and return the iron-heel of communism. Hmm, maybe I did help a little. Who knows?

Now, since both my American and Russian publishers have asked me to say something about myself, rather than just chatting about the books here goes. Gang, if you read my books, then you know me. My heart, blood, and guts are in every one. Let me explain. A long time ago I heard a recorded interview with Frank Sinatra on the radio from 1955, and the disc jockey was trying to bust Frank's chops with snide remarks, but Sinatra was cool and answered every question with panache and humor. Finally, the DJ asked if Sinatra had a philosophy that he followed and Frank said yes. He did everything, every song, every performance, every movie, as if he was going to drop dead instantly after it was finished, and it would be by this one last act that he would be remembered forever—or forgotten completely. I was floored by that and turned off the rest of the interview to memorize his words. Now I have the phrase framed on the wall of my studio.

"By this one book be remembered, or forgotten, forever." That's it, folks, win, lose or draw, every book is all that I got. I hold nothing back.

For those who want more, I'm half Sicilian and half Scottish, which means I occasional put on a dress and kill people with a pepperoni haggis. I used to be a stand-up comic in Manhattan, a martial arts instructor, an armed high security courier, owned a used bookstore, did voice-overs for TV commercials, and was a video store clerk. Now I write novels and am truly happy, living with my beautiful wife in a small town north of Chicago where there is a park named after Ray Bradbury, who was born and raised here, and I am only blocks away from a barbecue pit with the best smoked ribs in the known universe. Case closed, I am home.

So now you know the backstory. For my returning readers, old friends await inside, facing new dangers, and battling even more impossible odds. But guts are always more important than guns, and those this FBI team have got in abundance.

For all of the new readers, come on in and grab a weapon. Plenty of M16 machine guns to the left, or magical wands to the right. The tide of evil is rising, and the world is facing a supernatural war beyond imagination. But there's always room for one more hero on the battlefield.

Welcome.

—Nick Pollotta
Chicago, Illinois, 2000

INITIATION

I finally found the murderer, and he was a lulu.

It had taken me months of freelance work to track down the guy who killed my partner, and if the truth be known I broke more than a few laws doing it. But I didn't give a damn. As far as I could tell, the sick bastard had slaughtered over forty people across a dozen states. Each done the same way he killed Bill Smithers, my partner in Chicago, slit their throats and drained the blood like he was a freaking vampire or something.

The castle was up on the old New York Palisades, deserted for years. I hid my car in the bushes, so nobody could spot the out of state plates. The lock on the front door was good, an expensive French model. Took me almost ten minutes to get through. Inside, the place was surprisingly clean, some of the rooms even carpeted. Not the usual thing for an undead. But playing on the Count Dracula routine, I checked in the basement.

The place was huge, large enough to land a plane, with a high vaulted ceiling and granite-block walls. More resembled an underground warehouse than a cellar. In a corner was a big-screen TV and a brace of DVD players. Overflowing bookcases lined the walls and in the middle of the place, on a marble pedestal, was a large stainless steel coffin, with US Army Claymore mines wired to the outside. Yikes. Ever so carefully, I snipped away the wires on the anti-personnel charges. All those years watching the Discovery channel finally paid off.

The lid was locked from the inside, so I filled the keyhole

with stiff wire from my keywire gun. A lazy locksmith's best friend. A simple twist and the coffin opened on silent hinges. So much for stereotypes. Magnum in hand, I was surprised to find it empty. As I bitterly cursed, a chuckle sounded from behind, I turned and there the bastard stood.

He resembled a computer hacker with that deathly pale skin and weird eyes. But he was sporting a natty Armani suit that was worth more than I had ever made, woven Italian shoes with tiny tassels, and a gold Rolex watch. What, no caviar-scented cell phone?

A cop would have arrested him and sent the kook to a lunatic asylum. But I wasn't planning on reading this guy his rights. As far as I was concerned, he didn't have any. Not an animal like him.

The murderer came at me with arms extended, as if greeting a long lost relative. His mouth full of those phony vampire teeth you can buy at any novelty store. Pitiful. I didn't have to draw my .357 Magnum; it was already in my hand. Without a qualm, I gunned the freak down, the thundering retorts of the Smith and Wesson echoing around the cellar. But he kept coming, as if my copper-jacketed hollow points had no effect. Must have been wearing a bulletproof vest.

We went hand-to-hand and he had me in a second. Loonies are always strong. Adrenaline, or something. Maybe he was on PCP. The Count dragged me kicking across the basement and chained me to the stone wall. The chains felt oiled and were spotted with red flakes. I had a bad feeling Nut Boy had used these often.

Chuckling, he went away and soon came back with two women. A blonde and a redhead. Real hot numbers wearing skimpy denim shorts, sleeveless T-shirts and also sporting those phony teeth. That was when I went cold. I sure hoped

JUDGMENT NIGHT

whatever they had wasn't a contagious disease. Death was infinitely preferable to insanity.

They gathered around and made the expected remarks on how tasty and juicy I looked. I invented a few curses, which they took in stride. Then the Count waved the women on and they came at me with hands raised, their fingernails glistened like steel. Probably razorblades glued underneath.

This was no time for finesse, so as they got close, I kicked the blonde in the left breast. She didn't bat an eye. That was impossible. There was no way a bra, much less a Kevlar vest, could be hidden under her T-shirt. Kicking a woman in the breast is like kicking a guy in the balls. Blondie should have dropped big time.

Smiling, Red grabbed my hair and twisted my head about as if I was a child. Then she opened her mouth wide, exposing every inch on those long white fangs. They actually looked like her own teeth. That's when I realized the freaks were really going to drink my blood. I had faced death lots of times in 'Nam as kid. In the back alleys of Chicago, too. But there was a big difference between a bullet in the chest, or a knife in the stomach, and having a trio of drugged out wackos suck me dry like a free cherry soda. That was no way for a nice PI to die.

My brain was whirling with escape plans, none of them worth a damn, when the door in the corner slammed open and in strode a SWAT team.

Or at least that's what they resembled. There were three of them, two men and a woman. All were dressed in camouflage outfits, with backpacks, satchels and dozens of weapons hanging off them. One guy was tall and skinny, like he hadn't had a good meal since his last birthday. The woman was kinda short, slim and muscular-looking in a nice way. The other guy was downright fat. But he had a genuine shit-eating grin on his face as he worked the bolt on the huge M60 machine gun in his hands. I could tell this was a man who enjoyed his work.

My three freaks spun about at the sound, and hissed louder than steam radiators. Geez, they were really putting in overtime on the old vampire act.

As two of the SWAT guys separated, Skinny pulled out of his shoulder bag a melon-sized crystal ball and smashed it on the floor. Instantly every door and window was covered with stonework sealing us in. In spite of the situation, I dropped my jaw. Impossible. Yet I had just seen it happen. Maybe the ball was actually some sort of electrical device, an EMP bomb maybe, whose command signal pulse triggered the control mechanism for hidden sliding panels. It sounded lame, but what the hell could have happened? Magic? At this point, I began to wonder if they were really a rescue squad, or merely more loonies in on the fun.

The vampires advanced slavering and growling. Red came at Fat Boy, and he let her have a full burst at point blank range. The heavy-duty combat rounds blew holes in her the size of Montana. She burst into flames and dropped to the ground, still screaming and trying to get at the lard bucket.

One tough bitch. *Incendiary bullets?* I wondered.

That was when I realized that the sphere must have contained BZ, military hallucinogenic gas, because everything started to get real funky.

The other two vampire types flapped their arms and turned into freaking bats! No smoke, no special effects. And not dinky little zoo bats, but great big mothers who soared into the air and began circling around the room as if this was Wild Kingdom and I was Marlin Perkins.

Suddenly, Chubby moved in front of me, his machine gun spraying hot lead protection. At least that was no halluci-

JUDGMENT NIGHT

nation. I felt the stinging blast of the blow-back gas, and a red-hot shell casing bounced off my hand burning the flesh.

The short lady jumped up on the coffin and, reaching behind her, pulled out a long curved sword so highly polished that the blade seemed to ripple with rainbows. Flipping it over, she knelt and buried the sword to the hilt into the rectangular box.

Big deal, I thought. But Batguy didn't care for the idea a bit. Rearing backwards, he opened his jaw and vomited a lance of fire at the swordswoman. She ducked, but it wasn't necessary. A river of ice launched from the cupped hands of Skinny and the two streams hit in midair with a deafening thunderclap worse than an overload at a rock concert.

As I shook the ringing from my ears, I suddenly noticed that Batgirl was gone. I couldn't see her anyplace, but a weird patch of fog was drifting towards Mandrake over by where the door used to be. Impulsively I shouted a warning.

However, the coffin was in the line of fire for Rambo and Ninja Girl was dancing with Igor the human hang glider, so Mr. Wizard was alone on this one.

Muttering something, in Latin I guess, he threw a fistful of sparkle dust at the cloud with no effect. What a surprise there. The cloud advanced. Quickly he pulled out a cross and a water pistol, and started chasing the cloud around, shooting streams of water at it. This is where I lost my tenuous hold on reality and started laughing. Chubby gave me a quizzical glance over his shoulder as he yanked a fresh belt of ammunition out of his shoulder bag and shoved it into the breech of his weapon.

"You okay?" he asked in a husky voice.

"Shit, no," I replied. "Must have hit my head on an overhang somewhere and I'm having one hell of a dream."

He seemed to accept that and dashed off. I kept laughing.

The two men managed to corner the cloud and let her have it. There was fire and water and lightning and screaming and explosions and gunshots. In the middle of all this, the cloud turned into a wolf, a giant rat, a bear, a beautiful nude blonde, a nightmarish thing with tentacles and finally a lump of oozing flesh. Then they set the mess on fire by sprinkling it with communion wafers.

It may have been nothing but a drug-induced illusion, but I rattled my chains at the victory and shouted wa-hoo, even though I don't like fantasy. If I had caught this show on cable, I would have turned to another channel. I prefer a good mystery, with plenty of conflicting clues and a hot seduction or two, that kind of stuff. But magic? I believe in hard facts, science, human dignity, cold beer and the Chicago Bears. Not mumbo-jumbo voodoo gumbo. That's crazy. Or at least it seemed crazy until tonight.

Meanwhile, Shorty had gotten into a bad way. She was flat against the wall with the Count moving in for the kill. A flurry of sword thrusts to his head missed, but instead of attacking, the nut just stood there and stared at her. His eyes started to glow a bright red. Hesitantly she began to lower her sword when an arrow took the ugly thing right in the ass. Where the arrow came from I have no idea.

He grabbed his butt and howled in pain. Coming awake, she charged forward, her sword slashing off a wing. Snarling, the bat raked her chest with his claws, the front of her uniform ripping away to expose molded body armor. Nice. These guys were definitely government. From the sidelines, Chubby angled the M60 so he wouldn't shoot the woman. The big machine gun stuttered away, Lardo riding the weapon like a professional, spent shells forming a glittering golden arc in the air.

JUDGMENT NIGHT

A net materialized above the one-armed bat and dropped onto him. But the Count ripped it apart without even trying. Across the room, Skinny cursed and started digging about in his shoulder pouch. I realized he was the source of the magic stunts.

In yammering fury, the machine gun finally blew away chunks of the Count's skull. The rainbow sword flashed and a clawed leg fell to the floor. That should have killed anybody, but the Count shimmered like bad TV reception and was a man again. Whole and undamaged. Instantly the three closed in as if this was what they had been waiting for. Now I was cheering them on wholeheartedly. Hallucination or not, the sonofabitch had killed my partner and I wanted him dead.

Laughing confidently, the Count unexpectedly doubled in size. His clothes too. A neat trick that. But the woman leapt into the air and thrust her rainbow sword straight through the guy's chest, as Skinny threw what resembled a wooden dagger into his throat and Chubby shoved a grenade down his pants. Then everybody but me took cover as the big guy fell face forward onto the stone floor and thunderously exploded.

In the enclosed space, the blast was so loud I couldn't hear it at first. Then sound painfully returned and the shock wave smacked me flat. Acrid smoke tore at my lungs. The ground quaked. The building shook. A rush of heat cooked me to the bone. The ceiling cracked, chunks of stone falling everywhere. I abruptly understood that this was no illusion and braced myself for death.

A short eternity later the rumbling world finally settled back into place. There was no sign of the Count except for a few smoking bones, and a melted cell phone. For the first time in three months I allowed myself to relax and said goodbye to my partner. *We got him, buddy. We got him.*

Rising from the rubble, Shorty, Chubby and Skinny dusted themselves off and came over carefully picking their way through the charred wreckage.

"I'm glad you survived, Mr. Alvarez," the skinny fellow said, offering me a canteen. "We have been following you since O'Hare Airport, Chicago."

I gagged on the water. "Huh?" I asked brilliantly.

"As you seemed to be tracking the vampires much better than we ever had, I saw no reason to interfere with your progress until some intervention was needed. Actually a most impressive job, considering your lack of formal training."

My thanks consisted mostly of four-letter words.

Unperturbed, he opened a leather wallet, showing me a badge and ID card. "FBI," he announced. "Special Agent Richard Anderson, on permanent assignment to Bureau 13. This is George Renault and Mindy Jennings."

They were feds. "Bureau 13?" I asked.

Wearily George rested the stock of his machine gun on the floor. "We're a covert division of the Justice Department."

Covert my ass. But not entirely stupid, I was getting the general idea. "And you handle criminals like these guys." I jerked a thumb at the smoking corpses.

"Yep," Mindy said, wiping her sword off with a bit of cloth before sheathing the rainbow blade. "But believe it or not, our biggest problem is personnel. Just can't find enough trained people who won't faint when facing vampire bank robbers, werewolf motorcycle gangs or toxic waste mutant assassins."

They waited. The next move was mine. What the hell. A short life, but a merry one.

"Okay, deal me in," I sighed.

Smiling, Richard flipped open another commission booklet. The ID card inside this had my driver's license picture and

JUDGMENT NIGHT

read: "Special Agent Edwardo Alvarez, FBI." It was dated two months ago. Smooth. I was going to like these guys. However, there was still one very important question that had to be answered immediately.

"Can I get down now?" I asked, rattling my chains.

INFORMATION

**TOPSECRETTOPSECRETTOPSECRETTOPSECRET
TOPSECRETTOPSECRETTOPSECRETTOPSECRET
TOPSECRETTOPSECRETTOPSECRETTOPSECRET
TOPSECRETTOPSECRETTOPSECRETTOPSECRET**

SECURITY LEVEL 10

**FOR THE PRESIDENT OF
THE UNITED STATES OF AMERICA**

Good morning, sir:

Following procedure, this report will appear on your desk within two days of your inauguration. Read it carefully, then place aside. The paper will self-destruct automatically when you finish. Please do not worry about starting a fire: we have done this many times and no damage yet.

FYI: Early in the nineteenth century, it was discovered that supernatural phenomenon were a reality and occurring with some frequency within the continental boundaries of the United States. Most of the phenomenon are harmless, some only annoying or inconvenient. However, a few are lethal in nature and required fast action.

As the FBI is charged with the internal defense of America, a subdivision was created specifically to handle these problems. Unique agents were armed and trained to neutralize any possible supernatural, dimensional or unearthly menace to the United States. Ever since the infamous Lincoln/werewolf inci-

JUDGMENT NIGHT

dent, Bureau 13 has faithfully fulfilled the duties with which they were charged.

Because public knowledge of this organization would cause tremendous unrest, the Bureau is totally covert. Even their own agents do not know the location of Bureau headquarters. Rather, the personnel work as independent field teams roaming the country, checking known trouble spots and maintaining the peace.

In deference, sir, you have little control over the Bureau, as contact with its agents is extremely difficult and they have their own sources of income. The Bureau actually contributes its excess funds yearly to help balance the national budget.

However, if a special situation should arise which you believe could best be handled by the Bureau, simply outline the pertinent details to the portrait of George Washington in the White House foyer. We'll get the message.

In conclusion: please remember that while monsters are not always the enemy, the weirdos are always Bureau personnel.

Godspeed and good luck.

                Horace Gordon
                Division Chief, Bureau 13

P.S.: Nice try, but this document will not photocopy.

**TOPSECRETTOPSECRETTOPSECRETTOPSECRET
TOPSECRETTOPSECRETTOPSECRETTOPSECRET
TOPSECRETTOPSECRETTOPSECRETTOPSECRET
TOPSECRETTOPSECRETTOPSECRETTOPSECRET
TOPSECRETTOPSECRETTOPSECRETTOPSECRET
*burn.*__

ACTIVATION

ONE

"Got one!" Mindy Jennings shouted, pulling back on the rod and reeling in the line, the ratchet whizzing away loudly.

Net in hand, Raul Horta crawled forward in the boat and soon another rainbow trout was added to the growing collection of edible prisoners in the old tin washtub in the middle of the rowboat.

I watched the whole thing with an air of resignation. It had been my idea for the team to come up here to the Catskill for our vacation and everybody was catching the limit, but me. Ah, what the hell. Didn't like fish. Not really. I was a meat-and-potatoes kind of guy. Thank god there was a freezer full of barbecued ribs waiting in the cabin.

Congratulations for the catch were tossed about from the rest of my crew, and in a polite array of plonks, the lines hit the water again in a neatly staged series.

Once more, the war twixt man and fish commenced. We had been out on the lake for half the morning, doing it up royal, each of us grimly determined to have fun. Mindy was in the rear of the rowboat battling the fish for supremacy. Next to her, Raul Horta was experimenting with some goofball mail-order electric fish catcher. Damn things never worked, but still he tried. Balancing the front of the boat, Father Michael Xavier Donaher and I were just drinking beer, swapping lies and occasionally summoning fat trout to their deaths. Alone as usual, Jessica Taylor was in a skimpy bikini and practicing dives off a floating wood platform. In an even skimpier red speedo, Richard Anderson was lying on the beach working on his always perfect tan. Dressed in Army fatigues, George Renault was reclining in a lawn chair on the dock, happily field stripping his M60 machine gun. For George, that was as close to fun as he got. The man simply liked our line of work too damn much. He was also paranoid. But for someone in the Bureau, that was a very healthy attitude.

The yellow sun was shining in an azure sky dotted with puffy white clouds. Birds were twittering in the lush green forest lining the shore. The lake was smooth and clear. I kind of felt that we were living in a postcard. All in all, we were doing a fine job of forgetting Jimmy's death.

I shook my head and cast again, the line whizzing out to hit amid the weeds, sending a splash into the air. A month ago in Chicago, we had finally tracked down a mad scientist with a poor copy of Victor Von Frankenstein's medical journal he had downloaded off the Internet. Didn't sound like much, but the doc had joined forces with the local Nazi Party to pay for his experiments. Frankenstein Nazis. Lord, what a fight that had been. Ended with the downtown Chicago convention center in flames, the Sears Tower listing three degrees towards the lake, a helicopter chase above Lake Shore Drive and a multiple bazooka battle that left most of us wounded, the doc and journal burned to a crisp and Jimmy Winslow catching a shell right in the chest. We wanted to try a Resurrect, but there hadn't been enough of him to mop up with a sponge. Our section chief had ordered us on vacation and here we are. Having as good a time as possible after the recent death of a close friend.

Feeling something in my eye, I laid my rod aside and popped the top on a beer from the plastic cooler. I'd really miss the stupid little bastard. For an incubus, a sex vampire, Jimmy had been an okay guy. In salute, I took a healthy sip.

JUDGMENT NIGHT

Although, of course, I never would have let him date my kid sister.

Suddenly, a truly thunderous belch from Father Donaher shattered the peaceful silence of the lake. Heads turned, somebody laughed, and the big Irishman blushed crimson.

"Faith, I do apologize," he said, that fake brogue of his dripping shamrocks off every syllable. "I fear Mr. Alvarez's lunchtime offering was a wee bit spicier than my delicate constitution can handle."

Raul offered sympathy, Mindy offered a beer and I told the lot of them to blow it out their ears. I had made that Chicken Ranchero mild enough for a newborn baby to eat, but to hear these sissies talk, you'd think I laced the thing with napalm. Geez, hadn't used more than three pounds of mutant habanero peppers.

Coming from the other side of the lake, a guy in a small dinghy continued rowing our way. Earlier, I had dismissed it as merely another fisherman heading for the deep water in the center of the lake. But I realized now that he was well past that point and coming towards us.

Automatically I stared at him through my sunglasses. When nothing happened, I muttered a curse and stuffed them into my shirt pocket. I'd forgotten that my Bureau sunglasses were in the luggage back at the cabin. These dopey things only blocked sunlight, nothing more.

"Anybody have their sunglasses with them?" Mindy asked in a very casual voice.

Everybody answered in the negative. George probably did, but he was a hundred feet away on the beach. Bureau sunglasses were good, but they do have limits. From that far away, anybody's Kirlian aura would be only a smeary blur.

Taking his sweet time, the guy rowed closer and closer. He

was slim, about my height, wearing denims and a cotton work shirt. Back-rowing, he came to a halt about fifty feet away, well clear of our lines.

"Ahoy, there!" he called, through cupped hands. "Have any of you seen a woman and little boy swimming around here today?"

I relaxed. Just a father looking for his misplaced family.

"Sorry," Raul shouted, casting again. "Been here since dawn and haven't seen a soul!"

"When did you last see them?" Father Donaher inquired.

The guy seemed to ignore that. "You sure?" he asked, sounding concerned, almost frightened. "Positive?"

"Absolutely," I answered loudly. "Lake's been deserted all day."

Strangely, that seemed to cheer him and he gave a big smile. "Boy, that's great news."

"Why?" Raul asked, before I could.

In response, the guy insanely stood in his boat. But it didn't rock or tip. Almost as if the thing was nailed to the water. Instinctively, I scratched at my stomach only an inch away from the S&W .357 Magnum in my belly holster. I was also a Bureau paranoid.

"Because," he said smiling, his tooth-filled mouth stretching from ear to ear. "That means there will be no witnesses!"

Not enough for a court of law, but good enough for me. I whipped out the old Smith & Wesson and put two thundering rounds into the dingy right at the water level. There was a blur to my right and a fishing knife thudded into the guy's face. Snarling, I turned around to curse the idiot who had done that. Guy might just have been a harmless loony. No sense killing him immediately. However, the expression on my friends' faces made me turn again and I dropped my jaw along with the rest of them.

JUDGMENT NIGHT

Standing on the water, the guy was already almost twice his original size, his torn clothes falling off him in strips. The skin was changing into scales, horns were sprouting from his head, and his face was splitting in half along the line of the knife, forming a vertical mouth.

"Tunafish!" Raul yelled, rolling up his loose sleeves.

We tightly closed our eyes. Even through the lids, I could faintly see the blinding light burst that our number two wizard generated. However, Water Boy was obviously not cognizant of our code phrases and screamed like a banshee. Made me wonder if the thing was a remote relative of the Irish monster?

Opening my eyes, I found "No Witnesses" clawing at the four eyes on stalks dangling from its bulbous head, its leathery wings beating the water beneath its cloven hooves into a froth. This bastard was definitely on its way to winning the Ugliest Monster of the Year contest.

I pumped a couple more rounds into the amorphous mess, doing no appreciable damage, when the boat suddenly lurched backwards to the sound of creaking oars.

"Pull!" Mindy ordered, fear quaking her voice. "In the name of God, pull for your lives!"

Now that was genuinely strange. I didn't know of anything that Mindy was afraid of, aside from agency paperwork. That was when I noticed that the shore appeared a lot closer than it had a few minutes ago. A hard lump formed in my throat. The water level was lowering. Our guest was draining the lake. Hoo boy. Sitting opposite Raul, I put my whole body into rowing. I was getting a bad feeling that this was no random encounter, but an assassin sent to eliminate our team. Anything strong enough to even attempt that feat was nothing to take lightly.

With ever-increasing velocity, the little craft speed away

from the monster. In the bow, I could hear Father Donaher muttering Latin. It sounded vaguely familiar. Exorcism? On the shore, Richard was kneeling on the sand rubbing two sticks together and fat George was hastily shoving an ammunition belt into his M60. God bless all paranoids.

"Describe," I ordered Mindy since she was looking in the correct direction.

"Four times original size," she grunted. "Tusks have been added, along with a chest full of tentacles, an elongated snout and ice."

"Ice?" I echoed.

Raul nodded, sweat glistening on his muscular chest. "Lake is freezing. Fast."

"Well, do something about it!"

He scowled. "Without my books and wand?"

A chill touched my skin and nobody had to tell me that the ice was getting closer. Momentarily it occurred to me that any onlookers would probably discount this whole thing as a movie, or a hallucination, as I would have only a few short years ago. Life was strange that way. But then, working for the Bureau was even stranger. Just ask Admiral Presley of our Space Defense Fleet.

"Michael, whatever you're doing, hurry it along!" I shouted.

"Sorry," the priest sighed, pocketing the Bible. "Didn't work."

"Exorcism?" Raul guessed, through clenched teeth.

"Yep."

A chattering burst of machine gun fire from the shore told me George was in action. I only hoped he had armor-piercing rounds, or something fancy in the belt. I had already tried simple lead to no effect.

"Here it comes!" Mindy shouted, and the boat jerked to a stop.

In a crackling wave, the entire surface of the lake solid ice. At first glance, it appeared relatively thin, but the thickness was visibly increasing by the second. Which gave me an idea. I checked and everybody was wearing sneakers. Raul's were orange with purple lightning bolts and blinking lights, but what the hey.

"Run for it!" I yelled, leaping from the rowboat and scampering cross the ice towards the swimming platform. At the very least, the wooden assembly would give us a stable base to fight from.

"Tunafish!" Raul cried once more, but it wasn't necessary. We were facing in the opposite direction and making time. The ice was smooth as glass and none of us were any too damn nimble, except for Mindy, who was gliding along with her usual ninja grace.

But a few feet away from the platform, Mindy cursed, dropped to her knees and hit the ice with a karate chop. It splintered to pieces, but quickly froze solid again.

"What?" I demanded, stopping alongside her.

She pointed. Swimming just below the surface was a human figure. The ice blurred the face, but I could tell it was Jessica. The beautiful telepath must have been trying to sneak up behind the creature when winter hit. The expression on her face told me there wasn't much time. A dozen plans went through my mind and I chose the fastest.

Pulling the .357, I blew a fast series of holes forming a rough circle. On cue, Mindy hit the ice with a closed fist and this time it cracked into tiny bobbing fragments. We pulled Jessica free and I slung the wet girl over my shoulder. With Mindy's help, we reached the platform. Dry wood sure felt good. As I gave the shivering Jess my shirt, I saw that Bozo Boy was even bigger, had four wings and two heads.

Madre mia, when would this thing stop growing? Silently I offered anybody paying attention my eternal soul for one loaded bazooka. There were no takers. Not surprising. Wasn't much of a soul.

Standing on the edge of the platform, Donaher had his pocket Bible open and was doing the Latin routine once more. I figured a blessing to help protect us from evil.

"Amen," he said pulling a tiny vial from inside his shirt and pouring the contents into the lake.

Holy water?

Instantly, a section of ice melted and a spiderweb of cracks exploded outward to spread across the lake with lightning speed. The chunks dissolved and as the open water reached Big Icky, its clawed hooves burst into flame and the dinghy disappeared. Howling and shrieking, the nightmarish thing flapped its way into the sky.

Arcing over us, a lance of fire reached out from shore to hose the beast from claws to horn. Keening in what sounded like real pain, the monster seriously beat wings and headed for the distant clouds.

"Its going to come back," Jessica warned, fingertips resting on temples.

"So swim for shore!" Mindy cried, diving into the water.

Pausing at the edge of the platform, Raul gave me a consoling look before he also dove. It was appreciated. Might have been only ten meters to shore, but I am perhaps the worst swimmer in North America since Rod "The Rock" Kinnison.

"Send the boat!" I suggested when Father Donaher pushed me from behind. I went under with a splash, and after a short eternity came to the surface blowing water out of my nose.

JUDGMENT NIGHT

Frantically dog paddling for the shore, I wondered what the penance was for killing a priest.

I sighed with relief when land was under my sneakers, and stumbling from the cold water I joined the rest of my team waiting impatiently on the grass. Then the seven of us sprinted for the log cabin where all of our stuff was kept. Or rather, everything we took on vacation. Our motor home and heavy weapons were parked safe in town some thirty miles away. Might as well have been on the moon.

Gathering on the porch, we kept a watchful scan on the sky.

"Run, or make a stand?" Richard asked, breathing hard. His red speedo had shrunk in the water to a shocking size, his right hand clenched at his side, feeling for a wizard wand not there.

Good question. Our jeep could easily hold the lot of us and boasted a top speed of sixty. However, its open sides offered us no protection, the road was laughable and the Winged Wonder could probably do sixty in its sleep.

Cracking open my exhausted weapon, I dropped the spent brass and slide in a speedloader of fresh rounds.

"Cabin," I decided.

Piling inside, we barricaded the doors with furniture, then closed and locked the wooden shutters and the windows. This was accomplished without conversation. We've done this sort of stuff before. But our next step was not so obvious.

"Council," I ordered, and they gathered around. "Summary. It resembles every nasty thing in the world combined, likes water and ice, dislikes fire and holy water."

"And it lies," Jessica added, tucking a pert breast back into the bikini top it had inadvertently popped out of while she ran. Feeling my face flush, I did my best to ignore the action.

"So it's demonic in nature," Mindy said eagerly, her eyes starting to brighten with the prospect of battle. "That's a start at least. Dick, Raul, did you recognize it?"

Both of the wizards shook heads. I knew how much they wished for their gear and once again I cursed myself for making the mages leave the stuff behind. But it was well known that if you don't sit on them occasionally, wizards would do nothing all day but play with their wands. No joke intended.

"Jessica, any chance of doing a Mind Blast?" I asked hopefully.

The lady psychic stared. "Against that behemoth? No way."

"Father?"

Over by the porch, Donaher let the window curtain drop back into place. "Sorry, Ed, did my best already."

True enough. Evil clerics might have more destructive spells than a Catholic priest, but they sure weren't the kind of folk you really wanted to pal around with. Or turn your back on.

"Okay," I said, biting a lip. "Then its physical weapons." Pulling out my .357 Magnum I checked the load. It was a combo load, two cold iron, two silver, and two steel-jacketed hollow point bullets. Damn.

"The thing doesn't like fire, so I'll light the fireplace," Jessica offered, moving across the living room. Defense was always her best talent.

"And the oven," Mindy reminded, flipping her sword through the air. "Hey, isn't there kerosene in the basement?"

I smiled. "Way to go, killer. There's a couple of ten gallon cans in storage."

Shouting a war whoop, Mindy sheathed her blade and disappeared down the stairs. Personally, I was pleased by her reaction. I knew the martial artist would have preferred to go hand-to-hand with the creature. But there are times when even her deadly fists and indestructible sword just won't do the job required.

JUDGMENT NIGHT

"We'll need soap powder and a funnel," Richard said, dashing into the kitchen. The mage knew exactly what we were doing. This was a recipe everybody had memorized. Basic Monster Fighting, Chapter One.

"There are soda bottles on the porch," Raul offered, "And some sheets that can be cut into fuses."

Filling a bucket with water, I told him not to bother. "Go assist Mindy with the kerosene. I have a plan, and we may get out of this yet. George, how many rounds remaining?"

"Fifty-seven," George replied from his position by the door, not bothering to count the length of linked shells dangling from his ungainly weapon. "Steel-tipped, armor-piercng."

"Save 'em."

"Check."

A click-clack sounded from the bedroom and out walked Donaher holding a pump-action 12-gauge shotgun. The antique was not ours, it had come with the cabin.

"Ten shells," he announced. "Double-ought buck."

Better and better. As the group got busy, I surveyed the cabin and tried to outline my battle plan. The exterior consisted of hundred year old oak logs cemented into place. The interior walls were lined with antique brick, the floor made of modern concrete. Wood beams thick as a Volvo supported the ceiling, and the roof itself was butt-braced slate, capable of carrying a winter's accumulated snowfall. I may have goofed on not letting the crew bring their toys along, but I sure wasn't stupid enough to bunk us in a place that would crumble at the first sign of trouble.

With the good Father's help, we shoved the bookcases in front of the windows and blocked the door with the big sofa bed. Yeah, perfect, if we can just finish in time we might stand a chance.

Just then, a tremendous thump sounded on the roof, the whole building gave a mighty creak and the windows shattered. Aw crap. Peeking through a shutter, I saw a couple of scaly lengths, thick as tree trunks, blocking the exit.

"Something is coiled about the place, trying to crush us," I announced as a rain of dust fell from the rafters and the cabin groaned. "Most likely Laughing Boy has polymorphed again."

"Thanks for the news flash," Mindy snorted, returning with the kerosene cans from the basement.

The containers sloshed full and Raul hauled them to the kitchen. While I kept guard with the Magnum, Mindy held the funnel steady so that Richard could pour laundry soap into the metal fuel containers. Styrofoam worked better, but we didn't have time to dice disposable coffee cups.

Father Donaher worked the pump on the shotgun, chambering a round. "Following the basic rules on demons, the beasty probably can not enter this dwelling without our permission. However, there is nothing to prevent it from crushing the place to ruins and then snacking on us like organic trail mix."

"Oh, shut up and do a prayer," Richard snapped, screwing the cap onto the finished can, placing it next to the other. For some reason, wizards get rather testy when their lives depend on non-magical solutions. The big sissies.

Solemnly Donaher crossed himself and lowered his head. "Lord, please don't let us die."

"Amen!" everybody chorused.

In a thunder of splintering wood, the porch collapsed. I took that as the cue to move.

"Michael, nine o'clock at the door," I shouted, and the priest took a position to the left of the jamb, his shotgun at the ready. "Raul, flip over the kitchen table. Jess, six o'clock with the cans. George, behind the table. Anybody got a Magic Marker?"

With a flourish, Richard pulled a felt-tip pen out of thin air and handed it to me. A magic marker, ha. I said thanks and ordered him to the living room with everybody else. As the skinny man raced to obey, it occurred to me how odd it felt giving orders to a person who had been in the Bureau so much longer than me. But over the years, the chief decided I was a natural leader. Especially in combat situations. I didn't consider myself smarter than Richard, just meaner and faster. Guess that amounted to the same thing.

Drawing a mark on the door, I stepped to the broken window and cocked the hammer on the .357 Magnum.

"This is gonna be tight, people!" I shouted over the groaning of the rafter beams. A crack appeared in the slate roof and a clutter of stones fell from the fireplace. "Ready? Three. Two. One, go!"

Crossing my fingers in a primitive luck ceremony, I emptied my Magnum at the snake body which was bending and cracking the woodwork on the window. The bullets merely ricocheted off the scales. But the muscular lengths instinctively tightened to block any escape attempt. Which meant the rest of its body would be shifting a bit to allow the contraction. Exactly what I was counting on.

"Now!" I cried, pointing at Donaher.

His shotgun booming a gaping hole appeared in the wooden door.

"Jess, go!"

As if reading my thoughts, the telepath hopped on the couch, lowered the two cans through the hole and placed them atop the coil just below the jagged opening.

"Scat!" I commanded, and they ran for the imagined safety of the living room. Soon as they were clear, I crouched behind the upturned table and hit George on the leg. In a stuttering roar, the M60 cut loose, tracing a line of holes through the sofa, the door and the cans beyond.

For almost a full second I thought the trick wouldn't work. Then the world exploded in flame as those twin ten-gallon Molotov cocktails outside did their favorite thing. The sofa, door and table offered us some protection from the blast, but the heat flash bellowed into the kitchen to cook the air from our lungs and we fell to our knees coughing. Lord, I would never be mean to a French fry again.

Above the noise of the detonation, we could hear a hideous screaming that wassailed and wailed. Violently, the cabin shook to its foundation, a roof beam cracked, the fireplace collapsed and then everything went terribly still.

Smoke was pouring into the kitchen, making it impossible to breathe. But that was no problem. We simply scampered through the gaping ruin of the porch and onto the lawn. The sight of the giant thing flapping into the horizon was more beautiful than any sunset I could remember.

"Well look at that," Richard muttered, crossing his arms. "I wonder why the kerosene is sticking to it so well?"

Sword in hand, Mindy smiled. "I added a tube of epoxy glue to the Molotovs as an added bonus."

Shifting position, George shouldered his ungainly machine gun to rest the stock on a hip. "Where the heck did you get epoxy from?"

"My purse," she replied, "Its perfect for repairing broken fingernails."

"Its secret girl stuff," Jessica explained.

We had a shaky laugh at that, and started slapping shoulders in triumphant. But the victory celebration was unexpect-

JUDGMENT NIGHT

edly cut short when our Bureau wristwatches began beeping the emergency recall signal.

TWO

Everybody glanced at a wrist, even Jessica, who had been swimming. Our watches were standard Bureau issue. The nifty devices were a combination watch and cell phone, 56k modem, VCR remote control and calculator that were proofed against shock, water, magnetism, fire, ethereal bombardment hard radiation, and toxic chemical chocolate fudge. Don't ask. Plus, they could be set to explode. Switzerland would have given a fortune for the design. Seiko tried once a year to steal them.

With a flip of my wrist, I turned the thing off. Okay, so there was an important message from headquarters waiting for us in the van. First we had a fire to extinguish. Luckily, the majority of the flames had departed along with our uninvited guest so it only took some brief work with garden hose to extinguish the blaze. None of our camping gear was damaged, just smelly with smoke. However, there was another problem. The garage had been reduced to a pile of smashed timbers and our jeep was gone.

Nudging an empty window frame with a tan toe, Richard sighed. "Apparently the creature ate it as an appetizer."

"Good thing it was a rental," Mindy noted, turning over a section of plywood to expose the cement flooring. "Ed, you get full coverage?"

"Of course."

"Whew."

George hitched his belt. "Guess we walk to town."

"Fifty miles?" Raul asked incredulously. "Get real."

"Faith, it's just a healthy stretch of the legs," Donaher said, primly stroking his bushy moustache.

The mage scowled. "You walk, I'll fly."

As I glanced over the battlefield of our vacation home, ideas came and went like riffling cards. Then finally, a winner. Yeah, that ought to do fine.

"Perhaps there is an alternative," I announced, thoughtfully rubbing my chin.

"Yes," Jessica said, her palms flat against her temples, eyes tightly closed. "They are not home, but it is there."

Expectantly, the team turned to look at the telepath. They had seen this routine many times before.

"Explain, please," Richard asked politely.

"Down the road about twenty miles is the Hayes place," I stated, sounding annoyed. Wish she would stop answering my questions before I ask them. "Bill and Louisa. They own a couple of four-by-four trucks and a cargo jeep."

"Sounds perfect. Want me to go steal the jeep?" Mindy asked, standing and dusting off her hands.

In silent fury, Father Donaher stared at the woman and her smile wilted fast.

"Er . . . that is, should I commandeer the vehicle as is my legal right as a federal law enforcement agent for the United States of America?"

The priest nodded. "Better."

"Don't go naked," I warned.

She winked. "Never."

Disappearing into the cabin, Mindy returned in a minute sporting camouflage-pattern pants and shirt, with a belt slung over her shoulder, a dozen kitchen knives of various lengths shoved through the leather, making a crude bandoleer.

"Holler if you need help," George said, checking the feed

on his M60. The ammunition belt was pitifully short, only a handful of rounds still dangling in view.

"Check," she announced settling the glittering strap about her shoulders. "On my way."

Dashing across the road, Mindy stepped into the bushes and was gone. Stoically, we returned to the salvage operation. Searching through the wreckage, Richard found a pile of tools and appropriated a crowbar. He then sharpened the end to a razor point on a small grinding wheel. Raul chose a double-headed axe, carefully wrapping sticky electrical tape about the handle for a sure grip. Jessica cobbled together a few more Molotov cocktails, in glass bottles this time. Donaher still had his shotgun with a pocketful of shells, and I had my trusty S&W .357 Magnum containing four mixed rounds. There had once been a chain saw in a toolbox near the woodpile, but that disappeared along with the porch. Too bad.

With a few spare minutes on our hands, the swimmers took the opportunity to get dressed while the rest of us stood guard. Jessica returned in a short black-and-pink flower print dress, which she filled delightfully. The telepath blushed at my thoughts. Richard appeared in tight leather pants and a sleeveless T-shirt that read, "It's not a job, it's an adventure!" Immune to this nonsense, we ignored him. Why do mages have to be so damn weird?

Time ticked by slowly, and it was a nervous three hours before a green cargo jeep rolled silently down the dirt road and came to a stop before the cabin. There was nobody behind the wheel.

"Mexican Holiday!" I shouted through cupped hands, announcing that the area was safe.

There was a rustle of leaves behind us, and Mindy stepped from the bushes on the other side of the cabin, a knife in each hand.

JUDGMENT NIGHT

"Hi guys," she called out merrily, sheathing the blades and strolling closer. "Sorry I took so long, but I stopped for a nap."

"No problem," Richard answered, visibly relaxing his grip on the crowbar. "We were just waiting for the bus."

"Well, here it is. Come and see."

Hardly more than a box on wheels, the open-back vehicle was quite large enough to carry the whole gang. What's more, the CB radio was in working order, gas tanks full, with a spare ten-gallon gas can strapped to the rear bumper, courtesy of the diligent Ms. Jennings, and a compass in the glove compartment. As a standard precaution, we pasted some mud onto the license plate and peeled off a window sticker to hinder identification. When satisfied, I had the team pile into the jeep with our meager possessions and took off for the village. Once again, I wished that we had been able to drive our van to this cabin, but the heavy armored vehicle never would have made it over some of the dinky bridges spanning the river that fed the mountain lake. Its imposing weight was the only flaw in our mobile command center.

The designated cook for this trip, I took the passenger seat, and dutifully started assembling sandwiches from a hamper on my lap. As each was finished, I passed them about. Everybody ate quickly, the food merely fuel, as they scanned the skies for trouble. It was a gorgeous morning, despite the faint smell of smoke tinting the atmosphere. The lush trees lining the road were emerald green and the sky the kind of blue you never see in a city. The road could have used some work though, being little more than a dirt path with rain gullies. But soon we bounced our way to a much smoother gravel road and started making decent time.

Between bites, we discussed the obvious security leak that had occurred for an enemy to find us, and exactly whose butt was going to get kicked about the matter. Suddenly, with a squeal of brakes the jeep jerked to a halt. Standing in the middle of the road, was a huge furry creature sharpening its claws on the rough surface.

In a practiced motion, Mindy pulled a butcher knife from her shoulder belt and expertly weighed the weapon in a palm. "Okay, what is it?" she asked. "Resembles a bear."

"Just a grizzly bear," I said, adjusting my Bureau sunglasses.

Relief was almost palpable. "Just a bear? Nothing more?"

"Just a bear."

Richard nodded. "Fine." With a gesture, a duplicate of the mage stepped through the jeep and advanced upon the animal, the image growing in size with every step.

"Scram!" the illusion bellowed, and the bear did a splendid impersonation of a hairy express train, plowing straight through a clump of bushes in its haste to leave the vicinity.

Continuing onward, we encountered the main road, a modern marvel of cracked concrete and really put the pedal to the metal. Alongside the highway, the trees seemed particularly thick, their gnarled branches almost appearing to reach out towards us with malevolent intent. Hopefully, that was just my imagination.

An hour later we passed the sign saying, "Pineville — 5 miles" and started to relax. Populated cities were pretty much a safe zone. Nobody fought in the middle of downtown anyplace. Too many bystanders with cameras, police with guns, stupid dogs, traffic, eager-beaver vigilantes and a thousand things that can turn a clockwork scheme into a total fiasco. We know that for a fact, it was a perfect description of our last mission.

Crossing the town line, Raul started scratching at his neck, so I checked out the horizon with my glasses. Even at

JUDGMENT NIGHT

this range, the reason he was itching was plainly apparent. Overshadowing the normal aura of a small town was a malignant cloud of pulsating ethereal vibrations. It almost dripped with slime.

"Magic up ahead," I announced coolly. "Big time and evil."

Jessica cursed and George worked the bolt on his M60. To everybody but us, the weapon appeared to be a banjo. The effect was a permanent illusion that had taken Raul and Richard working together a full week to accomplish. Sure scared the hell out of airport security guards.

"How dark an aura?" Father Donaher asked, fumbling in his coat pocket for shells.

"Purple, with splotches of black."

That was bad, sure enough, but nowhere near as vile as the monstrosity we had vanquished at the lake. This was starting to have the feel of a concentrated effort by somebody seriously to eliminate us. Which wasn't an entirely bad thing. Saved us the trouble of having to hunt down the monsters. Also, definitely removed the question of whether they were friendly or not.

If George had been driving, we would have charged straight into town and announced our presence on a bullhorn. But wisely Jessica was at the wheel, so instead we parked by a bait'n'tackle store and proceeded on foot.

Pineville was laid out in square strips, the center of a town a traffic circle and small park with the obligatory bronze statue of some pioneer guy holding a rusty musket. Only now the statue was gone, and in its place was a small tornado, a twenty-foot-tall whirlwind dancing on the pedestal. Nearby were several people lying on the sidewalk, their heads a pulpy mass of brains and blood. Two of the corpses were police officers.

Through my sunglasses, I could see the cause for their deaths. Inside the twister was a four-armed demon brandishing the bronze statue like a club. The hellspawn would be invisible to ordinary vision: the poor townsfolk died without even knowing what hit them.

The streets were clear of traffic and the creature hadn't spotted us yet, so we could probably swing round the creature and get to our van without incident. But the still bodies on the ground asked for better than that and I knew my team would agree. It was payback time.

Unable to shout above the wind, I beeped my watch four times. In response, the team spread out in attack pattern number four, pulling handkerchiefs over the lower halves of their faces. We hated to work in public.

Spearheading the assault, George went straight in with the M60, the big blaster chugging away on its last belt of ammo. We knew standard AP rounds would do no good against this sort of creature. This was a feint, to allow the dangerous people to get close. In a series of banging impacts, the armor-piercing rounds tore the bronze statue to shreds. The snarling demon dropped the ruined club and stepped off the pedestal.

Father Donaher approached from the west, shotgun under one arm, the other holding a Bible, ready to administer a withering blast or a deadly blessing. I had always admired the man's raw courage. Moving to the sidewalk, the whirlwind ripped free a bench and hurled it at the priest. Donaher dodged and the bench hit George sideways with a sickening crunch. He dropped the M60 and hit the ground staying very still.

A twirling baton of steel and wood, the double-headed axe came out of the north and plowed into the tornado, knocking the demon off its hooves. That made the wind slow and a Molotov cocktail arched in to smash on the demon, spreading into a pool of flame. Frantically, the creature rolled away from the fire and a crowbar twirled by, just missing its face by a scant half inch.

On command, Jessica was by my side and she mentally relayed my orders. Now our attack coalesced. As the others circled about the creature to hold it in position, the fierce wind tore at our clothes, bits of dirt and leaves hitting us with stinging impact.

I fired off my last two bullets, the brutal currents deflecting the heavy rounds, but I still managed to wound the demon in the shoulder, the silver slug withering the limb into a stick. Ha! Raul gestured and a duplicate of each of us stood next to the original. Richard fired an arrow from the ornate ring on his index finger. Donaher pulled out a silver-edged knife. I grabbed my pistol by the barrel and got ready to throw. Jess raised another Molotov. We advanced slowly as it braced for our attack.

Then from out of the sky, Mindy came swinging by overhead at the end of an electric power cable. Halfway across the street, she dropped away and the cable sailed on, sucked in by the very protective force of the vortex. The demon tried to dodge, but with the same success as George. The end of the cable caught it in the chest and lightning erupted from the contact. Fat sparks crackled and danced over the galvanized hellspawn, its misshapen body jerking about madly.

Trying to get free, it expanded the tornado to completely engulf the town. Windows shattered and cars flipped over as the screaming hurricane increased in force and volume, until the whole world seemed to be filled with the throbbing maelstrom.

Latching onto a fireplug, I hugged it with all of my strength, desperately trying not to be blown away. Leaves plastered my face, loose items bounced off my arms and legs. The sidewalk cracked, the fireplug began to rise and then just as fast as it started, the buffeting winds abruptly ceased.

I bellyflopped onto the concrete, and painfully struggled to my feet. With gun in hand, I started for the traffic circle, the rest of my team close behind. This could be a trick, but when we arrived there was only a greasy smudge on the ground where the demon had been standing. Aw right, electricity. It was the only way to stop demons or extra-terrestrial carrots. However, sprawled nearby was George, motionless underneath the bench.

It took three of us to move the bench, but a cursory examination by Donaher showed that George was alive, just badly bruised and with several broken ribs. No prob. Once in the van we could fix minor wounds such as those easily.

With Donaher and Richard supporting the man, we made our way through the debris-strewn streets and past the growing crowd of civilians. A local reporter tried to take our picture and Jessica tripped, accidentally breaking his camera. Such a clumsy gal is our Jess.

Do my best, chief.

Two corners later we reached the parking garage by City Hall. A sign by the kiosk said they were open twenty-four hours, but the attendant was nowhere in sight. As a precaution, the team fanned out while Mindy and I checked the wooden booth. There was nothing suspicious, except for a tipped cup of coffee on the table that was dripping liquid onto the tiled floor. I followed a drop down to a pair of battered shoes underneath. Then blinked in shock. The shoes were not empty, feet were inside neatly cut off at the ankles. Yuck. This was becoming mondo bizzarro.

Our van was on level two, the middle level. We had specially chosen it for security reasons, not readily accessible from

JUDGMENT NIGHT

the ground, not directly exposed to the sky. But now it meant our unknown adversary had lots of shadows to hide in.

Keeping to the center of the main ramp, we reached level two, and, big surprise, the lights were out. In a standard two on two defensive formation, we edged along to the middle line of cars. Sure enough, there was the attendant, checking license plate numbers on a clipboard. His feet, however, were strategically hidden behind a cement bumper.

"Hi, guys," he said showing a big smile and giving a wave. "Finished with ya fishing already?"

"Black!" I shouted adjusting my sunglasses. "Get black!"

He obviously thought I said "Get back!" which was the general idea. But the team heard me correctly and Donaher cut loose with his shotgun, blowing the man-thing to crimson bits. Even as the body fell, the tattered flesh parted with a horrid sucking sound and out stepped a transparent skeleton. Smeared with blood, the bones were bluish, appearing very similar to ice.

"Tunafish!" Raul cried, gesturing. We blinked, it didn't.

As the thing clawed blindly at its skull, Richard hit the skeleton with an arrow from his ring. No effect. I decided to play hardball.

"Timex!" I commanded, undoing the strap of my wristwatch.

Tearing off their timepieces, everybody twisted the dials and tossed the devices towards the shambling mockery. It walked right over them and the resulting explosion of the self-destruct mechanisms rocked the garage, setting off a hundred goddamn car alarms. We waited, and when the smoke cleared away there was nothing remaining but a charred patch on the cracked concrete.

Mindy tried to speak, but the alarms drowned her out.

Jessica nudged Raul, he gestured and silence returned.

"Never seen the species before," Richard commented, mopping some blue moisture off his T-shirt with a handkerchief. "Anybody snatch a picture?"

Jessica silently displayed her pocket camera for an answer.

"Atta, girl!"

You're welcome, Edwardo, dear.

"Come on," Father Donaher snorted, impatiently. "Let's get to the van."

The rest of us agreed wholeheartedly and we raced across the parking level in double-time. Nestled between a RV and a delivery truck, we found our vehicle safe and unharmed. Twenty-two feet long and eight feet high, the van was more a mobile home than anything else. Or rather, mobile fort. The windows were inch-thick Armorlite plastic, the hull armored to withstand .50 rounds. All ten of the tires were military-grade self-repairing radials. The RV was airtight, with a twelve hour supply of oxygen, carried more electrical surveillance equipment than Air Force One and had a missile pod disguised as an air-conditioner unit on the roof. We stole that idea from a Mack Bolan novel. At the present, we lacked missiles. Those weren't normally considered standard supplies for a vacation. Although they would be from now on.

Reaching the van, we carefully turned off the antipersonnel devices, canceled the magical barrier and unlocked the doors. Following procedure for being away for this long, we ran a security check, but the vehicle was clean. The only bugs were the crickets in a cage to feed our pet watchdog. A fat little lizard we called Amigo. He didn't appear dangerous, but the carnivorous Gila had a tiny magical necklace about its throat and God help the poor thief who broke into our van. 'Nuff said.

JUDGMENT NIGHT

Firmly locking the doors, we gently laid George on a bunk that folded out from the wall. He was white and sweaty, but did not complain of our rough handling. In short order, I had his shirt off and the mages were taping his chest with a soft golden cloth, muttering steadily. As we watched, the exposed bruises started to pale and the fat man heaved a mighty sigh.

Convinced he was going to be fine, I made my way to the rear of the van. Already, Donaher was elbow-deep in the weapon locker reloading his shotgun and getting a belt of mixed ammo for George. Mindy had her rainbow sword strapped to her waist and was testing the balance on a handful of razor-sharp oriental throwing stars. They have a name, but I forget. Jessica was checking the action on a double-barrel taser stun pistol. I helped myself to a couple of reloads for the Magnum and a satchel of grenades. Everybody took a new watch.

We then exchanged positions with the mages, who cycled open the special cabinet containing their wands and books. Raul's wand was about a foot long and made of steel. Richard's was three feet long, and solid silver tipped with gold. Apparently the better the wizard, the fancier the staff. Guess they started off with wood and ended with diamond. Jimmy used to tease Raul about the length of his staff, until the mage turned him into a toad for an afternoon and that sort of took the fun out of it.

Preliminaries over, the two wizards took seats at the back of the van well away from the radio, which had a habit of not working in their immediate presence; as did firearms, VCRs and computers, but not fax machines. Once they tried to explain why, but I got lost as they dove into quantum mechanics and the nature of flux reality.

Jessica was in the swivel chair before the communications console, her nimble fingers tapping authorizations and such into the mainframe computer. The laser printer came to life with a whine, sliding out the finished paper into view when done.

"Hmm, it's in code," she said, offering me the sheet. That was odd. Sitting in the passenger seat, I stared at the paper, letting the garbled words enter my mind and re-arrange themselves into coherent sentences. "Identification code, yes, that's correct, from the office of Horace Gordon, the big boss himself, in reference to blah, blah, blah . . ." As I finished reading the message, the paper dropped to the floor. "Holy shit!"

"What is it?" Jessica asked, snatching the paper but the ink was already gone

"Holy shit!" I repeated, unable to express myself any more clearly or precisely.

"I think we may need more information than that, chief," Richard said, sounding amused.

"And watch the language," Donaher scolded, working the pump action of the shotgun.

Moaning, George sat upright on the bunk appearing much better. "Talk, Ed," he whispered hoarsely, herbal smoke billowing from his mouth.

A swallow cleared my throat. "We," I paused to cough. "We've been ordered to Bureau headquarters."

Silence thick as lead filled the van. Then Father Donaher mumbled something in Latin, and the rest of the team nodded assent.

Holy shit, indeed.

THREE

Mindy opened and closed her mouth a few times as if to chew air into her lungs. "Bureau headquarters?" she asked, stressing the last word.

"B-but nobody even knows where it is!" Raul stammered, spreading his arms wide. "We've been under maximum security since 1987!"

The slaughter of '87, I called it. A bloodbath when over eighty percent of the total Bureau personnel were killed within a four hour period. To this day we still had no exact knowledge of who, or how, it was done. But we were still looking and would do so forever.

Brushing back his wild crop of hair, Richard licked dry lips. "So where is it?" he asked excitedly.

"Manhattan, New York," I announced. "Thirty-third Street and Third Avenue. The Gunderson Building. We're to get there ASAP, pronto and fast."

"Why?" Donaher asked, getting to the heart of the matter.

Already behind the wheel, George was starting the engines and doing a systems check. This was a time I didn't mind having Mr. Speed-Limits-Are-Only-a-Suggestion-and-Not-The-Law doing the driving.

"Don't know," I said truthfully, buckling in tight. "They'll tell us when we get there."

Without further discussion, the group started strapping on seat belts and George backed out of our parking space at 90 mph.

* * *

We were an hour outside Pineville on Route 95 south when flashing lights and sirens sounded from behind us. George paid them no attention and maintained speed. As the police car pulled alongside, I gave the officers a fast scan with my Kirlian sunglasses.

"Human," I announced.

From inside the other car, an angry police officer motioned us to pull over. Jessica started twisting dials on the radio until she found their frequency. Should have seen their faces when we broke into their conversation with the local police station. We identified ourselves as FBI agents on a priority mission, with absolutely no time to spare. Through the window, I showed them a fistful of federal ID badges. The station was loath to accept this, but the patrol bought the story, slowed and let us pass.

A Bureau 13 deluxe model, the radio was equipped to work on nigh every frequency in the spectrum. Including a couple of military channels. But none of the top secret frequencies, of course. That would be illegal. Only the NSA was chartered for such activity. In fact, my team could chant in unison: "No, sir, we did not have access to any top secret military channels. Uh-uh."

A few hours later, George spotted some hitchhikers standing on the berm, looking forlorn and waggling thumbs. Both of the women were amazingly beautiful, with ample young breasts almost bursting out of those skimpy halter tops, and cut-off jeans that only accented the sort of legs that made a man drop to his knees and thank God for his Y chromosome. Not that Mindy and Jessica were lacking anything in aesthetic quality. Ms. Jennings was nicely attractive, in a muscular sort of way, and Jess a total fox. Hubba hubba. But these two buxom babes were outstanding.

JUDGMENT NIGHT

As we came near, I checked them over with my sunglasses and got nominal readings. The human aura of the women meant nothing in this business. They could be brainwashed assassins, or artificial constructs, just about anything. Then again, maybe they were exactly what they seemed to be, two women lost in upstate New York needing a ride back to civilization.

Only where was a broken car, camping gear, roller skates, or parachutes? Just how did a couple of dainty beach bunnies reach this glorious middle of nowhere? Walk? Yeah, right.

Now suspicious as hell, I drew my trusty S&W .357 Magnum and clicked back the hammer while dialing for computer enhancement on my Bureau sunglasses. Ya never know, ya know? Suddenly the magical illusion of the sexy human females faded away to reveal a stack of crates bearing the military designation for C4, high explosive plastique.

Oh crap. "It's a trap!" I shouted, over the roar of our racing engines.

Savagely twisting the steering wheel, George tried to swerve away from the hellspawn centerfolds just as the crates violently detonated.

Thunder filled the universe, the RV was thrown off the road and went flying into the sky over the median. Encased in boiling fire, my team could only hang on for dear life as we went ass over teakettle, every loose item in the vehicle went shotgunning from side to side, as we rolled over and over. It felt as if we were airborne forever before the van finally slammed into the pavement with a bone-jarring crash. The windows cracked, airbags punched us against our seats, the fire alarm went off, Amigo dropped from the ceiling, the lockers erupted supplies onto the floor, the radio switched to AM, and our spare tire went rolling by outside.

Steadily cursing, George used a combat knife hidden in his boot to stab himself free from the airbag, noisily sneezing at the powdery discharge from inside the safety balloons, then shifted gears, gunned the engines, and the van roared away on smoking tires. Ha ha! Alive and still kicking! Although our little armored chariot was now shaking so badly it made the bullets in my gun rattle.

"SSttoopp tthhee vvaann!!" I ordered as my glasses headed south for Miami.

"NNoo wwaayy," George replied, fighting the madly bucking steeringwheel. "MMaayybbee mmoorree!!"

That was true enough. But this could not go on for long before we started breaking things not already damaged by the blast. Such as our internal organs, and other non-essentials. Tightening my seat belt, I killed the alarm and motioned for Raul to come up front. After an aborted attempt to walk, he resorted to crawling on hands and knees. Flying was seriously of the question, what with the floor and the ceiling attempting to touch each other at the present moment.

"AAnnyy rruubbbbeerr ssttiillll oonn ttiirree??" I asked all nine of him.

Raul touched the interior wheelwell and furrowed his brow. After a minute, he nodded yes. A wizard's "inner sight" lets him see through a lot of things. Quite handy on a mission, but reason number one why you never play poker with a mage.

"FFiixx iitt," I ordered, cheeks wabbling madly.

Brandishing his wand, Raul touched the metal rod to the wheelwell, but it kept bouncing off. Gritting his teeth, the wizard held it in place with his other hand and starting harshly muttering. A thin stream of sparkles flowed from the tip of the wand and seeped into the floor. Immediately our ride began to smooth and soon we were running straight and even.

JUDGMENT NIGHT

Doing ninety plus on the wrong side of the highway.

George corrected that by bouncing over the median again. The sharp jostles a mere waltz after our recent slam dance.

"Whew," Raul sighed, slumping in a chair, the auto-massage refusing to function for the mage as usual. "I've fixed flat tires before, but never on a moving vehicle."

"Cup of tea?" Mindy asked, moving to the kitchenette.

"Make it a brandy."

She glanced at me and I gave a hesitant okay. Raul had a possible problem in that area and we kept a watch on his drinking. On the other hand . . .

"Make that two," I said, licking my lips.

* * *

A short while later, we entered a "Falling Rock" zone, a towering cliff of veined granite edging the highway on our side. I was driving at the time and on a hunch hit the nitrous oxide injector.

In a roar, the engine revved to overload, the dashboard meters hit the red and we rocketed through the area at 150 mph with flame coming out of our twin tail pipes. Nothing else happened, but it was always smart to play it safe.

* * *

Six hours later, I knew we were in New York City before reading the sign, because we were slammed to halt reaching bumper-to-bumper traffic.

"Parade?" Richard asked, craning his neck for a better view.

In the passenger seat, Donaher scowled from under his fishing hat. "No, just rush hour."

"Rush hour on a weekend?"

A shrug. "Welcome to New York."

Not amused, I watched as a snail raced by on the berm. Some of our fellow prisoners were starting to read books, or begin jigsaw puzzles. Guess this was old hat to them. Then an odd movement amid the traffic caught my attention. A gasoline truck was starting down the up ramp of the expressway, forcing cars out of its way to reach the motionless river of vehicles.

"Drunk driver?" Mindy asked, gesturing in that direction.

"Just a New Yorker," Raul said grumpily, polishing his wand with a chamois cloth.

My sunglasses had broken during our recent sojourn, so all I had now was a single lens to peer through. As I dialed for enhancement, I could see the driver had a human aura, but on his forehead was clearly visible the tattoo of a silver knife stabbing through the moon. Hoo boy. That was the symbol of the Scion of the Silver Dagger, a lunatic group dedicated to the destruction of the world for no particular reason that the Bureau could ever discover.

"It's the Scion!" I shouted, drawing my Magnum.

Everybody grabbed weapons, George even flipped the switch arming our missile pod before remembering it was empty. "Shit," he growled, glaring at the roof.

Rolling down a window, Richard gestured with his staff and a low stone wall appeared directly in front of the truck. A split second later, the tanker smashed through the barrier as if it was paper mache.

"Looks bad," Raul said grimly, his wand glowing with power.

"Its worse!" Jessica added, staring to our left.

On the other side of the expressway, another tanker marked "Liquid Hydrogen" was proceeding down that ramp. A dozen plans flipped through my mind, each critically flawed by the fact we could not move the van an inch. Only one thing left to do.

JUDGMENT NIGHT

"Abandon ship!" I yelled and kicked open the door. There was only a slim chance for escape, but we had to try. I hit the ground running and slammed directly into a green wall.

Turning about, I saw that the van was now surround by a shimmering green ball of force that encased us completely. I had seen its like before, but never on this grand a scale. Damn thing must be thirty feet in diameter! Tingling with an adrenaline rush, I hesitantly climbed back inside. We exchanged nervous glances. What was happening outside the sphere around us was impossible to say. This spell blocked all vision, noise, vibrations, everything short of a nuclear bomb.

Think they have one? Jessica sent nervously.

I shrugged. With the Scion, it was anybody's guess.

On the couch in the back, the two wizards were holding their wands in clenched hands, eyes closed, muscles tightened and sweat pouring off their bodies. I could almost feel the ethereal vibrations in the air.

"How long can they hold the shield?" I whispered, fearful of breaking their concentration. This was not an easy spell to conjure, I knew that from past experience.

"Uncertain," Donaher said softly, mopping their brows with a soft cloth. "They are both pretty fresh, but this shield is huge. Biggest I've ever seen."

As we waited in green silence, faint age lines began to appear around the eyes of Raul, and Richard's hair began to gray at the temples. Minutes passed and we started to fear for their lives, when the wizards broke apart gasping for breath. They limply slumped to the floor, wands still tight in their grips. As Donaher and Jessica moved in with oxygen masks, I went to a window bursting with the desire to know what the hell had happened.

The RV was sitting in a clear patch of floor, surrounded by

a pile of brick and plasterboard that filled the room to the ceiling and spilled through the side doorway and down the stairs. In front of us, was a ragged tunnel the size of the van leading through a series of smashed walls. With sudden understanding, I realized that the blast resulting from the colliding trucks must have thrown us off the highway and inside an apartment building. And from the dilapidated condition of the room about us, obviously an abandoned one. Nothing unusual there. The Bronx was full of vacant buildings. Hundreds of them waiting for a promised renovation that would never come.

Pushing open the door, I wadded through the wreckage to reach a section of clear floor and proceeded down the tunnel. It ended in a crumbling hole through the outer brick wall of the building. Watching my step, I took a position near the edge of the floor and trained a pair of inflatable binoculars on the distant elevated highway. Looking through the cool glass, I actually felt my heart stop.

The field of debris stretched as far as I could see, the twisted burning wrecks were strewn everywhere. It would take a forensic team months to determine how many died in the titanic blast. Nothing visible was larger than a smoking tire; cars and people included. As I relayed this information via my watch, I did not need Jessica's talent to read the minds of my companions. Somebody was going to pay dearly for this senseless massacre. Attacking us was expected, just part of the job, but this kind of wholesale slaughter of civilians was intolerable.

Supporting the pale wizards, the rest of the team joined me at the rim of the hole. Mindy kicked a chunk of brick off and watched it drop to the garbage strewn lot below. "How are we going to get down?"

"The stairs," I said, tossing the binoculars to Donaher.

JUDGMENT NIGHT

Mindy gestured. "But the van . . ."

"Stays here," I interrupted.

This statement raised a flurry of comments and I saw an explanation was necessary. "We have been tracked and pursued since the lake. We've managed to stay one jump ahead of our faceless enemy, but they're using the big guns now and there isn't enough clearance. Civilians are getting murdered."

"But I thought the van could scramble any electronic surveillance," Raul stated weakly, his face almost white in color. He looked years older and reeked of sour sweat.

"Correct."

Trembling, Richard gestured in the air, his fingers leaving trails of light behind. "There are no magical tracers on us," he announced.

Jessica tilted her head. "Psyonics, clear."

I scowled darkly. "Goddamn it, you're forgetting the obvious."

Crossing her arms, Mindy asked, "Visual tracking?"

"Why not?"

"So what do we do?" George asked, tapping a finger on the long vented barrel of his machine gun.

"Take advantage of a golden opportunity," I stated. "The blast that hurled the van here, also masked our escape. If we play this quiet, our enemy will never know we survived until its too late."

They murmured hesitant approval. I went on. "We leave the van here and split up. First into groups of two, then individually. The plan is to scatter and converge. That way, at least some of us will get to Bureau headquarters."

"On 33rd and 3rd," Raul said grimly. He sounded stronger by the minute, but mages were known to be fast healers. Already there was a faint aroma of Old Spice aftershave around the man.

"As far as we know, that is the place," I agreed.

Returning to the van, I opened a small safe under the drivers seat and pulled out a wad of money. It was a bit dusty, but still serviceable. "Here's five thousand for each of you. Remember, use cash only, no credit cards. Sign nothing and never give your real name."

"What about you?" asked Jessica asked in concern. "How will you operate without funds?"

I patted her hand. It was nice to know there were some thing she couldn't read. "Thanks for the concern. But if I need more than fifty bucks to get from here to there, I've lost my touch."

"Special private eye training?" Richard asked curiously.

"Nope," I lied. "Just cheap."

Climbing into the swivel chair before the console, Jessica got busy with the document forger. A fantastic device built by Dr. Roberston, the Bureau's pet genius. The compact machine was a combination computer, printer, embosser with the precise details of over 20,000 government documents in storage; passports, library cards, federal weapon permits, security passes, military ID, arrest warrants, drivers licenses, tax stamps, diplomas, writs of habeas corpus, stays of execution, season Yankee tickets, you-name-it. In short order, she made an assortment of documents and identification cards for each member of the team, ending with a new drivers license for me under the name of Joe Smith. I like a challenge.

"What about Amigo?" Raul asked, swiveling his chair around. The lizard waddled closer and he ran a finger over the scaly head of our tiny guardian who rumbled in pleasure.

"Take him with you," I suggested, cleaning my wallet of

unwanted material. I fed the cards into the ash tray where they burst into ash. "We can't leave him here, or let him loose."

"Fair enough." Smiling, Raul slipped the lizard into a side jacket pocket. Amigo poked his head out and flicked his forked tongue as if to say goodbye, then withdrew and began squirming about to get comfortable. Mindy handed the mage a matchbox of chirping crickets.

After a brief dissertation on the practical uses of greasepaint, our disguise trunk was emptied of supplies and everybody changed their hair color, donned glasses and/or moustaches and stuffed clothing packs into pockets. In deadly silence, Donaher shaved his moustache off, his only consolation was the near weeping of George as he left his M60/Banjo on the floorboards. There was nothing silly about it. Took a soldier a long time to know the particular idiosyncrasies of a favored weapon. George was consoled with a MAC 10 assault pistol with infra-red laser spotter, flip-clips and Mark IV Glaser Sure-Kill Safety Slugs. The rest of us were satisfied with less exotic weaponry.

Each team member departed when they were ready. Deliberately stalling, I was the last to leave. Setting the van's self-destruct mechanism for fifteen minutes, I hurried out of the ruins. Sensors had shown the building empty of human life, so the maneuver was a safe act. There was too much important information and valuable weapons in the vehicle to chance letting it fall into enemy hands. Or worse, the hated press. The forty five pounds of strategically placed thermite charges would reduce the van to a memory in exactly 2.4 seconds. And I knew that for a solid fact. This was our third van.

Taking the rat-dropping covered stairs, we soon reached ground level. Removing the boards covering the front door, the group raced into the courtyard when came was a mighty whump above us and long tongues of flame gushed from the windows of the ninth, tenth and eleventh stories.

"So long number three," Raul said, giving a brief salute.

Leaving the growing conflagration behind, we crossed the street, pushing our way through the crowd of people staring at the distant highway. Faintly, we could hear the wail of ambulances. Father Donaher said a quick prayer for the dead, and we moved past the crumbling overpass. Down here on the street level, larger wreckage dotted the sidewalk; a melted car door, an intact engine, the charred husk of something small, but we paid it no attention and moved steadily on. I think Mindy wiped a tear from her eye, but I couldn't be sure, as something was blurring my own vision. Dust perhaps. Yeah, dust.

Together, we entered a bar on 175th Street and separated throughout the establishment, within minutes each pair departed via the bathroom windows, back door, or cellar. Dressed as gothic punks, Donaher and I strolled out of the garbage strewn alley and hailed a cab. Paying the driver early, we jumped out halfway to the ordered destination and took off zigzagging through a weed infested empty lot. Thirty minutes later, two bearded police officers boldly strolled into the George Washington Bridge Port Authority Terminal. In a utility closet, I became a rastafarian and openly bought a ticket for Philadelphia. Across the concourse, I spotted Donaher hobbling out of the lavatory as a naval lieutenant with only one leg. How did he do that? As the priest headed for the subway platforms, I adjusted the brim of my cap to disguise a wave and the naval officer scratched his nose, then brushed some lint off his stomach, left and right shoulders, giving me a brief benediction. Every little bit helps.

JUDGMENT NIGHT

At the Meadowlands Arena in north New Jersey, I left early again with a bunch of yowling sports fans, stole a car from the parking lot and drove south on the Jersey Turnpike to the Lincoln Tunnel and then back into New York City. Pulling into a sleazy motel on 10th Street, I dodged an army of ugly hookers and took the service elevator to the basement, raided a locker and exited as a cigar smoking African janitor.

* * *

A few hours later, I was leaning against the mouth of the alley at Thirty Second Street.

Belching loudly at the passing crowds, I took another sip from the empty whiskey bottle concealed within a rumpled paper bag. Ninety-nine per cent of the whiskey had been poured over my tattered, filthy clothes, the other one percent sloshed about in my mouth to flavor my breath. Maybe a random sip had accidentally flowed down my throat, but no more than a sip. Singing an obscene song about sheep, I scratched at pretend fleas and waited for the rest of my team to show.

George was the first to arrive, hopping out of the trunk of a moving cab as the vehicle turned a corner. This being Manhattan, nobody paid the incident the slightest attention. Dressed as a yuppie, he took a position near the hotdog cart on the corner and that was when I realized the redheaded vendor wearing the dark glasses was Jessica. She sent a telepathic laugh my way and I tipped a mental hat in appreciation of a job well done. Damn she was good.

Thanks!

In the street, a manhole cover nosily slid aside and out of the sewer crawled a skinny utility worker in grimy overalls. Richard clicked off the light on his hardhat and joined us cool as could be. Didn't know the mage had it in him.

With a sputtering roar, a huge motorcycle pulled to the curb.

The driver was an amazingly buxom blonde whose physical charms many porno magazines would have considered overwhelming. She was dressed in black latex body suit cut down to the ohmigod level, fishnet stockings, boots, and a slick black leather jacket. She sure looked familiar. Maybe I saw her on the internet.

Climbing down from behind her, was Father Donaher, bare chested, in a chainmail vest, studded denims and sandals. He gave her a complicated hand shake, and whispered something too soft to hear.

She beamed a smile, and gunning the big 1700cc engine, popped a wheely to roar off into Manhattan traffic.

As the motorcycle departed, a stretch limousine parked in its place. I watched the rear door, but instead, Mindy stepped out from the front in chauffeurs livery. We formed a ragged line at hot dog cart, munching the fare in sincere appreciation, each paying no attention to the others.

The clock in the window of a local restaurant caught my attention, so I nudged Jess and she made telepathic contact.

Everybody here? I asked her inside my head.

No, came the soft reply. Her voice always felt soft to me.

Who's missing?

Raul.

Check the bystanders, I suggested, squirting mustard on my dog and getting my sleeve in the process. After all, I was playing a drunk.

Jessica made change for Mindy. *Already did. Not here.*

Parked cars? Alley ways?

I said, he is not here.

Which meant Jessica had done a total sweep of the area to the maximum range of her abilities. I didn't like this. The mage was late, but only by a few minutes. *Jess, please ask George what was his last move?*

A few ticks later, she reported, *When last seen, he was disguised as a rabbi, heading for Brooklyn on the M19 bus.*

The long way, eh? We'll give him an extra ten minutes.

Sounds good.

But he still did not appear. The team waited as long as we dared, a full half-hour, but Raul never showed. Finally, we had to move and with a heavy heart I counted our friend dead. My only hope was that he took a bunch of the bastards with him to the grave. In our next fight, if any of the enemy was wounded, I'd chalk it up to last licks from Raul Horta. Then taking a breath, I forced the matter aside. Mourning for a fallen comrade could come later. We still had a job to do.

Reaching 33rd Street, we walked round the corner to third Avenue expecting anything but what we saw. The sidewalks were blocked with wooden saw horses, the street filled with heavily armed soldiers and concrete tripods. *Tank traps,* George identified. Army helicopters hovered above a ten story building and the roof was lined with more armed troops.

On the corner was a film production crew, with cameras, boom mikes, huge arc lights, cue card girls, best boys, gaffers, dozens of extras and a young wag in riding breeches sitting in a director's chair, shouting orders to everybody and not liking the answers.

My team bobbed their heads in approval. This was a gag the Bureau used often. The organization actually owned a motion picture production company in Los Angeles. Filming a movie was a great cover. Anything strange would simply be chalked up to special effects. Many new agents were shocked to discover how many famous monster movies were actually live footage of Bureau 13 battles. It sure saved money on costumes and make-up. Plus, since movies sometimes take years to be released, most of the idle curious would have forgotten about the incident, or attribute it to the vagaries of Hollywood. We had used something similar ourselves once. Pretended to be a TV news team to gain entrance to a ghoul infested yacht race in Malibu Beach. Nasty job. Crack addict ghouls, that was about as bad as it got.

At the barricade, our disreputable dress caused a commotion among the soldiers until we showed our FBI cards to a corporal. As she inspected them, the rifles of her companions never wavered from our direction. It was nice to see professionals at work.

Finally, the corporal summoned a sergeant, who ignored our identification cards and asked what our favorite food was. I leaned close and whispered into his ear, "Tunafish."

Grudgingly, he accepted that and walked us past the multiple defense rings to the front revolving door of the building. We couldn't see through the glass panels as heavy cloth had been taped over the windows. One at a time, we were placed inside a section of the door. It would revolve halfway, stop, and a brilliant yellow light flooded the area, seeming to illuminate us from the bones out.

"I've heard about those," Richard said on the sly. "Its a molecular scanner. They now know everything we're carrying, what we had for lunch and probably the color of our underwear."

Jess started to toss off a snappy remark, but stopped and frowned. I understood. We could all feel the emptiness in our midst. That terrible vacant space between Richard and Mindy. Lord knows humor has its place, but a joke now would have been more than inappropriate. It would have been vulgar.

Once inside, we were frisked and our weapons taken. A lieutenant informed us the assorted devices would be returned

JUDGMENT NIGHT

later. The unspoken message being they didn't quite trust us yet. If these people had any working knowledge of Bureau agents, they'd never trust us. In our hands, paperclips and napkins are deadly weapons.

The foyer was a zigzag maze of sandbags topped with concertina wire. The next generation of barbed wire, it was nothing more than an endless coiled razor blade. The steel band could slice through leather gloves as if they were made of toilet tissue.

Walking slowly, we reached the receptionist desk—which was now a machine gun nest, boasting a huge electric driven .50 Vulcan Mini-Gun. Our Bureau cards were asked for this time, and we complied. The blank plastic rectangles were a mixture of technology and magic. Only in our willing presence would they show our picture, thumb print, ID number and real name. Very rarely did we ever have to use them. The lieutenant in charge placed them on a glowing sheet of glass set in a black metal box.

As we waited, I casually checked the place over. So this was our HQ, eh? Steel bars lined with electrical conductors closed off the side corridors. A pair of siege arbalists, giant six foot wide crossbows carrying ten foot long, 200 lb. arrows, protected the main corridor from unauthorized passage. Surreptitiously, I did a quick check through my one lens, and spotted an invisible something holding a bazooka over by the broom closet. Whew. If I ever got an assignment to invade this place, I'd quit.

Finally, the box beeped and the expression on her face said we could live. For awhile, anyway. We were given our cards back and under armed guard the team was escorted to an elevator with a small machine gun nest filling the rear and taken to the fifth floor. The elevator doors separated with a musical ding to display a squad of people in radiation suits holding something that resembled a common leaf blower. I had no desire to ask what it was. They might show me.

Flashing something in her palm to the squad, they saluted as we passed and the lieutenant directed us to a door marked Conference Room #1. My team entered and the doors closed, then automatically locked behind us. As the lights came on, we glanced around. It was a curved room, with three sections of theater-style seats facing in towards the center stage. A lecture podium was there, behind which stood a beefy, white haired man. He was dressed in combat fatigues, the insignia sporting the rank of brigadier general. An oddly built pistol was strapped to his left hip, a gold wizard's wand in a holster on the right. We could read the name badge on his breast pocket, but it wasn't necessary. Only one person we knew of fit this description.

"Horace Gordon," George whispered in unabashed reverence.

Mindy arched an eyebrow, Richard stood at attention and Father Donaher crossed himself. It was the first time any of us had ever seen the chief of Bureau 13. He was an elusive individual, more famous than J.P. Withers, the very first Bureau agent from 1880, who supposedly was still in service as an immortal werewolf. But then, you know how company legends grow. Yes, I had gotten drunk at the last Christmas party, but I did not email a jpeg of my ass to the Kremlin. Lies, it was all lies.

"Hello, sir. What's the problem?" I asked taking a seat in the front row.

"The end of the world," Gordon said, in the deep gravelly voice we knew so well from our wristwatches.

"Or rather, the end of the world as we know it," he added after a moments hesitation.

FOUR

As we reacted to that news in various ways, Gordon slit open a manila envelope and pulled out a blank sheet of paper. As he held it for a moment words slowly appeared. I was impressed. That was technology, not magic, usually only reserved for security level 10 Top Secret documents.

"Edwardo Alvarez Jr.," Gordon read aloud from the paper. "Mindy Jennings, Jessica Taylor, Richard Anderson, George Renault, Father Michael Xavier Donaher." He looked at us, patiently sitting and listening. "A private investigator, a martial artist, a telepath, a wizard, a weapons expert and a priest."

"That's a good mix. Nicely balanced." He paused. "My condolences about Raul Horta. He was a good agent."

"Thanks," I said, crossing my legs at the knees. "Come on, chief, the only reason we're not out there searching for him is the priority summons. Just tell us what's happening, so we can get on with it."

Horace seemed to appreciate the bluntness. "At approximately 0600 Tuesday morning, just twenty hours ago, a dense fog formed at sea, about 100 miles outside New York. Normal shipping operations were seriously disrupted and a state of emergency declared."

We waited patiently as a three dimensional map appeared floating in the air behind him. A weird fog at sea was nothing for us to get excited about, there must be more. The map showed the greater eastern seaboard of America with a rather large swirling airmass about fifty miles off the coast of New York state, stretching from Mystic, Connecticut to Perth

Amboy, New Jersey, with Manhattan right in the middle. Ominous.

His head haloed by the map, Gordon went on, "As you can see it is getting closer, fast. And since the appearance of the cloud, there has been an unprecedented surge of paranormal activity across the country. Mass attacks of werewolves in Los Angeles, vampires in New Orleans, ghouls in Miami, dragons in Chicago, gargoyles in Boston and countless single encounters of everything from ancient astronauts to zombies. Apparently, its an all out attack on Bureau 13 agents, aided and abetted by every nutcase group and organization of evil that we know of and maybe a few that we don't."

He rolled a hand. "The New American Thugee Cult, The Sixth Reich, the Project, Brotherhood of Darkness, you name it."

This we had already suspected from our own troubles in getting here. It was, however, disheartening to know the fighting was pandemic. Whoever the enemy was, they knew alarming amounts of information about our supposedly supersecret organization.

"In our effort to maintain the peace and protect American citizens, the Bureau has been placed in dire jeopardy of exposure," Gordon said grimly. "As this is obviously a coordinated effort, we do not consider it a coincidence that the cloud is heading for our New York headquarters."

We perked up our ears at that.

"So this is our main HQ?" Mindy asked eagerly.

The chief scowled. "That's Need-To-Know information only, Miss. Let's just say this is one of the Bureau headquarters and leave it at that."

"Any details on the cloud available yet?" I inquired, changing the subject away from the breach of etiquette.

He nodded. "Lots. None of them good. Satellite photos

show the area of the fog is some sixty miles in diameter, steadily growing and will reach land in 36 hours. Radar stops dead at the edge of the cloud. As does sonar, CAT scan, X-rays, radio waves, lasers and masers. Some of the fog was trapped in a jar, but it defies chemical analyses. Kirlian photos show the cloud to have a solid black aura, laced with green."

Evil and magic. Swell.

Turning the page over, words faded away and more replaced them. That was a new trick.

"Scout ships were sent in to investigate and never came out again. They are presumed sunk. An AWAK reconnaissance plane was sent in. It disappeared. Next, an armored jet fighter tried for a penetration and vanished. As did a Blackbird stealth bomber. A submarine nosed in close and was heard of no more. So the Navy tried a stealth sub, one of the best we have, same thing. NASA even dropped an unmanned probe, to the same result. When anything vanishes from normal vision within the cloud, or crosses that line of effect—" Gordon snapped his fingers. "That's it. You're gone."

"Maybe just rendered temporally inert," Richard suggested, leaning forward in his chair.

"We thought of a time status and had our people run a chronometric density test."

"The result?" Jessica prompted.

"Reports show a perfectly normal time flow."

I was surprised. So far, it was the first normal thing about this cloud. At least it wasn't an invasion of dinosaurs from the past. But then again, maybe it was. Time is a funny thing.

"Sir, has the Bermuda Triangle moved?" George asked.

"We checked that. No."

"At this point, I would assume the military got tough," Father Donaher remarked, reclining in his seat. "And decided to have a quote, incident, end quote."

"Affirmative. SAC was consulted and tried high altitude bombing. No go. They even attempted an air burst using a state-of-the-art multiple ton blockbuster thermite bomb, hoping to disperse the cloud. Then a gas vapor bomb was tried. Both useless. Alerting NORAD, an ultra-fast, stealth missile was launched. It went into the cloud, and that was that. No explosion, no heat flash, no . . . nothing."

Heroically, I refrained from mentioning the double negative as this was more important than proper grammar. This cloud was really something.

"Naval gun fire? Torpedoes? Rail Guns?" George queried hopefully, his voice plainly stating that military ordinance could not possibly fail to solve the problem.

"Ditto," Gordon said, resting a hand on the pistol in his belt holster. "After trying everything they could think of, the Pentagon finally reported to the president, who immediately alerted us. But of course, we already knew about the problem."

"What about nukes?" I asked, not really sure I wanted to hear the answer. But thankfully, the chief said those were being saved as an absolute last resort.

Politely, Richard raised a finger. "How much of this is hearsay and how much confirmed from official sources?"

"Its the truth. Straight from the portrait of Washington."

Good enough for me.

"What have we tried so far?" I asked, meaning the Bureau, not America. Our techs had a lot of stuff the Pentagon would hemorrhage over if they knew it existed.

"Divination, telepathy, and magical probes. We even tried talking to the local fish. But from flounders to whales, they want nothing to do with the cloud. Scares them silly. Our best telepaths can't even get a glimpse of the cloud, much less see

JUDGMENT NIGHT

inside. However, for a brief second, our top mage managed to use her crystal ball and penetrate the cloud to see an island in the middle of the fog bank."

"An island," Mindy mused thoughtfully.

"Or at least a land mass of some kind," Gordon corrected.

"Has anybody tried www.mysteriousisland.com?" Richard asked.

Mages! Sheesh.

Crossing her slim legs, Jessica asked. "Any history, or legend, of an island in the area?"

"No."

I had a feeling he had gone over this material many times before and was simply waiting for us to review the data and reach the appropriate foregone conclusion.

"How big an island?"

"Not very, only about five miles wide."

That left over thirty miles of fog for protection. A lot of things could happen in thirty miles.

"Has the mage been able to get any additional information on the island?" Donaher asked.

"Can't."

"Why?"

"Dead."

"How?"

"Brain blasted."

Brief, but to the point. Hoo boy.

Clearing his throat, Gordon pulled a silvery envelope from inside his fatigue jacket, broke the seal and lifted a single sheet of paper from inside. It was covered with official looking seals and multiple ribbons.

'Here it comes,' I thought and Jessica shushed me.

"Your mission is to reach the island, evaluate the situation and deal with it accordingly," Gordon formally read. The paper then burst into ash and was gone.

"That's it?" I asked confused.

"Yes."

That was rather vague and I openly said so. The chief agreed, but said it was the best the Council could do with the limited information at hand. The Council? Who the hell was the council? I made a mental note to check into that when we got back.

"You have roughly 36 hours before that cloud reaches land. So give yourselves time to depart. Because in 35 hours, 30 minutes, the missiles fly."

Missiles meant the Pentagon, so we didn't have to ask what kind. Atomic, nuclear, thermonuclear, was there really a difference? Not when you're standing on Ground Zero.

"Faith, and just how do we reach this wee island?" Father Donaher asked, going Irish on us. "Are we to swim?"

Not amused, Gordon grunted. "Prof. Robertson, in cooperation with Naval Intelligence and SAC, has designed a special plane that they believe should get through the mist intact."

"The operational word here beings hould,'" Jessica noted, with a sour expression.

Reluctantly, our chief agreed that was correct.

"Why us?" Mindy interjected, crossing her arms. "Convenient, or expendable?"

Ah, Ms. Tact strikes again.

Gordon turned red. "None of my goddamn people are expendable," he snapped. "I chose your team, because you're the best we have! The absolute best! Had it been necessary, we would have flown you clowns in from Tasmania!"

That was nice to hear, until I realized that in case of trouble there was nobody better to come and rescue our butts. Bummer.

JUDGMENT NIGHT

"Mission limitations?" I asked, already starting to list possible ways to get around them.

"None," the man sighed, and for a second he looked bone weary. I wondered for how long he had been awake and busy working. Was that cup of coffee by his side number two, or two hundred?

"The Bureau has been given presidential authorization for us to run amuck. You can terminate with extreme prejudice anybody encountered, buy them off with the national treasury, offer political asylum, or negotiate a treaty. Whatever is necessary. Just don't do anything stupid. Muck-up, you'll have to answer to me for it. Personally."

Now that was a threat we respected.

"What about military equipment?" Donaher asked, tilting his head. "Additional weapons? In case of trouble, I'll want more than my trusty snub nose .32 police special."

"Your team has been given carte blanche, full and total access to the Bureau's armory. That includes SWAT, RECON and the Experimental weapon sections."

At this news, George took on a feral expression and I wondered if we would have to tranquilize the boy to get any work done.

Impatiently, Gordon glanced at his wrist and a watch appeared. "You are scheduled to leave within the hour. There's an emergency transport tube located in the armory that will take you directly to the Hudson Bay loading dock. There, you'll find a sea plane waiting. An unmarked DC-3. Pilot's name is Hassan. Lt. Captain Abduhl Benny Hassan. Average height, black hair, dark skin. Identification code: Raincloud."

Or at least that's what it sounded like he said as the last syllable of the word was cut off by a howling siren. A wave of icy cold swept over the room, frost appearing on the walls, and instinctively we leapt to our feet, reaching for weapons not there. The siren dropped in volume, but the bitter cold stayed.

"Report," Gordon said into his wristwatch.

"We are under attack," replied a tiny voice from the glowing instrument. "Large, winged creature is on the roof attempting to claw its way through. Kirlian scanners indicate a solid black aura, laced with purple and gray. Two dead."

"Raise magic shields," the chief said as calmly as ordering tea.

"Pentagram up and holding. But not for long, sir."

Faintly in the background, we could hear gunfire, explosions, the crash of lightning and a loud animal roar. Sounded worse than our fandango at the lake if that was possible.

"Close the steel shutters, activate intruder defensives, alert the camera crew and prime the stun cannon. Whatever it is, we want it alive for questioning! I'm on the way." In a bound, he left the stage, but we blocked his way in the aisle.

"Orders, sir?" I asked, snapping off a salute.

"You already have 'em," Horace growled, checking the power magazine in his laser pistol. "Now get out of here. You have a plane to catch. We'll handle this."

The building chose that moment to give a shudder as if something tremendous in size had slammed into the structure. It reminded me of the attack at our cabin and I opened my mouth to speak.

"We know about the Catskill incident," Gordon bellowed, sprinting for the door. "Now get going!"

So go we did, but we didn't have to like it.

FIVE

Dashing into the hallway, Gordon went to the right, and we went to the left. The siren was soon replaced by a soothing voice telling specific people where to go and what to do.

As we ran for the elevator bank at the end of the hall, I noticed every doorway was now closed with a steel grill that slid out of the thick walls. This place must have cost a fortune to build. Luckily the Bureau was rolling in funds. With so many wizards on the staff, a bit of lead-to-gold was no big bother. Of course, we wisely kept it low key so as not to totally disrupt the world's economy.

Reaching the elevator, we passed on by and took the stairs. If any of my people had been dumb enough to even try the elevator, I would have personally shot them dead to save the embarrassment of having to take Agent 101 over again.

"Just had an idea," Richard said, as we danced down the steps in a group. "Let's solidify our weapons."

"Meaning what exactly?" Jessica asked, suspiciously.

Didn't blame her reticence. We had all heard his great ideas before, and carried the scars to prove it.

He smiled. "Nothing serious. But rather than George carrying a .45 pistol, Ed a .357 and Donaher a .32, they each take 10mm automatics, so in case of an emergency we can pool our ammunition."

"Ten millimeter?" Jessica asked puzzled. "I thought nine was state-of-the-art."

George fought back a laugh. "Not anymore."

"Unified weapons sounds good," I said, trying to keep

pace. "Hate to leave the old girl behind, but in this particular instance, it makes sense."

Not missing a step, Mindy turned and arched an eyebrow at me. "The old girl?" she repeated.

"Faith, lass, be taking no insult from the remark," Donaher said, rallying to my defense. "We laddies use the female possessive on all things of beauty; sunrises, ocean liners, spaceships, guns, pizza, the superbowl . . ."

"I get the picture," she growled. "And quit while you're ahead."

At the proper level, we hit the doors running and entered the Bureau armory. I assumed that Gordon had tuned the security system to our ID cards for we made it inside the room alive.

As the armored doors cycled closed, despite our severe time limitation we paused to catch our breath. The place was staggering in size. Colossal! It strongly resembled an ordinary warehouse, with a steel girder roof, cinderblock walls and lack of internal divisions. The armory was just a huge room with acres upon acres filled with weapons. Thousands of racks and tables and crates and boxes of weapons. Swords, guns, pistols, rifles, suits of armor, shields, lances, knives, bazookas, machine guns. Sitting on the floor, hanging from the ceiling or standing on clusters. There was even a World War II Tiger tank and a NASA space shuttle in dry dock. It was a military supermarket! I think George had an orgasm. Felt kind of flushed myself.

Quickly, the team spread out, each to their own interests. But I clapped my hands for their attention.

"The basics first," I ordered brusquely. "George, grab that hand cart and let's load up."

There were premade haversacks of camping supplies: tents, sleeping bags, cooking utensils, survival tools, canteens, compasses, knives, entrenching tools, waterproof matches, steel and flint, flashlights with wind-up generators in the handle, toilet tissue, all-purpose soap, tooth brushes and such. We took one for every member of the party, then Donaher added an extra for the pilot. Smart man.

A red cross on a white circle indicated first-aid packs. We even located some field surgery kits. Along with a couple of packs of magical healing supplies, cloth, pills and potions of a quality that made our mage dance with joy. We took two of each.

Under a tarpaulin, we found cases of MRE packs, prepared and dehydrated food, dried meat, fruit rolls, canned bread, powdered milk, vitamin pills and fortified high energy snack bars, both vanilla and dark chocolate with almonds.

"Don't forget water," Jessica advised, dragging a sack of mess kits over to the heavily laden cart.

George snorted and pointed. "Four ten gallon cans, one fifty gallon drum, water purification tablets and a small distillation unit."

"How the hell are we going to carry that load?" Richard demanded from behind a stack of mylar blankets.

"A second cart," Father Donaher announced, pushing another wheeled platform beside the first.

Two sets of scuba gear and some mountain climbing equipment were added to the pile. The gang started to take a short breather when the building shook to its very foundations and we returned to work. Binoculars, infrared night scopes, two inflatable rafts and shark repellant. Lord, how much of this stuff were we going to need and what critical equipment were we forgetting to bring along?

Moving to a wall rack holding combat fatigues, Mindy ripped open her blouse. The contrast of the white sports bra against her dark skin was a lovely sight, but I stopped her anyway.

"Don't waste time," I shouted. "We'll change on the plane. Just grab the correct size!"

As this was almost definitely a combat mission, not a simple seek-and-isolate, we started with army boots that had steel plates in the soles, toes and heels. A person could kick their way through a wall with these babies. Following Gordon's example, we appropriated military jumpsuits of bullet resistant cloth. Cushioned steel helmets were added to the growing collection, along with light cloth caps. It was George who tossed in socks, underwear and T-shirts, god bless him.

At last, the team turned its attention to weapons. Rushing to a nearby rack, Father Donaher grabbed a pump action 12 gauge shotgun and two loaded banderoles of shells. Moving quick, I slapped the ammo bands out of his hands.

"Stop thinking small," I said, grabbing a carton of shells and tossed them to him. "We take a case, or don't even bother."

A grin exploded on his face. "Faith, its Christmas!"

"Hanukkah!" somebody corrected from behind a stack of wooden crates containing Claymore mines.

"My birthday!"

"K-Mart!"

We ignored that last remark.

A table full of Bureau wristwatches was cleaned in a second, with everybody taking spare batteries. Bypassing the full suits of medieval armor and shields, Mindy grabbed a brace of crossbows and two quivers of arrows. One standard, the other marked as Bureau Specials.

"Bracelets!" Richard cried in joy, displaying a small wooden box. The inside was lined with velvet on which rested six rather plain copper bands.

"Yeah?" I grunted, slinging a satchel charge of C4 over my

shoulder. Damn thing must weigh 30 pounds.

He seemed surprised at my lack of understanding. "I'll explain later, but these are wonderful! Fabulous!"

"Great. Take all of them you find."

"I will!"

As for sidearms, I chose Heckler Koch 10mm automatic pistols, holding 15 rounds with combat triggers and ambidextrous grips. I decided five cases of mixed bullets was enough, then got smart and added a case of spare clips. I searched for silencers, but didn't find any for this type weapon, until I moved a carton of homogenized oil and there they were. They were acoustical, not material silencers, so I only took ten, along with a box of belts and holsters.

A third cart had been allocated and the pile of loot grew constantly. Ten cases of assorted grenades, a flare gun and a case of flares, two combo backpacks of LAW and HAFLA rockets, a mixed case of tear gas, BZ gas, vomit gas and garlic vapor canisters, a box of wire garrotes and a bundle of switchblades. We also took a crate of brand new Uzi 10mm submachine guns, as they accepted the same caliber ammunition as our pistols. The laser-guided Thompson machine guns were nice, but they only fired .22 rounds, meant to wound, not kill. Somebody had added a crate of M16/M79 combination rifles, along with cases of ammo and shells. I let them stay. The Kevlar vests we passed over, as our own body armor was better, lighter and we were already wearing the stuff. I only hoped somebody brought along deodorant as this might be a long campaign.

There was a rack of MR1 Delta Force rifles, and I plugged the cable from the stock into the goggles. The lenses glowed into life and now I saw a crosshair floating in the air before me, and it moved to wherever the barrel of the MR1 was pointed. Nice for shooting around corners, but the battery pack weighed a ton and those damn computerized helmets chafed like a bastard, so I decided to leave it behind.

At last, I found the Special Weapons cabinet I had been looking for and tore the doors open. Inside were four shelves, three of them empty. Damn. So much for the laser pistols and lightning wands. But there was still good stuff remaining. Snatching a box of Experimental class derringers, I also grabbed a leather briefcase tagged with the symbol for radiation. Pausing, I doublechecked to make doubly sure the instruction book was still attached to the handle/trigger.

"What about this flamethrower?" Mindy asked, pointing to the backpack canister, hose and spray rod assembly.

"Is it charged?" George asked, fumbling with the lock on a wire enclosed area.

She kicked it and got an answering slosh. "Yep."

With a yank, George got the wire gate open and was inside. "Take it. We can always use the thing to toast weenies."

"Check!"

"Found the weenies!" somebody added gaily.

Sighing, I said goodbye to the Wichataw Thunderbolt pistol laying in plain sight on a nearby table. The single shot, bolt action, pistol fired a .569 Magnum Express round that could blow the head off an elephant. But the stupid thing weighed ten pounds and each bullet was an additional pound. Besides, I had never heard of anybody managing to hit their target because of the weapons incredible recoil. I decided to stick to the 10mm and a few grenades.

Wise move, sent Jessica, busy in a cabinet.

Triumphantly, George stepped out of the wire cage wearing a bulky backpack, supported by padded shoulder hooks, chest straps and a belt about the waist. Whatever it was, must be pretty heavy. An enclosed metal belt extended from the top and curved down to enter the stock of a stubby machine gun with an oversized maw. From the grin on his face, I wondered if the weapon launched atomic missiles, or a disintegrator beam.

Father Donaher returned carrying an arm load of crosses, Holy Water pistols, wooden stakes and a Bureau standard issue shoulder bag that I knew held garlic powder, communion wafers, a Bible, wooden stakes and a scapula.

Jess appeared toting a Quija board, Tarot cards, candles, a crystal pyramid, a bolt-action taser rifle and a box of Bureau sunglasses. Then and there, I decided to marry the woman.

I added a stack of gold and silver coins and we were ready.

Under Richard's adroit direction, the team started securing everything into position with canvas and rope, making damn sure the wheels were free to turn. Having an ex-Boy Scout in the group sometimes came in handy.

"That everything?" Mindy asked, finishing off a clove hitch knot.

George jerked a thumb towards the wire cage. "There's still a Dragon missile system and a semi-portable, 40mm, Vulcan mini-gun in there."

"Why didn't you take them?" Richard asked surprised.

"The Dragon is too heavy and takes a trained four man crew two hours to assemble," George explained. "And the Vulcan can empty a truck full of shells in less than a minute. Its a weapon for established ground fortifications, not field units."

The mage nodded, as if understanding the military babble.

"There's also an Atchisson, but I figured Michael would already have one."

The father straightened with a groan. "What is it?"

"An assault rifle system that fires 12 gauge shotgun shells," George said impatiently. "ROF, 800."

"ROF, rate of fire," the priest translated. "Eight hundred shotgun shells a minute? Can it handle stun bags?"

"Of course."

"Sounds mighty useful. Is there room on the cart?"

"No," Richard stated, tucking in a flap.

Donaher pouted, then grinned. "Well, let's get another cart!"

The building shook again just then and the lights dimmed, returned, then died away completely leaving us in pitch black.

"Time to go," I announced, clicking on a flashlight. The brilliant white beam illuminating half the team and only a chunk of the piled supplies. More flashlights came to life brightening the darkness. On the floor, a series of pale yellow arrows flickered into life indicating the direction of the elevator.

"And how do we find the transport tube," Mindy asked, coming closer. As she spoke those words, the arrows changed direction and pointed towards a different wall.

"Come on," I said glancing at my new watch. "The plane leaves in fifteen minutes. Let's skidaddle."

Richard had done a fine job of balancing the loads on the carts, and it was relatively easy for us to push the wheeled mountains along the path of the arrows. After about a hundred feet, they ended at a blank cinder block wall. Searching about, Jess found a card slot in the wall and tried inserting her FBI card. There was a hum, a click and a section of the wall disengaged and swung away on hidden hinges.

Inside was a well-lit cubicle of burnished metal, just barely large enough to take us and the piles of stuff. We had to hoist Mindy on top of a cart to make room, but the gang made it inside and I pushed the sole button on the wall. The doors closed with a soft hush and locked tight.

A steady rumble started below us and then suddenly we

were floating in the air, the floor of the lift inches below our feet. There was an odd feeling in my stomach, and George looked as if he might toss lunch. Stretching an arm, Richard touched him on the head and the fat man visibly calmed, color returning to his cheeks.

"Thanks," he croaked.

"No problem," the mage smiled.

The rushing, falling, sensation continued and after a minute our feet returned to the floor in time for it to tilt slightly on an angle. Ugh. Now we were going sideways.

"Hey, this must be a pneumatic tube," Richard exclaimed with a broad grin.

"Wow! Neat!" Mindy added, obviously enjoying the ride.

"Swell," I contributed, meaning every word.

"Ed, I just realized something," Donaher said, sounding very serious.

I swallowed lunch and focused my eyes on him. "What?"

"At present, we don't have a single functional weapon or defense prepared. Better do something about that."

Words of wisdom, indeed. In frantic haste, the 10mm pistols were retrieved and loaded. As we thumbed off safeties, Richard pulled a long, curved knife from out of the air. Our swift journey continued, and just as I was beginning to swear off food forever, the transport leveled, then slowed and finally started to rise upward like a proper elevator. Thank god. After a minute, the cubicle came to a gentle stop, the door separated and we stumbled into a dank, smelly garage, a horde of very startled rats scampering for safety away from the harsh light of the transport.

Fanning out in a standard pattern, we did a fast sweep of the place to secure the perimeter. It was clean, or rather the dump contained nothing more dangerous than rabid rats, broken glass and old copies of the New York Post.

Wiping the dirt off a window, I saw that the garage was situated on the waterfront, a battered wooden dock directly in front. Moored at the pylons, was an ordinary DC-3, twin prop, sea plane. Lounging by her side, smoking a cigarette, was a dark skinned man of average height and black hair. He was dressed in tan slacks, deck shoes and a white shirt that had been painted on by a close friend.

"Nice," Mindy purred in frank appraisal.

"Yeah," George agreed happily. "The DC-3 is a classic."

Donaher and I exchanged glances and sighed. Sometimes, our Mr. Renault was a bit of a muttonhead.

There were four doors leading from the place. Three were bricked closed, the fourth lined with steel plating and bolted shut. Trust Gordon to think of everything. Undoing the lock, the garage door swung noiselessly aside and we moved to the loading platform. An inclined cement ramp led to the dock and we forcibly pushed, pulled, and dragged our semi-portable department store of survival supplies to the waiting airship.

In the distance, the horizon was a featureless expanse of gray fog. But it behooved nobody to mention that.

As we approached the plane, the pilot ambled towards us, a hand dangerously near a holstered Wesley .44 revolver that I hadn't noticed before.

"Ah, raincloud," I said hopefully.

At that, the fellow relaxed and offered his hand. We shook. "Mr. Alvarez? Captain Hassan, awaiting your orders."

"Howdy-do. Open the cargo hatch, and let's boogie."

"Fair enough."

Glancing at the team, he started for the front of the plane when he saw Mindy and gasped. "Good lord miss, are you okay?" he asked in concern.

Puzzled, Mindy looked at the guy as if he was crazy, but then noticed her ripped shirt and the amount of skin showing. He probably thought she had been saved from a fate worse than death. The white, seamless, sports bra only served to accentuate her trim figure.

"Yeah, I'm fine. Thanks. Did it myself." Openly, she looked over the man's square jaw, piercing black eyes and muscular build. Then she dimpled in a manner that almost made me jealous.

"But your concern is most appreciated," Mindy smiled daintily.

He stepped closer. "My pleasure."

She stepped closer. "That can be arranged. Jennings."

The man blinked. "What?"

"Mindy Jennings."

A toothy smile. "Abduhl Benny Hassan."

"Hump later, work now," I said from the end of the dock heaving a box of grenades towards them.

Mindy turned in time to catch the box and carried it inside the plane. The pilot went off to the cockpit and we got to work. Briefly, I wondered how she did things like that? Hear the air currents moving around the box, or what?

"Yes," Jessica said, loosening a knot.

"Stop reading my mind," I snarled.

"Old habit," she replied casually. "And I accept your earlier proposal of marriage."

I dropped a crate of canned goods on my foot. "Now wait a damn minute . . ."

"Alert!" Donaher shouted, his HK 10mm pistol doing a steady pattern of barking discharges. "Incoming, three o'clock!"

Everybody turned to the right with a weapon in hand. I did also, but then nearly dropped mine. The water tower on top of the garage had broken free and was presently climbing down off the building to walk our way.

"A water tower?" Jessica squeaked. "What the hell can that do?"

Richard frowned. "You wanna find out?"

"Ignore the water tower and load the plane!" I commanded in my patented top sergeant voice. "Don't bother to stack the stuff anymore, just sling it in fast." Personally, I hoped nothing broke and blew us out of the water before we even left the dock.

"George?" I barked.

"Ed?" he replied calmly.

"Kill that thing!"

Coolly, the chubby soldier spun about on the balls of his feet, the squat rifle in his hands spitting flame in a stuttering series of soft chugs, nowhere near as loud as his old M60. But the metal pipe legs of the water tank were torn apart in a near continuous series of sharp explosions and it collapsed sideways into an alley. Not satisfied, George kept up the barrage, the discharge of his weapon ripping the structure to pieces until it fell apart in a great gush of water.

"Anything else you want killed?" he asked smugly, the flow of liquid from the tank stretching out towards the dock, but only succeeding in drowning a rat or two.

I thought fast. "My IRS agent."

George took a firing stance. "Name the bastard."

"Hey!" Donaher snapped from the cargo hatch. "Help load the plane, ya bums."

We joined the busy work force. In a matter of minutes, the carts were empty and the hatch closed. Hassan cast off the mooring lines from inside the plane. The huge prop motors started with a growl and we pulled away from the dock, taxiing for takeoff.

In the style of a troop transport, the seats lined the walls, leaving the center clear. Sitting down, I put my feet up on crate of canned goods and breathed a sigh of relief. "Time for a ten minute break."

"Guess again, chief," George contradicted, his face pressed against the glass of a window.

Joining him, I could see half a dozen transparent blue speedboats behind us. Apparently made of ice, the boats were rising from the water of the bay. Steering each craft was a robed figure clutching the wheel with bony blue hands. Checking them with my replacement sunglasses, these guys registered so black that I couldn't even discern details.

"Lock and load, people," I announced, grabbing an assault rifle from a stack and rummaging for ammunition.

"Whatever happened to the good old days of talk first, shoot later?" Richard asked petulantly, sliding a copper bracelet onto his wrist. "When we were more of an investigation unit, than a SWAT team?"

Slamming a clip into my M16, I pulled the bolt. "Its the way of the world, my friend. Some people make garbage, some cart it away."

"Want me to take care of them?" George asked, hefting his bizarre rifle cannon.

I shook my head. "Naw, shouldn't need any heavy artillery to take out a couple of speedboats. Auras are black, but don't look very powerful."

He shrugged. "If you say so."

Forcing the hatch open against the wind, I hooked an arm around a stanchion and let the lead boat have a full clip, putting a line of holes along the craft at the water line. But the vessel neither sank, nor slowed.

"Interesting. Do you think its too late to try diplomacy?"

Mindy asked, extending the tube on a LAW as a preparation for launch.

Before I could answer, she leaned out the hatch and fired. Smoke erupted from the aft end of the tube and a finger of flame stretched from the front to impact directly on a robed figure. In a thunderclap, it disappeared in a ball of rolling flame. But as the smoke cleared, the pilotless boat was still plowing on towards us, steadily increasing in speed.

Both of the wing motors of the DC-3 roared with power and the plane skimmed along the water, hopping from wave crest to wave crest, but never truly becoming airborne.

Father Donaher was praying. Richard and Mindy were head to head conferring. Jessica was sitting crosslegged on the floor, knuckles to her temples. George waited for orders and I thought like crazy while the water boats zoomed ever closer.

"Hassan!" I yelled up the aisle of the plane.

"What?" he answered from the cockpit.

"Take off, now!"

"Can't!"

"Why?"

"Too heavily loaded," Abduhl cried. "I can't get enough speed!"

I moved to the hatch. "Okay, what can we throw out?"

"Wait," Richard cried, blocking my way. "Captain Hassan, would lightening the plane by a couple of hundred pounds be sufficient?"

"Maybe," he relented. "Whacha got in mind?"

Richard scrunched his face in that secret wizard way and nodded. Pulling his wand, the mage got a good grip, muttered something and he floated off the deck into the air. Instantly, the engines increased their noise and the plane left the water rising smoothly into the sky.

JUDGMENT NIGHT

Watching from a window, porthole, or whatever the hell it is they call the thing, I saw the six boats converge on our last position, to collide and violently explode, a geyser of water reaching towards the sky and just missing our tail section.

"Whew," Mindy exhaled, wiping imaginary sweat off her brow. "Close one."

Smiling broadly, Richard agreed. "Safe, at last."

Furious, George turned on them. "Bullshit!" he bellowed, spittle spraying from his mouth. "They found us again! After all the security precautions of headquarters itself. They found us again!"

The mage looked chastised, but Mindy rallied. "Yeah, well—"

George interrupted. "Yeah, well, if it isn't science, magic, psyonics or plain old fashioned tracking. Then what does that leave, eh? What? You damn well know what!"

What remained was something almost too unpleasant to contemplate.

"A traitor?" Father Donaher asked softly, his Irish green eyes round with disbelief.

Jessica dismissed the idea with a haughty hrumph. "There are no traitors in our group," she announced.

"That you know of," George countered grimly.

"I know," Jess said, poking herself in the chest with a finger, the tone of voice daring anybody to challenge her statement.

Graciously, George relented. "Okay, then tell me how. How?"

Unfortunately, that was a question nobody could answer. Yet.

SIX

Breaking the debate, I got the group hustling. We had thirty minutes before entering the cloud and a lot of work to get done. Question & Answer time could come later.

Reluctantly, the team members busied themselves sorting and doing inventory on the equipment. Had to move fast, as Richard was determined to stay afloat wasting power until we thinned down the cargo and tossed enough overboard to guarantee flight. I damn well knew that we couldn't heave anything away after reaching the cloud, because opening a window would probably reduce us to smoking skeletons. Which would seriously hinder our fighting abilities.

The culling went smoothly, with only a few oddball items needing a group vote or an executive override, like the electric wok—which went, and the pocket encyclopedia—which stayed, until I encountered a prize.

"What the hell are these?" I asked, raising the molded metal casting into view. "Silver-plated brass knuckles in case we have to punch a werewolf to death?"

Sheepishly, George replied yes.

I tossed them into the discard pile. "Get real."

Soon enough the group was pared down to six back packs, seven jumpsuits with sidearms and four trunks holding our secondary equipment. Everything else was jettisoned without ceremony. I roughly figured that over a million bucks of stuff fed the fish that day. Good thing we're covert, or Congress would have shit kittens over the waste.

JUDGMENT NIGHT

As Mindy dogged the hatch shut, Richard tentatively rejoined us on the deck, ready for instant flight. But the plane maintained a level keel and he stood in relief.

"Flying while flying is a weird sensation," the mage, said, quickly changing into fatigues. "Sort of like . . . um—"

"Getting drunk while you're stoned?" Jessica offered.

"Close."

"Swimming up a waterfall?" Father Donaher suggested.

"Closer."

George squinted. "Dancing in an earthquake?"

"Bingo!" Richard cried, and shook the man's hand.

I whistled. "Now that is weird."

Sealing the velcro seam on his Army fatigues, Richard wrapped a white silk ascot about his neck and tucked a violet carnation into the stiff lapel of his uniform. Next, he requested the carved wooden box found in the armory and presented it to us with a flourish. We applauded and then asked what the hell the ugly copper bracelets did?

He happily explained. The bracelets were ethereal batteries, a brand new Bureau invention. The slim bands not only held enough matrixal power for a medium grade conjure, but also a kind of molecular circuit printed inside to cast the spell for you. Not just mages and wizards could use one of these, anybody could. Simply don the bracelet and when you thought the activation phrase, the spell would conjure.

In order, the six copper bracelets contained: a Lightning Bolt, Fire Blast, Meld, Invisibility, Flight and Jump Start. The last was our pet name for this healing spell which could snatch you from death's door and put you back on your feet ready, able and totally healed. The limitations were, it could not be done more than twice in your whole lifetime and only worked when you were at the very edge of life. A split second late in activation and you took the big dirt nap. As it says in the Bureau manual, nothing could actually bring the dead back to life. And believe me, Technical Services has really tried.

However, Meld was the real bizarre spell for we had been unaware that anybody had ever gotten the freak conjure to work correctly. In essence, Meld allowed a person to dematerialize and, ghost-like, phase through an object, wall, door, floor. Once you got to the other side, shazam, you were solid flesh again. Limitations were it only lasted for two minutes and god help you if it wore off while you were still inside something. Your molecular structure would then violently intermingle with that of the barrier, each molecule-in-a-molecule tearing itself apart into sub-atomic particles. Such a catastrophe had actually occurred once, but luckily at the nuclear bomb test site in White Sands, New Mexico, so nobody even noticed the blast. Except the Pentagon, and us.

Excluding Father Donaher, everybody got a bracelet. For perfectly understandable reasons, he did not care to have magical items on his person. Even though we only used white magic, the Catholic Church had decreed that magic was, at best, questionable in origin, and the priest disliked to ever go against the dictates of his religion. The team occasionally sneaked a Heal or Invisibility his way, but we kept it to a minimum, and Donaher would rather die than ask. Literally.

Sporting the Invisibility bracelet, I showed the wizard the box full of derringers. A modified version of the Belgium 9, the tiny gun possessed four short barrels and one trigger, which fired every barrel at once. Chambered for .22 rounds, the pocket pistol held: a silver bullet, a wooden bullet, a cold iron and a phosphorus tracer round as an incendiary. Sort of a general, stop-anything barrage. For a power-drained mage it would be a perfect last ditch weapon.

JUDGMENT NIGHT

But more importantly, the pistol did not use gunpowder, or fulminating cotton, or any of the standard munition chemicals as a charge that normally refused to work near a mage. So the derringers would work in the hand of a full charged wizard. Richard demanded to know what was this marvelous substance. Having no idea, I told him it was need-to-know data. He accepted the fib, Jessica bit her tongue and everybody tucked the diminutive weapon into a boot holster designed for the pistol.

Testing the draw on the tiny gun, George glanced at it and his shiny new bracelet. Fire Blast, of course. Nothing subtle about Sgt. Renault.

"Techno-mage," he said with a grin. "I like it."

For some reason, Richard went still at those words.

"Techno-mage," the wizard repeated, slowly straightening. "Technological magic... could it... maybe... yes, that's it!"

The team gathered around, finding seats where we could on the deck and equipment trunks, his tone and stance informing us that the wizard was having a revelation.

"Its really crazy," he said, cracking the knuckles on a hand and pacing within our circle. "But do you know what would happen if, say, somebody magical activated a radar scanner?"

"What?" Jess asked eagerly. "What would it do?"

"Such a construct would indicate the position, hell it would pinpoint the location, of any combined techno-magic devices. Whether they were electrical/alchemy, or chemical/ethereal."

"Like seeks like," Mindy rationalized, her brow furrowed. "How very zen."

"Exactly! And that's a problem."

"Why?" George asked, not sounding very interested. Our jargon bored him as much as his did us.

Donaher slammed his bible shut. "Our Bureau ID cards!"
Now George was as interested as the rest of us.
Richard nodded. "Precisely. Our cards."
"Is such a detection device possible?" I demanded.
"Theoretically. Raul would have known more about such research than me. He was fascinated by obscure and esoteric conjures. Horta was one really weird mage."

A wizard calling another weird? Oh kettle, thou art black.

"Can you do it?" Jessica asked. "Let us find our mysterious enemy?"

"Or jam it?" George added. "So they can't find us?"

"No way. Take a diamond wizard, maybe better."

I blinked. "Better? I thought that was the top."

"That is the general belief," Richard hedged. "But there are those who postulate that once you reach that high a level of proficiency, the wand will resemble anything you want."

Mindy chewed that over. "That means an ultra-powerful wizard might seem be a rank beginner with only a wooden stick?"

"Yep."

George gave a shiver for all of us. What a horrid thought.

But magical radar . . . . Sheesh. Certainly would explain how the enemy has been able to focus their attacks on Bureau agents and find our HQ. The place probably resembled a fireworks display on their screens.

Frowning, Mindy touched my sleeve. "Ed, any chance we might need our cards on the island?"

"None," I stated pulling a lighter from my pocket. With a flick, the tiny flame came alive. "Burn 'em."

We did it in the lavatory and started to flush when I noticed there was no handle. This was a chemical toilet, without access to the outside. Those TechServ folks think of everything.

"This may be what we will be facing on the island, you know," Richard said, as we single filed back to the main compartment. "Combined science/magic."

"Gonna make it tough," George observed practically.

"And strange," Mindy added.

Jessica gave a laugh.

"What's so funny?" Donaher asked.

"Any sufficiently advanced technology is indistinguishable from magic," she said, as if quoting from memory.

"That sounds familiar," I said. "What is it from?"

"A sci-fi writer named Arthur Clarke."

"Yes, I remember it now," Richard said. "Raul used to jokingly add that any sufficient advanced magic is indistinguishable from technology."

"I buy that."

"Have to. You're wearing some."

Just then, the PA system bleeped and Hassan gave us the five minute warning. This was not and never would be a job for people who go slow, hate pressure, or wish to live beyond forty. As we strapped ourselves into the seats, George raised the possibility that the cloud and island were not related. The island might be fugitive good guys trapped by the evil cloud. Or maybe the cloud, although bad, was trying to contain and even greater evil. Pretty heavy thinking for Mr. Renault. I logged both possibilities away and decided to keep an open mind on the matter.

The ride started getting bumpy as we neared the edge of the fog bank. I was forced to remove my sunglasses, as ever time I glanced out the window, I got a stabbing pain from the awful blackness of its aura.

"Almost there," the wall speaker announced cheerfully. "Please refrain from smoking and place seat backs in an upright position. Today's movie will be, 'Lifeboat'."

"In your hat," Mindy growled, hunching low in her seat.

Suddenly, the plane went dark as metal shutters closed over the windows. The glass had been triple thick Plexiglas, built strong enough to resist a rhino charge, but I suppose it never hurt to play it safe.

As the overhead lights brightened to compensate, Donaher frowned. "If the front windshield is the same, then how is Hassan flying? By instrument?"

"Correct," Jessica answered, her eyes closed, hands neatly folded in her lap.

"But with the cloud, how can he be sure of the readings?"

"I don't need to be," the wall speaker replied. "A shipboard computer checks the flight course against a battery of internal navigational devices; gyroscopes, inertial guidance system, gravity plates and the like. Very similar to the way ICBMs stay on target."

His voice changed tone, became less conversational. "We are closing fast. Mark at 200, 150, 100 meters, 50 . . ."

Through my combat boots, I could feel a faint vibration build in the deck. Steadily it increased.

"Here we go," Mindy said, bracing her legs against the seat before her.

"In!" crackled the speaker.

Instantly, there was an awful, ripping, tearing sensation in every fiber of my body, similar to a muscle cramp, only a thousand times worse. My brain swelled within the confines of my head, the bones starting to crack from the pressure. I fell forward, trying to hold my head together, supported only by my safety belt. Violently, the plane bucked and bounced through a thunderstorm that sounded like every storm that had ever existed mixed together. Then the motors died, to be replaced by a steady throbbing noise. Chemical wing jets, I rationalized in some recess of my brain. Fantastically powerful and too damn simple to foul or break.

If we accelerated, or slowed, I had no idea. Struggling with lunch and sanity, I felt older, younger, bigger, smaller. Blood erupted from my nose and I fouled myself. Static electricity snapped and crawled with painful bites over every inch of my flesh. In some horrible fashion, my guts twisted into grotesque new forms, writhing beneath my skin with a life of their own. My senses, mixed in random order and I could smell the bitter artificial light in the plane, hear the rancid clothing on my body, and feel the tangible odors of fear, hatred and courage. Then my equilibrium crumbled, the world spun dizzily round and round—and it started all over again.

This went on for years, building to the pinnacle, then the torture abruptly stopped and we were normal again. Sitting limp in my chair, the steady purr of the jets told me we were still flying. Grudgingly, I was forced to appreciate the effectiveness of the cloud barrier. Any unwanted intruder would be a sitting duck as they danced through that little slice of hell, totally unable to protect themselves. How Captain Hassan had maintained control through that was beyond my understanding. He must be a robot. Or from the planet Krypton.

"Kowabunga," Mindy groaned, only her legs showing from behind the crumbled mass of a seat. "Haven't had a trip that bad since we mixed LSD and uranium at the Duke University lab."

"What happened?" Richard gasped weakly.

"We blew our minds."

George moaned in reply. I moaned back at him. Then we moaned in unison.

"The . . . pilot," Father Donaher croaked, struggling to get loose. "Gotta . . . see . . ."

"He's fine," Jess breathed, wiping vomit from her mouth. "As a precaution, Abduhl turned on the auto-pilot just before we entered."

"Wise move," Richard said, staring motionless at the ceiling.

"That's why I get the big money," croaked the PA system.

In a truly Herculean effort, George lifted himself from the passenger seat, then dropped out of sight with a thump. "See the island yet?" his voice asked from the deck.

"No way, Jose," replied the PA, in one of my least favorite phrases. "We're still in the cloud."

Weakly, Mindy asked, "But we're through the worst of it?"

"Hell, no! The automatic defensive systems on this ship are going crazy! I have a dozen gauges in the red and we're on emergency power."

"Recommendations?" I requested.

"Prayer," came the curt reply. "The ship does the rest of the fighting for us from here onward. Either it succeeds, or we die."

Prudently, I let the gang rest for a few minutes and then started cleaning operations. Sponging our fatigues off and using towels to mop up the worst of the mess on the deck. I knew that Richard could cast a spell that would make us and the place spotless. But I had no intention of having my only mage waste precious energy on housekeeping in the midst of a fight.

Because this was war. Machine against nature in a battle royale. A struggle of wits between the gang at Technical Services and whatever was on the island. I don't know about the rest of the group, but I hated this passive acceptance. I would have felt enormously better if there was someway to help Captain Hassan. Even a flock of flying monsters would at least give us something to do.

JUDGMENT NIGHT

"Alert!" barked the wall speaker. "There's some leakage coming through!"

Mindy was on her feet, sword drawn. "What does that mean?" she demanded. But there was no answer and none of us felt inclined to knock on the closed door that led to the cockpit.

"Conference!" I called, and the gang gathered round. "Okay, if the first layer of the cloud attacks the people, then the next should attack the vehicle."

"Sounds reasonable," Donaher said. "What can we expect?"

"Eddy currents in the metal?" George suggested.

I snorted. "For what purpose?"

"Enough of them would induce sufficient heat to melt the plane."

"Too damn fancy," Mindy retorted, adjusting her grip on the sword. "It would only work on things made of conductive metals. A wooden rowboat, or stealth missile would get right through."

"Agreed," Jess said, sweeping back her hair. "The longer we're in the cloud, the greater the danger, so it will probably be something to slow us down." She then repeated the words, as her breath was visible mist.

"Cold. How simple," Richard noted, buttoning up his uniform.

"Depends upon how cold it gets," Donaher observed, pulling spare blankets out of seat locker.

Rapidly the atmosphere became cool, chilly, uncomfortable, freezing. Quartz heaters built into the hull started to glow, trying to relieve the bitter cold, but soon we were wearing every piece of our clothing and gathered into a huddle, the outer members draping blankets round themselves.

"W-what b-bout, H-hassan?" George stammered past chattering teeth.

"L-lectric flyingsuit," Jessica mumbled, from with her wool cocoon.

"And t-the engines?"

Mindy lowered a blanket and cocked an ear. "S-sound f-fine to me."

A loud crack made us jump. It was followed by another, and then a regular pounding came from the outside. Hail the size of baseballs, the pilot informed us briefly. Now I understood why this craft was so heavy. Must be armor plated.

"Cold to make you hold still, then hail to pound holes through you and the hull," George said shivering. "Death by drowning. Primitive, but clever."

"Useless against this plane," Donaher boasted.

The muscles in my shoulders relaxed a bit with the knowledge that the statement was true. We had a good inch of military grade, steel alloy protecting us from the ravages of the cloud.

Then the left wall near the camping supplies exploded and the plane jerked as a piece of hail punched its way through. With a screaming whistle, wisps of the fog entered the compartment. The huddle broke fast. I grabbed a blanket to stuff in the hole, but Donaher stood and sprayed the ragged puncture with the flamethrower, the chemical fire annihilating every trace of the vile fumes.

"Saints above, get a blessed patch!" the priest shouted over the roaring stream, the light of the flamethrower turning the interior of the plane blood red.

Quickly, Mindy used her sword to carve a metal square from the steel lining of a seat and Richard levitated it into position on the hull under the stream of flame. Took us only a minute to weld the patch down with a small acetylene torch and Donaher cut the big weapon off. The place stunk horribly of jellied gasoline fumes, but we were alive and I made a note to put the good Father in for a raise.

"That was almost too easy," Richard said suspiciously, brushing some frost off his carnation. It was pink now.

"However, it is warmer," Jessica noted positively.

True enough. The plane was nowhere near as cold.

"Heat is next," George deduced, loosening the front of his khaki jumpsuit. "Logical. Make the weak faint, set fire to wood, maybe even explode our fuel supplies."

Doffing the parka over her rain coat, Mindy snorted. "Thank you, Sister Mary Sunshine."

Soon the temperature was quite comfortable. But the heat built and we realized George had been correct and heat was the next phase. Steadily, it rose from balmy, to toasty, past warm, through uncomfortable and settled in for keeps at hot. We stripped to our underwear, sweat pouring off our glistening bodies. A small box bolted to the ceiling blew cool air into the cabin, and we used half our water supply splashing each other. There was quite a bit of flesh showing, and not all of it attractive. Standing on a haversack to protect my naked feet from the scalding deck, I was down to boxer shorts and shoulder holster, with the boxer shorts going next, but the temperature thankfully held at medium broil. It was pretty bad, but a summer picnic in comparison to the initial boundary effect.

"Is this the best they can do?" George scoffed, tying a camouflage bandana about his head. In only briefs and boots, you could see the hard muscle beneath the flab on the man.

"What a bunch of amateurs," Jess agreed, sloshing some water from a canteen over her trim figure. "No hard radiation, or ultra-sonics. Reality hasn't altered, and nothing polymorphed."

Damp with moisture, her bra and panties were becoming

transparent. Suddenly, I had to face the outer wall and think about baseball, no, doing my taxes, professional golf!

"Remember, this is not the brunt of the attack," stated the stark naked Richard, skinny arms folded across his perfectly tanned chest. He was displaying some curious tattoos in very odd places, and we struggled to keep from directly staring. "Only some minor leakage past our material and magical shields."

Father Donaher nodded. In only briefs and rosary, his great hairy form dripped sweat. "True enough. In an open ship, we would all be dead by now. But so far, this has been a cake walk."

As if on cue, every primed weapon we had discharged.

Bullets flew everywhere, the shotgun blew a seat to shreds, and the flamethrower incinerated the sleeping bags. Ricochets rattled off the metal walls, striking Mindy in the arm and grazed me in the chest, the force of the slug knocked me flat. No serious damage was done to anything important though, as neither the LAW rockets, the satchel charge, or my briefcase had been armed yet.

"Thank god," Jessica said, and Father Donaher did.

With Richard's assistance, Mindy and I were healed in no time, and settled down to wait for new developments. Slowly, the temperature cooled to a reasonable level and we gratefully donned our body armor and fatigues. Being naked can be lots of fun, but not in battle.

In time, the noise of the jets eased in volume and the throbbing power of the propeller engines replaced their smooth humming. Quiet reigned for awhile, when the shutters on the windows raised and security door to the cockpit flew open. There stood a bedraggled Captain Hassan, showing us exactly how many teeth he had and their excellent condition.

"We're through!" he cried joyously.

JUDGMENT NIGHT

The team didn't cheer, we ran to the windows. There was a minor traffic jam of bodies, so I claimed executive privilege and went to join our pilot at the front of the plane.

The cockpit possessed twice as many controls as a plane of this size should have, a lot of them unfamiliar to me. The chart locker was blackened by fire, the co-pilot's seat was gone—ripped from the deck apparently and there were numerous spent .45 shells littering the floor. Obviously, the good captain had seen a bit of action himself. But more importantly there was a beautifully undamaged windshield which gave me a panoramic view of our goal, the island.

Below us was a dirty sea, that appeared more polluted than possible, above and to our sides was that damn swirling cloud sealing out the world. But directly before us, was a smooth cliff of tan stone which rose from the churning water to enter the deadly fog high overhead. As far as I could see, there were no beaches, coves, or bays where we might land. Nor any caves, fissures, or ledges on the cliff that even suggested climbing might produce results.

Keeping one hand on the wheel, Hassan tilted his cap and looked at me. "Suggestions?"

"Circle around till we see a beach, or bay where we can land. If we don't find a place, well, that's why they gave us a sea plane. We'll park on the water, taxi up the cliff and moor ourselves with pitons and rope."

"Then what?"

"Beats me. But we'll think of something."

The navy pilot curled a lip. "I can do better than that."

"What do you mean?"

"Watch," he said flipping a switch and pressing a few buttons on the dashboard.

Amid the complex array of controls, a section of the broad

separated and a video screen lifted into view. Sluggishly, the screen lit up with a vector graphic of the island. The glowing green outline showed the landmass to be a near perfect circle, but the southern tip was cut flat by a small beach and cove. No details of the interior were discernible, but I was still damn impressed.

"This is great!" I complemented, patting him on the shoulder. "What is it? Some sort of laser scanner? A relay from a NSA Keyhole satellite in low orbit?""

"Better," he replied proudly. "A special device built by your own Technical Services. It combines science and magic into a sort of super-radar."

I think my eyeballs momentarily left my head before I was able to move and slap the machine off. "Jesus Christ! Didn't you listen to our early conversation?"

Hassan stared at me blankly. "Not all the time, no. I had work to do. Why, something wrong?"

"Battle stations!" I cried dashing into the aft compartment searching for the parachutes. But I was still in the short service corridor that separated the two sections when I was nearly deafened by a terrible silence.

"What the hell happened?" Mindy demanded from the aft compartment, her sword at the ready.

"Engines died," Hassan announced, busy flipping switches and adjusting dials.

Bitterly, I cursed the enemy for their efficiency. "Richard, fix'em!"

Wordless, the wizard nodded and rose from his seat. But he was back in seconds with a strange expression on his face. "Fix what?" the mage asked, his voice cracking like a nervous schoolboy.

I grabbed his jacket in a fist. "Explain."

"There's only black smoking craters where the engines used to be on the wings." He paused. "Rimmed with teeth marks."

Hoo boy.

"We're going in!" Hassan shouted, the words echoing over the PA. "Prepare for a crash!"

The deck tilted and the plane banked. I lost my footing and flew off into a jumble of noise and pain. Trying to stand, I hit my head on something and lost consciousness. My last vague thought was a valiant try to shout, "Aim for the beach!"

SEVEN

Swimming through a warm sea of blackest ink, I slowly came awake with somebody tugging at my clothes. Summoning what strength I could muster, I rammed a fist at the dimly seen figure. Somehow, they dodged the expert attack, so I brought my knee up to crush testicles and only succeeded in smacking myself in the jaw. Ow. As my vision focused, I found myself sitting on one of our equipment trunks on a sandy beach, the booming surf spraying me with a mist of salt water.

"Yo," I said to the blur.

"Hi," Mindy said, offering a canteen. "You always wake up this way?"

"Always," I replied after drinking deeply. "Ever since a nasty man stole candy from me as baby."

"Hmm, that could be dangerous to any intimate associates. Jessica, I suggest you be careful in the future."

Sitting on top of a nearby rocky outcropping, Jess blushed and I turned red in the face from anger and embarrassment. Was it that obvious?

"Everybody okay?" I said, trying to stand and succeeding.

Mindy said, "Just fine. You were the worst injury."

"Injury?" I repeated shocked, looking over my fatigues. "Where was I hurt?"

"It was your groin," she said pointing. "There was something there red and swollen. Looked dangerous. We decided to remove it."

"Ha. Very funny. You're fired."

"Oh no! But what about my pension?"

JUDGMENT NIGHT

"Never had one."

"Well, that was lucky."

Turning around, I saw that we were on a little half-circle of beach made of fine white sand, so pure it had a silvery sheen to the grains, the kind you only find in movies. Curving about us on three sides, like a tan glass wall, was the cliff. It reached some thirty or forty meters into the ocean before arcing out of sight. Soaring impossibly high above us, the light brown rock of the cliff was indecently smooth, without a single crack or fissure to mar its facade.

Forming a dome over everything in view was the ever present cloud, thick and gray as an old man's nightmare. It gave me the feeling of being confined in a bell jar. Personally, I had no doubt this cliff was of artificial construction and not a natural formation. We had seen similar when the team took care of a nasty voodoo problem in the Virgin Islands. However, that brought up a good point. Was it built to keep others out, or something in? We'd have to answer that question the hard way.

Only a short walk away, the DC-3 had pancaked into the cliff, its nose crushed flat against the stone. Behind the plane, trailing off down the beach, irregular skid marks told the story of a frantic, but successful, battle to bring the aircraft to an emergency halt.

Favoring my right knee a bit, I ambled over to where the team was busy unloading the plane; bags and backpacks piled about like canvas mountains. The main body of the seaplane seemed okay. But one of the flotation pods was smashed to kindling, and the right wing had a rend in it large enough to stuff Father Donaher through. Which was no exaggeration, as he was standing in the rift studying the inside.

"Struts are okay," he announced stooping down and walking away. "But the fuel tanks are empty. Even if we find the engines, she'll never fly."

"Nonsense," Richard stated, tossing a duffel bag to the sand. "What a negative attitude. We can always make fuel, and find a replacement engine, from a car or speedboat. My old station wagon had a huge 400 horsepower monster under the hood. I used to joke that with a set of wings she'd fly." He raised his head. "Hey, Abduhl what kind of engines were they? Six cylinder? Eight cylinder?"

Glancing at us from the open window of the cockpit, the pilot reversed his cap and spit into the distance. "Two thousand horsepower, supercharged, 24 cylinder, Pratt & Whitney Double Wasp with a top speed of eight hundred miles per hour."

The wizard slumped. "Okay, we're trapped."

Mindy slapped him on the shoulder. "Come on, Rich. Don't worry about it. We'll probably never leave alive anyway. Not against combined science and magic."

"That's the first thing we should do," Donaher said brusquely. "Shut off any combination stuff still operating in the hold."

"Check," Abduhl said, and he did something on the control panel. There was an odd noise from the belly of the plane and a puff of smoke rose into view from around the seam of the external hatch.

"Fire in the hold!" I yelled dashing forward. Instantly, George was at my heels.

Undoing the hatch, we climbed into the subcompartment. Inside, a small fire was burning in the corner of the amassed equipment and the place was stuffed full of every scientific and magical defense I had ever heard of or seen. There were banks of NASA fuel cells powering radar scramblers,

JUDGMENT NIGHT

pulse generators, field distorters and a collection of sealed black boxes erected in the style of a miniature Stonehenge.

A huge copper bracelet hung from the ceiling, glowing crystal pyramids dotted the floor and at odd angles, endlessly turning mobius strips were mounted on silver rods. Plus, the walls were lined with crucifixes, Mogen David's, ankhs, pentagrams, astrological signs, a delightful Kathi Somer bikini calendar, dollar bills, horse shoes and rabbit feet. This collection in the cargo hold is obviously what had gotten us through the cloud. TechServ hadn't missed a trick.

From the top hatch, Hassan passed down some CO_2 extinguishers and we put the blaze out. It had been nothing serious. A short circuit in a relay set fire to a transformer. No magic involved, we were safe.

Exiting, I dusted off my hands and called for a council. They gathered round. "Mindy, do an inventory. Rich and Jessica, prep our stuff for immediate departure. Abduhl ready the plane for lock down, and see about jerry-rigging a self-destruct. Michael keep guard with the flamethrower. George grab your super rifle. We're going to do a perimeter sweep."

"Its a Masterson Assault Cannon," George, replied falling into step alongside. "Mark IV."

"Lovely," I nodded. "But I don't care if you call it 'Tootsie,' just make damn sure the thing is loaded."

"That's good," he said.

"What?"

"Tootsie."

"Oh geez."

Following the skid marks in the sand we traced the plane back to its initial approach. Staying clear of the waves washing on the west shore, I studied the ocean. Sure enough, there was something jagged just under the surface, momentarily exposed with the crest and gully of the waves. I pointed it out to George and asked for his opinion.

Adjusting a set of folding binoculars, George scrutinized the formations. "Too regular to be natural," he decided. "And yet too irregular to be a trap."

"Conclusion?"

"A waterfront dock in extremely bad condition. See? Those are the pylons, and out there, the breakers."

That alleviated my fears of us hitting a sea serpent. A little bit, anyway. Proceeding along the edge of the beach, we encountered nothing interesting until the far east end. The thing was mostly hidden by a mass of seaweed, but enough showed. It was the body of a human male in a scuba suit laying face down on the shore. Since he was making no effort to turn over, his lifeless condition was self-evident. Even more so when we moved the seaweed to find only half of the body. From the hips down, he was gone. His wet suit ending in a ghastly view of bones and intestines. There were pressurized airtanks strapped to his back, the breathing hose still in his mouth, and a cracked mask on his face. A bulky sealed bag was over a shoulder and an underwater equipment belt encircled his waist.

I beeped the team on my wristwatch, and they came a running, weapons at the ready. At a safe distance, the group halted and inspected the beach before moving closer. But there was nothing dangerous or suspicious showing, so they joined us with the corpse.

Carefully turning him over, George removed the diving mask. Not a friendly face. Looked like the kind of guy who wouldn't smile without written permission from the boss. He had been a big man, with the kind of a muscular build that comes from hard manual labor, not a gymnasium. His hands were heavily callused, especially along the edge of the palms. I pointed this out to Mindy, who checked the tips of his fingers and thumbnails.

"A fellow martial artist, without a doubt," she declared. "Definitely a student of karate, with a high probability of something else."

"Strong and trained. A formidable opponent. Father?" I requested pointing to the lower extremities.

"Bitten," the priest said kneeling, inspecting the wound with a pocket medical probe. "But not by a shark. There's no ripping or tearing of the tissues. This is a single clean slice, almost as if done with a guillotine."

"Interesting. Hypothesis?"

"None."

"Hasn't been dead long, either," Richard remarked, pressing the pale skin on a forearm with the tip of his staff. "No rigor mortis and the flesh hasn't become bloated with water."

This was hardly dinner conversation, but then we weren't first-timers to this sort of thing. Dead bodies were an occupational hazard. Happily, Abduhl seemed unperturbed. Good man.

"Let's check his stuff," I directed.

In the waterproof holster at his hip was a 10mm automatic pistol filled with explosive bullets. The manufacturer's name and serial number had been filed off. Odd. An ammo pouch in his belt held ten additional clips, a silver edged combat knife, and four thermite grenades. The bag contained nothing more than the expected spare clothes without labels, generic compressed food and assorted no-name camping gear. But hidden inside a pair of rolled socks, we found a small book in an unknown language. I passed it to our resident scholar.

"That's Greek," Father Donaher identified, thumbing through the pages.

"Can you read it?"

He gazed at me askance. "I am a Catholic priest."

"So?"

"The original version of the New Testament is in ancient Greek."

"I thought it was in Latin," Mindy said puzzled.

Donaher scowled mightily. "The Old Testament was written in Hebrew, New Testament in Greek. They were both converted into Latin about 200 AD."

"Oh."

Under his breath, the priest muttered something about dullards and heretics. Better not have been talking about me.

Callously, we stripped the body, searching for additional clues. He wore only swim trunks under the wet suit, as was standard practice. There were no tattoos, but his body was a mass of thin scars, mostly on the back. On a hunch, I checked about his neck and sure enough found a set of invisible dogtags. Setting my sunglasses to maximum, I was able to dimly perceive some flowing script on the metallic ovals.

"Machlokta d'Sitna," I said, wiping my fingers off in the sand.

"Satan Department," Richard translated, taking a step away.

Jessica hawked and spit on the corpse.

"Who?" Captain Hassan asked, hooking both thumbs into his wide belt.

We explained. Satan Department was an old and bitter enemy of ours. Operating as a counterpart to the Bureau, they did not neutralize, or subdue evil supernaturals. But instead, tried to enlist and, if necessary, brainwash, the creatures into becoming spies and assassins for their government. In addition, we strongly believed them to be the masterminds of the slaughter of '87. If we ever got any proof, we'd find their headquarters in the Elburz Mountains and reduce it to a smoking hole. We held them in lower esteem than used car dealers.

"My own people," Hassan said in disgust. "Well, come on, Father. Get it over with."

Raising a hairy eyebrow, Donaher scowled. "What?"

"The last rites, or whatever you call them."

"You are joking," the priest said coldly.

Abduhl appeared flustered. "You . . . you aren't going to lay his soul to rest?"

"A Satan Department agent?" Donaher said, his voice rising in timber. "A murderer, heretic and worse? One of the people who tried to assassinate his holiness, the Pope, and stole the Shroud of Turin, leaving that awful copy in its place? Never! May he burn in hell for all eternity!" An awkward silence followed, as the priest turned and walked towards the plane.

"You guys play hardball," Hassan softly said.

Mindy kicked sand on the body. "And don't you forget it."

"What about meat-boy here?" George asked, nudging the body with the barrel of his rifle.

"Let his bones bleach in the sun," Richard snarled in raw hatred.

"And his weapons?"

"Leave them. We have more than enough. Besides they might be booby trapped."

"Good point." I clapped my hands. "Okay, people, spread out. Let's see what other delights we can find."

Fanning out in a standard search pattern, the team poked and prodded their way along the beach. I followed the shoreline to the plane and was working my way back along the bottom of the cliff where I found Mindy and Michael talking in animated conversation.

"Find something?" I asked, joining them.

"We're just studying this door," she said, pointing to the blank wall.

Confused, I looked at the cliff with my Bureau sunglasses. It appeared perfectly normal. "What door?"

Father Donaher gestured. "Step closer."

As I did, a door appeared in the cliff. A sharp cut rectangle set in a recessed alcove. Pretty high flouting illusion to beat my glasses. This beach was becoming a plethora of surprises. On the lintel above the portal there was an arcane symbol of some sort and a collection of tiny squares set in staggered horizontal lines. Interesting. Ornamental design, or message?

"Jess, can you get any impressions?" I asked hopefully.

Occasionally by holding an object the telepath could tell us a wide variety of things about the owner; age, sex, disposition, inclination, political affiliations, all sorts of stuff.

"Just old," she said, hugging herself. "Very, very old. Two thousand, three thousand years. Maybe more."

That was something anyway. Going with the theory of Occam's Razor, I tried the obvious first. The simplest answer is often correct. But no hinges or handle were readily apparent. I checked in the usual places for hidden levers, or counterweights, to no avail. I could see why they called for me. Pulling out an old fashioned magnifying glass from my fatigue jacket pocket, I examined the portal from top to bottom and side to side. The smooth flowing grain of the stone was almost hypnotizing in its dull regularity.

"Well?" Donaher asked eagerly.

"Beats me," I admitted stepping away and brushing sand

JUDGMENT NIGHT

off my knees. "Couldn't locate a pinhole for physical manipulation and the doorjamb is too fine for jimmying."

"Try something else," Mindy suggested helpfully.

"What a grand notion. Unfortunately, I can think of any number of ways it may be unlocked; a magnetic key waved over the correct spot, radio message beamed in code, vocal command like 'Open Sesame.'" I waited. Nothing happened. Oh well. "Whoever built this knew what they were doing."

The rest of the team had gathered round by then and were brought up to date.

"Blast it open," George said, reaching into a canvas bag over his shoulder. "We have plenty of C4."

Judiciously, I decided to give Richard a try first.

Drawing his wand, the wizard chose a page from his book and gave a short incantation. A stream of sparkles flowed from the tip to dash against the portal in a pyrotechnic display of multi-colored lights and nothing more.

"Sealed," he said at last, lowering the wand. "There was a faint indication of an internal mechanism, so it is a doorway. But the thing is so heavily magic shielded, we may have to use dynamite."

"C4," George corrected with a smile.

"Hopefully not," Father Donaher drawled. "That would only preclude us from closing it again behind us, and might just inform the whole damn island that we're here." There was general agreement to that.

I addressed Mindy and George. "Bring the supplies. When we get this open, it may only be so for a short time and we better be ready to move."

"Good idea," she said, and they departed.

The sea breeze tugging at her hair, Jessica worried a knuckle. "Too bad we can't leave a radio beacon, or broadcast a message, to the Bureau in case this cloud lifts."

"The radio is in working order," Hassan said, sliding back his cap. "But much too cumbersome to bring along."

"Then leave it inside the plane," I decided curtly. "Can you key it to broadcast a short message every hour?"

"Easily. But the set is powered by the engines, with them gone, the batteries won't last for more than a day."

I frowned. "Damn."

"Excuse me, but we have electrical power coming out of our ears," Richard said, rolling up sleeves.

"Whatchamean?" the pilot asked.

"The NASA fuel cells," he said simply.

Hassan and I exchanged glances declaring our total abject stupidity. Quiet and efficient, the fuel cells were what NASA used to power space shuttles. Utilizing ionic polarization to chemically convert methane into electricity, the fuel cells would calmly sit there generating power for the next month, whether we used them or not.

"Right," Hassan chuckled, starting to run off. "I'll get right to work re-wiring the—"

With a startled cry, Captain Hassan lurched, red blood spraying from his neck. As we rushed forward, a watery something behind him yanked a crystal spear from his neck and the pilot dropped to the sand.

Standing brazen, the translucent creature was vaguely humanoid in shape, but totally devoid of any details; facial, bodily or otherwise. Nothing more than an outline. Ridiculous as it sounded, the thing appeared to be made of fluid water, for its body sloshed as the creature waddled toward us and threw the ice spear in a three fingered hand. I ducked and Richard knocked the spear out of the air with his staff.

"Take it alive for questioning," I ordered, drawing my pistol.

Going into a marksmen stance, Father Donaher snapped off a shot with his pistol, hitting the thing in the shoulder and the water creature burst apart in a gush, the liquid contents flowing into the beach. I watched for treachery in the sand, but apparently it was gone. Maybe they were specifically vulnerable to lead. What a nice change that would be from wooden stakes, silver bullets or depleted uranium slugs.

Then Jessica cried an alarm and I saw several more of the creatures coming from the west. We tried wounding them, but a single shot and poof.

"These guys are wimps," Richard declared, as a ray from his wand blasted the last and it dissolved into the sand.

Sadly, Jessica agreed. Even her stun rifle had killed them.

A wave from the sea washed onto the shore and four more of the water creatures were formed. Relentlessly, they started waddling forward, ice spears and axes glittering in their chubby mitts.

"Yeah, but there's an ocean of them to seven of us," I noted. "They will just keep coming until we run out of ammo and eventually keel over from exhaustion."

"Any suggestions?" Jessica asked, holstering her taser and sliding a shotgun off her shoulder. She jacked the pump with one hand, chambering a cartridge.

Another wave. Six, this time.

"Keep firing for the present. Michael, check Hassan."

The priest thumped over to the sprawled form and reached to turn him over. Steam arose at the touch and he jumped back.

"Dead," the big man said, painfully flexing his fingers. "Frozen solid. I nearly got frostbite just touching his clothes."

I gazed at Richard. "Wimps, huh?" He shrugged.

At this point, Mindy and George returned loaded with

our packs, gainfully pushing a wheeled cart over the hard packed sand. Thank God we hadn't tossed both of them overboard. At the end of the beach, I could see a dozen or so of the water demons beating on the plane with their axes. Rapidly, the fuselage started to cake over with ice and I kissed the rest of our supplies goodbye. Even if we fought our way to the DC-3, there was no way we could defrost an aircraft and protect ourselves simultaneously.

Yanking aside the canvas covering the cart, I snatched a bag of ammo and an M16/M79 assault rifle. Half machine gun, half grenade launcher, it combined spray-and-pray firepower with big punch capability and was my favorite thing in times of trouble this side of Not Being There In The First Place.

"How's Abduhl?" Mindy demanded, tossing Donaher a pack.

The priest made the catch. "Dead. For keeps."

Stringing her bow, Mindy spat an oath that could have raised a bloodblister on boot leather. Wow. Guess she had really liked the pilot a lot. Too bad.

"George!" I barked, shoving a 40mm shell into the breech of the bottom-slung grenade launcher. The upper machine gun already had a fully loaded 30 round clip in it.

"Ed?" the soldier panted, as he helped Richard don a bulky backpack twice the size of the others.

"Get the door."

"Check."

Grabbing a sealed plastic tube, he pulled the arming pin, extended the muzzle, flipped up the sights, released the safety, aimed and fired. On a lance of fire, the Light Anti-Tank Weapon rocket impacted directly on the rock and detonated with spectacular results. We rushed forward, but halted as the smoke cleared and could see that the surface was undamaged, not even a scratch.

"Have to try something else," he sighed tossing the exhausted rocket launcher aside.

Watching the beach, Mindy notched an arrow from her double-quiver. "There's no time!"

"Don't be an idiot," George snapped. "We have plenty of time." Taking a grenade from a carton on the cart, he pulled the pin, flipped the handle and tossed the canister on the shore, where it bounced along the beach and splashed into the water. A split second later, the ocean jumped and formed a geyser of boiling steam. The process continued as George lined the shore every few meters with the canisters.

"Those are thermite grenades," he explained lugubriously. "A non-stoppable chemical reaction which burns at 3,000 degrees Kelvin, the surface temperature of the sun. The ocean won't put it out. Can't. On the contrary, the oxygen in the water will only act as additional fuel, maybe doubling the burning time."

George glanced at his watch. "Okay, I just bought us five minutes. Now you brainy types solve the door."

"Three on three," I ordered. "Group A, the door."

Father Donaher, Richard and Mindy returned their attention to the problem, as George, Jessica and I assumed a defensive position to protect their rear.

Racking the bolt on my machine gun, I spoke to Jessica. "Sometimes, I wonder if we shouldn't put George in charge."

"I think he already is," she replied in a stage whisper.

More water babies tried to rise from the sea, and departed this world with a minimum of fuss.

The scholars nosily debated the virtues of the portal, arguing pedantically over this and that. The sea was starting to cool, when a cry of victory cut through the verbal morass.

"Details," I snapped.

Father Donaher spoke, "Those squares above the door can be depressed in the manner of a keyboard. They must be the way in."

"Great!"

"Not really," Richard added over his shoulder. "With almost a hundred squares, there's over eight hundred thousand possible three digit combinations, and the entrance code might be a four, ten, or even a hundred integers."

Triggering the M16, I mowed down a fresh group of waddling wonders coming in from the east. "Doing the gambit would take longer than we have, that's for damn sure."

"Wait, I got an idea," Jessica said, punctuating each word with a shotgun blast.

"Okay, switch!" I cried.

The two groups changed positions.

"Talk fast, lady," I suggested as we gathered around the door.

She pointed to the symbol on the lintel above the rectangle. "Might that not be an icon for water?"

"What if it is?" George asked, resting the butt of his rifle on a hip.

"Well, you must have observed the definite water motif in every attack on us."

"And?" I snapped impatiently.

"I'm betting the key for entrance is water."

"Okay, spell water."

"How?" Jessica demanded. "There's no letters."

An easy problem. "Anybody touch type?" I asked above the gunfire. Donaher could. He and George moved and the priest tried the ploy. Results, negative.

JUDGMENT NIGHT

"Try Greek," Mindy suggested, loosening a Bureau arrow with violent results.

That also failed. As did Latin, Hebrew, French, Russian, Spanish, Morse Code and computer binary.

"This is a complete waste of time and effort," Richard declared, a golden ray from his wand flashing the liquid demons into vapor at its slightest touch. "These squares are not in the order of any alphabet I know."

"Still, there is something faintly familiar about that array of squares," I said, raking my brain for what it was. There was a fleeting memory from my past just outside of range, I could sense it was there, but not quite clearly enough to get even a brief glance.

"Want me to help?" Jessica offered.

In spite of our situation, I hesitated before saying yes. It was no easy thing to allow another person access to your mind, even a close friend like Jess. But this was an emergency, so I said yes and shouldered my weapon. Stepping close, Jessica cupped my face in her warm hands and our gaze locked. Involuntarily, I stiffened as her thoughts gently slid into my mind, then completely relaxed under a soothing caress softer than a lover's kiss.

Instantly, the years flowed backwards like the fluttering pages of a book in the wind. I was a PI in Chicago, a cop on the South Side, a security officer for my father's trucking firm, in high school, a sophomore, November, 14, Tuesday, 11:45 am, in Chemistry, my teacher droned on about something incredibly dull . . .

"Got it!" I cried as we broke apart. "Its the periodic table."

"Nonsense," George snorted, working the bolt on his weapon to clear a jam. "Doesn't resemble it a bit."

"Not the new, modern version, but the old original.

Dimitri Mendeleef's simple one, circa 1869."

He got the idea. A couple of thousand years ago, the molecular structure of water would be big juju. Forbidden knowledge. Far beyond the understanding of most common folk, who thought everything was made of the four elements. And sometimes they got those confused.

Reaching above the door, I pressed the first square—hydrogen. It sank, but rose again as soon as I let go. I pressed it once more and now it locked into place with a click. Holding my breath, I counted to the eighth square that should be oxygen and depressed it. The square sank, locked into position and noiselessly the massive stone door swung inward.

"Retreat!" Mindy shouted, charging through the open doorway.

Maintaining defensive fire to protect our rear, the team moved into an antechamber, a seamless cavern of natural stone only a few yards wide. There was no other exit in sight.

"Close the door, please," Jessica said, taking cover behind the wall and shoving fresh shells into her weapon. Countless waves of the water demons were washing onto the shore, marching at us in nightmarish precision.

"Now would be good!" George shouted, firing a stream of caseless HE from his bulky assault cannon.

Confidently, I searched on the other side of the door, but saw only smooth blank stone. No symbol, no keyboard. No nothing.

EIGHT

"Find another keyboard!" I ordered, searching the walls.

Rosary dangling from his gunbelt, Father Donaher took a position in the doorway alongside George and hosed the front ranks of the creatures with his flamethrower. In a loud hiss, they disintegrated, only to be replaced by dozens more.

"This is getting serious," he shouted above the roar of the burning spray. "Close the freaking door!"

Jessica dramatically touched it with a single finger and Mindy gave it a roundhouse kick. "We're trying!"

"No time for halfway measure!" Richard shouted, rolling up his sleeves. "Stand back!"

We cleared away fast. Gesturing wildly, the wizard shouted in a foreign language and the chamber was instantly immersed in total blackness.

"Did the spell work?" somebody asked from the dark.

"Yep," a smug voice replied.

Flashlights clicked and in the bright white beams we saw that the doorway was closed solid with a stout wall of red fireplace bricks.

"Good work, man!" I said, slapping him on the shoulder.

He smiled. "Thanks."

"Why bricks?" Jessica asked curiously.

"First thing that came to mind."

Father Donaher adjusted the pre-burner on the sizzling nozzle of his weapon. "Come on, George. Let's form a firing line just in case they can get through."

Grimly, George nodded. "Check."

But as the soldier stepped away from the brick wall and the toe of his boot cleared the swing line of the door, the stone mass promptly closed and locked. Stunned silence followed.

"A regulated door," Mindy gasped in sudden understanding. "The damn thing won't close as long as somebody is in the way."

Growling a curse, Richard grabbed our chubby gunman by the collar. "You almost got me killed, Renault!" he snarled.

"Won't be the first time, Anderson!" George snarled back.

They bumped chests for awhile, making dangerous-sounding threats, then broke apart laughing.

Strange as it sounds, I have heard of some military leaders who don't allow this kind of horseplay by soldiers. In my opinion, they're the kind of idiots who are either easily defeated by the enemy, or else get killed from friendly fire. Humor relieves tension and improves morale. Besides, it was the first time anybody had actually joked since the disappearance of Raul. We were starting to pull together again.

"Hey, look!" Richard cried, pointing his wand.

We turned and on the cavern wall behind us was a tunnel not there before. Ten feet wide and high, the passage led deeper into the cliff, the end beyond the range of our flashlights.

Mindy angled her beam around for a better look, but nothing new was shown. "Must have formed when the outer door closed."

"Makes sense," Donaher agreed, stroking his moustache. "Typical security arrangement."

"Security infers they have enemies."

"They do now," George said gruffly, taping his flashlight to the end of the barrel on his assault cannon.

I was going to immediately proceed into the tunnel, when I noticed the slightly hangdog appearance of the group and remembered that we had been on the go since 4am this morning. Fifteen straight hours. This was no place to pitch camp, but a short rest couldn't hurt.

"We'll hold here for ten minutes," I said, checking the load on my grenade launcher. "If the water guys haven't gotten through the door by then, we break for lunch."

"Here?" Jessica asked, arching an eyebrow. "I thought we would at least go down the tunnel a ways."

"Why?" Mindy replied. "This way, we know one direction we won't be attacked from."

Jess gave a slow nod. "True enough."

Everybody assumed an attack position, weapons ready and the ten minutes passed with agonizing slowness. As the second hand on my watch swept to twelve, I breathed a sigh of relief. My innards were gnawing on each other and my head still hurt from the plane crash. Luckily, this double barrier did the trick.

"Okay, short break," I said. "Water and MRE packs only. No cooking, no fire. Standard guard rotation."

Gratefully, the group allowed their packs to slide to the ground and set about opening food packages. I took the first shift, dry swallowing aspirins from my pocket med kit and keeping my butt to the wall where I could watch the door and tunnel.

For a few minutes there was no sound except ripping mylar, crinkling plastic wrap, munching and slurping. Wolfing down his food, George relieved me and I happily joined them. Aspirins make very poor luncheon fare.

Chewing a military meatloaf sandwich, Donaher was busy with the flamethrower, checking gauges and thumping tanks. "I'm afraid this is pretty much drained," he announced sadly. "No more than a ten second charge left in it. Hardly worth carrying anymore."

"Then here," Jessica said, offering the pump-action shotgun. "Take this."

He hesitated. "But, Jess . . ."

"It is your preferred weapon, correct?"

"Well, yes."

"Then take the shotgun. There are plenty of stun bags, and I'll use one of the M16 rifles. Doesn't make much difference to me. I hate all weapons."

That was certainly true. On just regular day-to-day living, I toted my S&W .357 Magnum into the shower. But even on a field assignment, Jessica only carried a taser. She once explained that it had something to do with the negative psychic vibrations of an offensive weapon disrupting her mental harmony. I chuckled to myself. Telepaths. Can't live with them, can't live without them.

"I heard that," sang out Jessica, removing the plastic wrapper from an apple.

Oops.

Lowering his canteen, Richard wiped his mouth and recapped the container. "Any ideas about that tunnel?" he asked the group at large.

"Probably a security corridor, similar to the one at our HQ," I said. "Once past the outer door, people who know what they're doing can stroll along without being molested. But a stranger will blunder about tripping alarms and other nasty stuff."

"There are an awful lot of assumptions in that," Mindy observed around a mouthful of candy bar. "We don't even know who we're dealing with yet. Animal, vegetable or mineral. Mortal, spirit or construct."

"Good, bad or neutral," Jessica added, finishing the litany.

"When do we ever know anything for certain?" Father

Donaher said. "Faith, lass, there's a bit of good in the most evil of men, and a touch of bad in each of us."

"But death is for keeps," Mindy snarled, teeth savaging her candy bar.

If they were getting this philosophical, I decided the group had rested enough. Standing, I brushed the crumbs from my khaki jumpsuit. Where was Armani when you needed him?

"Okay, break over," I announced. "Let's check the supplies and get going."

By reflex, we cleaned the site and packed the refuse. Feeling immensely refreshed, I stood guard again while the rest of the team routed through the mounds of supplies in a fast inventory. Work would keep their minds off our recent loses. As the Eskimos say, food is sleep. Smart folks.

"So what are we missing?" I asked, when they were done.

Checking a list in her hand, Jessica reported. "The barrel of water, the big tent, all of the mountain climbing gear, the inflatable raft, the flare gun and the scuba outfits."

"No loss on the last," Donaher said, loudly blowing his nose on a bandana.

"Thank you, Elephant Man. How about weapons?"

"The Surface-to-Air Missiles are gone," George said glumly. "And so are two of our satchel charges. We have all of the Uzi machine guns and plenty of ammo, but no clips for them."

Swell. "Dump the guns next to the flamethrower, but keep the ammunition. It'll fit our pistols. Anything else? How 'bout my briefcase?"

"Not here," Richard frowned, poking at the stony ground with his staff.

I spat an oath.

"Was it something good" Mindy asked. "Or merely useful?"

"Very useful," I replied sadly. "Extremely so. It was a miniature atomic bomb."

Silence.

"A Snoopy?" George asked in awe.

I nodded. He whistled.

"We had a nuke?" Jessica asked, her voice rising in pitch.

"Yep. A miniature atomic bomb, about half a kiloton yield. Not enough to destroy the whole island, but more than sufficient to convince anybody that we mean business."

"Damn," Mindy said, grinding a fist into her palm. "That is a major loss. Should we try and go get it?"

After a moment's thought, I shook my head. "Too darn dangerous. We'll just have to solve the situation, or leave before zero hour in . . ." I checked my watch. "Twenty two hours."

There were murmurs of approval. Horace Gordon had said, that none of his people are expendable. Well, usually not.

While George booby-trapped the collection of useless weapons we piled by the door, the rest of us distributed the remaining ammunition and explosives on the cart for easy access. Then Richard tightly tied down the canvas sheet with easy-open slip knots, as Mindy oiled the wheels.

Finally, we gathered in front of the mouth of the tunnel. Checking the entrance for traps, it proved to be clean and I proceeded carefully inside. The smooth walls of the tunnel curved to become ceiling, the rock strangely warm to the touch.

However, the floor was properly cold, smooth and very clean. There was no way of telling if anybody had ever gone this way, or we were the first. Comforting thought.

"Two meter spread," I whispered, gently working the bolt on my machine gun and easing off the safety. "Silent penetration. Single file. Mindy take the point position, George cover the rear."

JUDGMENT NIGHT

"Check."

"Gotcha."

The air in the tunnel was deathly still and the noise of our boots echoed slightly. Nothing we could do about that. Our sneakers were in the frozen sea plane. The team only penetrated a short distance when we confronted a T intersection. Peeking to the left, Mindy reported a Y branching and Richard said he saw another T to the right.

"It's a Phoenician maze," Donaher said scowling, resting the shotgun on a shoulder.

At once, I was suspicious. This was almost too easy. "The Egyptian solution?" I asked the priest and he agreed.

About three thousand years ago, the Egyptians started building pyramids protected by mazes filled with deathtraps. Now, it was too much to ask of anybody to expect them to remember a hundred specific twist and turns through the maze, so the builders settled upon the simple solution of the left wall. Never let your hand off the left wall and, eventually, you will reach the end of the maze alive and safe. Of course, this is a well-known trick nowadays, but if this place really was thousands of years old, the people who constructed the maze might think the solution still secret. The ploy had worked once before for us in Peru, when we went after the Aztec Book of the Damned and it just might work today.

With a sigh of steel on steel, Mindy drew her sword, the rainbow effect of the blade casting crazed shadows on the walls. "Let's go," she said and we followed close behind, our fingertips brushing stone.

Three hours later, tired and dusty, we reached the end of the maze. Nothing to it. The last turn put us on a barren ledge facing a large empty room. The walls and ceiling were rough hewn, barely squared off, but the floor was a network of perfectly formed, one meter rectangles, seven in a row, ten long. At the far end of the room was a simple wooden door. Personally, I was wondering why the owners just didn't erect a sign here saying; "Beware, Death Trap. Please Advance and Die. Thank you."

"Want me to fly over and check the door?" Jessica asked, brandishing a bracelet.

"Don't waste it on this," I said. "Might need it later."

"Want me to?" Richard offered, sniffing his flower.

"No. You're going to lead us across."

In defense, he held up a hand. "Whoa there, pardner. I did that radioactive morgue in Dallas."

"Correct, and I did the trans-dimensional mansion in Atlanta, and George did the hat store in Miami, so it is your turn again."

"Damn."

"Fair's fair."

The wizard started removing his backpack. "Yeah, yeah, just give me a minute. I hate this part of the job."

"As do we all."

Rid of his excess baggage, Richard experimentally gave the front seven squares a good hard rap with his wand. Nothing happened. Extending an arm, he tapped the next line of squares. Still nothing. But that was normal. The squares were probably set to activate on a weight limit, or body temperature, or mass proximity.

George uncoiled some rope from the haversack and starting tying it about Richard's waist. That was so we could pull the wizard back if there was trouble. However, George and Donaher held the rope loosely in their hands, just in case whatever got the man threatened to haul them in also. This was a most unforgiving business we were in.

JUDGMENT NIGHT

Rummaging through his pockets, Richard came up empty. "Anybody have some change?" he asked.

"Are you nuts?" Mindy asked. "Carry loose change in battle? Might as well put a bell around my neck."

Richard looked at George, looked at me and I extended a hand to George. "Gimme."

"What? Give you, what?" he asked innocently.

Impatiently, I snapped my fingers. Grumbling, George dug into a pocket and unearthed a small bag of cookies. Our soldier boy did not retain his manly shape without constant effort.

Properly equipped, his staff held horizontally in both hands, Richard moved to the right and gingerly stepped on the first square. When there was no reaction, he exerted more pressure with his leg, then shifted his weight until he was standing fully on the square. Satisfied, he placed a cookie on the square to mark it. Kneeling, he examined the squares in front of him and chose the one on a diagonal. Step, pause, weight, shift, stand. Another success. He repeated the process on the square directly in front of him. Success.

It was strange thing, but there was no real rhyme, or reason to a job like this. You had to move almost entirely by feel, on instinct. I used to think this would be a piece of cake for Jess. She could simply read the feelings of victory where somebody made it through and easily detect the sense of horror where a person had failed and died. But actually, the reverse is true. The two feelings were separated by mere inches, spaced so close together, occasionally overlapping, that often she would boldly walk right into the death traps and avoid the safe regions at any cost.

Again, the wizard stepped carefully ahead. But this time as he shifted his weight, the square gave a creak and then dropped from view. A hideous grinding noise rose the exposed hole and stone dust flew up to pepper the shoes of the wizard who was floating in the air above the hole, both hands firmly wrapped around his staff.

Levitating to the right, Richard chanced a landing. No problem. As we watched, the stones closed over the opening and the floor was whole once more.

"What was down there?" I asked.

"A set of whirling blades," he replied in a croak. "Resembled the insides of a blender."

"Nasty," Jessica muttered. Donaher agreed.

Exercising extreme caution, Richard moved ahead another square, then went diagonal again. Of the five squares available to him, the wizard obviously didn't like the looks of any of them, but chanced straight ahead. As his foot touched the stone, it depressed with a click. Simultaneously, the wizard was airborne backwards and a column of stone rose from the floor upward to resoundingly impact on the ceiling. The square pillar and ceiling ground against each other for a minute, then the column sank to floor level and all was as before.

His limbs shaking, Richard stood on the safe square and thanked us with his eyes. Priest and soldier tipped imaginary hats in return.

Crossing his fingers, Richard tried the square to his left and survived the experience. He moved diagonally and then diagonally again. That stone took his weight for a few seconds then broke clean down the middle. Frantic, Richard hopped to the left against the wall as the last square folded upon itself with the strident sound of colliding anvils. But the square he was on now shimmed and Richard dive rolled forward as it tilted away from the wall in an effort to throw him to the right.

JUDGMENT NIGHT

Pausing a moment to catch his breath, the wizard placed a cookie on the stone he was in and then floated back to the earlier safe square. It was a step backwards, but he had to complete the path. Leaving sweat stains on the stone, Richard twice more went straight ahead.

Now, he was facing the wooden door only a single stone away. It made sense that the square directly in front of the door would be safe, for ease of entrance. But the door swung outward, towards the room, so the stone to either side gave limited access.

It was a tough choice. Three squares, one almost certain death. Going for broke, the wizard stepped onto the middle stone. Nothing happened.

Beaming pleasure, Richard placed a cookie there and had one himself. He then released the rope about his waist and tossed the bag to George.

"These are great!" the wizard said happily. "Just like mother used to bake."

George made the catch. "Your mother worked for Nabisco?"

"Shaddup."

"What about the door?" Father Donaher asked, coiling the rope about hand and elbow. "Locked?"

Richard worked the latch. "Unlocked."

"Check for traps," Jessica suggested warily.

The wizard did by running the tip of his staff along the edge of the door. "Clear," he announced.

"Any vibrations, sounds, smells?" Mindy asked anxiously.

Richard placed his head to the door and listened. "I hear big breathing."

Big breathing? "Human, or animal?"

"Can't tell."

"Clear the avenue of attack," I ordered quietly and the team split, moving to the side of the ledge. "On the mark, throw open the door. Rich, stay hidden behind it in case we need a surprise."

He nodded and thumbed the latch on the handle.

"Ready, set, go!"

Pulling the door on top himself, we could see a small room, and completely filling the far wall of the cubicle was a giant face. A huge distorted face, some twelve feet tall. It appeared mostly human, but with odd muscle arrangements and weird peaked eyebrows. Broadly, the thing smiled at us in unabashed pleasure.

"SALUTATIONS!" he boomed cheerfully.

That startled the lot of us. It spoke English?

"It has some kind of a built-in translator," Jessica said, touching her forehead. "I sense no hostile thoughts, only a tremendous desire to serve."

Friendly, eh? Swell. I cleared my throat. "Ah . . . hi there."

"GREETINGS! LONG HAS IT BEEN SINCE I HAVE TALKED TO OTHERS."

"And who are you?" Mindy asked politely.

"I AM, THE GATE."

"The gate to what?"

"BEYOND."

"Beyond what?"

"ME."

This was almost too weird for words, and as the conversation could go on till the sun cooled, I decided to speed things along.

"Acknowledged," I said pretending to force back a yawn. I know a flunky when I see one, and this guy had butler written all over him. "Please, inform us as to your exact purpose and be quick about it."

"YES, SIR. THE MASTERS MADE ME A LIVING BARRIER, DESIGNED TO ALLOW THE ENTRY OF ONLY THE DESERVING."

"And who are the deserving?" Jessica inquired curiously.

I could have cheerfully shot her for saying that. Geez, you never give a servant or guard, a chance to think. Talk fast, move fast. That was my motto.

"YOURSELVES," he said to our relief. "MY NOSE CAN EASILY SMELL THE MAGIC, THICK AND SWEET, FROM EACH OF YOU."

Huh? Ah! The bracelets. Course, Donaher didn't have one, but then he was a cleric and magic in his own way. Sorta. Kinda. The masters liked magicians, eh? I made a note of that.

Father Donaher raised his voice, "How do you function?"

"STEPPING INTO MY MOUTH GIVES PASSAGE TO THE OTHER SIDE."

Oh brother. Tell me another.

"He has got to be kidding," the priest muttered, fingering the rosary in his pocket.

Surreptitiously, George tapped his fingers on the satchel charge and I shook him off. Time for that later.

"PLEASE, COME," the face begged. "WHO SHALL BE FIRST?"

"Me," Mindy said, stepping forward.

A chorus of disbelief rose from everybody in the room, including Richard behind the door.

Roughly, I pulled her aside. "Are you insane?" I snarled softly. "My glasses give a reading of pure green. That's neutral magic, it may do anything."

"Jess said the face only wants to serve," she reminded patiently. "Besides, I have the Meld. If there's any trouble, such as, he tries to eat me, I'll activate the bracelet and walk out. Then George can waste him."

"Darn tootin,'" George said, giving a wink.

Crazy? Yes. But the idea had merit. "Sounds okay, first we should . . ."

However, Mindy was already crossing the floor, following the trail of cookies. "See you soon," she called over a shoulder.

Approaching the Gate, the face smiled and opened his jaw wide. Daintily, she stepped onto the tongue and the mouth closed. Watching, I nervously clenched and unclenched my fists. Risk taking was part of the job, but this bordered on suicide.

"Hey, its okay, chief," George said, offering the bag of cookies in a friendly manner.

"Tell me why," I asked coldly, ignoring the confection.

"Mindy has a grenade in her hand with the pin pulled. If she has to make a fast exit, I bet the pineapple stays. And eight ounces of exploding plastique in your head will seriously ruin anybody's day."

That made me feel better. Then my watch beeped. I pressed the talk switch. "Mindy? You okay?"

"Sure, safe and sound," her voice replied. "I'm on the other side of the cliff. You have to see this place. We really have our work cut out for us."

This code was old. I hoped Mindy remembered. "King's knight three to queen's rook four, check."

There was a pause. "Oh shit, I used to know this. Ah . . . queen's pawn five to king's bishop two, checkmate."

"Really?" I asked impulsively.

Yes, she is fine, Jessica said inside my head. *Now shut up and get somebody else there.*

JUDGMENT NIGHT

We sent George over next and, one at a time, I had Richard float our two carts of equipment into the mouth. The wizard followed, then Jessica and Father Donaher. But as the priest entered the cubicle, the face sniffed loudly, its features contorting into a scowl of rage and disgust.

"HOLD!" the Gate bellowed. "THIS SMELLS AS NO MAGE, BUT A . . . A CLERIC!"

Oh crap. Massed together, Michael must have been lost in the crowd, masked by our aura of magic. But standing alone, the priest was far too noticeable.

"Nonsense," Father Donaher scoffed, doing an excellent impersonation of being amused. "I? A cleric? Why, I simply carry a holy talisman."

"DIE CLERIC!" the face screeched, as burning rays leap from its devil eyes and Father Donaher fell to the floor a screaming torch.

NINE

Caught off-guard, I didn't have anything prepared. But it took only a second to click off the safety on the M16 and let Gate have the full thirty round clip, the armor piercing rounds stitching the pale flesh. Then I triggered the grenade launcher and put 40mm of high explosives right between those damn cat eyes.

Black blood flew everywhere, hot gore pumping from the ruin of the face like a fountain in hell. The nose and left eye were completely gone, exposing bone, ganglia and electronic circuits. Damaged but not dead, the Gate glared hatefully at me from its remaining orb and as I ducked to avoid the death ray, the face exploded.

Noise and flame filled the room, gobbets of flesh smacking into the walls. As the reverberations ceased, I stood and saw faint figures moving through the swirling smoke. Slamming in a fresh clip, I stopped from firing just in time when I recognized George and Jessica moving across the floor. Behind them was a gaping hole ringed with tattered shred of bleeding flesh.

"What the heck went wrong?" George demanded, hopping off the last square to the ledge. His satchel charge was not evident.

"Medical, stat!" I cried, heading for the burning Donaher.

Together, we raced to the priest and beat out the flames with our jackets. His screams were only low moans by now. Jess emptied her canteen on the man, while George took the smoking shotgun from his black hands and removed the shells from the pockets of the smoldering jumpsuit.

JUDGMENT NIGHT

Appearing by my side, Richard gasped at the sight on the floor and knelt to force some powder into the priest's throat. Then he liberally poured the contents of a small vial over the man. From my pocket medical kit, I gave Michael an injection of morphine for the pain: 5cc, 10cc, more. Finally, at 20cc, the priest went unconscious. The poor man had my deepest sympathy. We had each been set on fire at one time or another. It's what gave us our true fear of Hell.

"I don't think he's going to make it," Richard said, moving his staff over the smoking body, bathing the man in a soft golden light. "Systemic shock, burns over half of his body, respiration down, blood pressure down, pulse 45 and dropping."

"Do a Jump Start," I ordered filling another syringe with digitalis.

The wizard slumped. "After everything I've already done today? Can't. Too drained."

"Well, do something!" George demanded, tenderly mopping the priest's face with a damp handkerchief.

"Sorry, my friend. But nothing I can cast will stop him from dying."

Jessica trust something into my hand. "Here."

It was a copper bracelet. I didn't have to ask which. First Raul, then Hassan. We'd be damned if another member of our group was going to die, not if there was anything we could do to help them. Tenderly, I slipped the band about his blackened wrist, the hot skin crumbling into flakes at the slight pressure and mentally shouted the activation phrase.

There was a flash of light and Father Michael Donaher sat up completely healthy. His freckled cheeks rosy, eyes bright and shiny. However, the priest was now bald as an egg, his thick thatch of red hair and eyebrows gone. He vaguely resembled somebody famous, but I couldn't quite tell who.

"Whew," Donaher exhaled, a wisp of smoke leaving his nostrils. "Thank you from the bottom of my heart."

We helped him to stand. "No problem, Mike."

"But please never do it again," he continued, in controlled anger. "If this was my time, perhaps you should have let me die. The Church does not approve of such things."

Jessica rested a hand on his crumbling uniform. "Then let the onus of saving a human life rest upon me, old friend."

The good father had no reply for that.

As we started across the floor, the stiff clothes of the priest cracked with every move. Though not overly fastidious, Donaher stopped and viewed the fatigues with displeasure. "Anybody have a spare outfit?"

"That trifling I can easily fix," Richard said happily. With a wave of his staff, the priest was properly clothed once more. The army fatigues looking freshly laundered, shirt pressed, boots polished.

Running a hand across his head, the priest was obviously shocked at the skin-to-skin contact and quickly ascertained his hairless condition. Guess we had forgotten to tell him. Anyway, it was a good swap. Your life for your hair. I'd take it any day.

"Dick, old pal, you forgot something," Father Donaher said hopefully, running a hand over his bare pate.

Somehow, the wizard hid a smile. "Sorry, nothing I can do about that. Besides, think how fast you will move minus that excess weight. Why, you're aerodynamically streamlined."

"Of course, the sun glinting off his head could give away our position to the enemy," I observed clinically.

Thoughtfully, Jess pursed her lips. "I might have some cosmetics that would tone down the mirror effect, or we could drape him with camouflage netting."

JUDGMENT NIGHT

Muttering something in Latin, the priest turned his back on us. Didn't sound like a prayer to me.

Chuckling, George returned the Father's shotgun and the weapon proved undamaged from the cooking, just dirty. We gathered the scattered shotgun shells, then moved past the booby-trapped floor and through the dripping hole in the wall, bits of dangling flesh brushing against our arms as we passed. Reaching the other side, I found an anxious Mindy guarding the pile of supplies. As the rest of the group apprised her of the situation, I took stock of our surroundings.

The nearby cliff stretched off to either side, rising impossibly upward to join the swirling gray cloud cover. Wow. It made me dizzy just to contemplate the sheer size of the thing.

Kneeling, I gave the road a cursory inspection. It was made of tiny hexagons of a ceramic material neatly joined together in the manner of a jigsaw puzzle. Dirt littered the surface and the road was badly cracked in several spots. But on the whole, the transit was in good shape. Good enough for us to wheel our carts along, that was what mattered.

The forest edging the road was thickly grown, but few leaves were on the branches and the bushes had seen better days. The grass was made of oddly shaped blades and was withered and brown.

Standing, I worked a few kinks out of my joints. In the far distance, was a single mountain rising majestically above the others, its snow capped peak almost reaching to the surface of the dome. A bird, or something, was flying around the rocky peak. Waitafreakingminute, just how big would a bird have to be for me to see it with unaided vision from this range. Answer: too goddamn big. I slipped on my sunglasses and immediately removed them. It was just like being in the cloud. The place was so permeated with ethereal power the glasses were overloaded and registered nothing. However, my binoculars showed the bird was coming this way fast.

"Red alert," I said softly. "Incoming. High noon."

Following the direction of my arm, the group saw the winged express train and they moved with practiced haste. Ramming the end of his staff into each of the equipment piles, Richard lifted them both from the ground and ran for the forest.

Not a blade of grass crackled beneath his boots, nor was a leaf disturbed by his passage into the woods. The rest of us followed as best we could. Gathered under a spreading tree, whose bare branches offered little shelter, we took each other's hands and breathlessly waited. The sky darkened as something blotted out the sunlight overhead.

"Emergency Invisibility now," I whispered and we vanished.

Totally vanished. Even the depressions of our boots heels in the soil were gone. Invisible was a rather simple spell, but it had many levels of operation. Total Invisibility meant that nobody could see, hear or smell you. Nor would radar, sonar, infra-red or even mass detectors indicate your location. The limitation was, to be that undetectable, the subject also became invisible to itself and walking across a flat empty field proved to be an adventure in moving.

Glancing upward, the gigantic form was only a black blob to me, but the sheer size of the thing made me wonder if this was our buddy from the lake, full grown and open for business.

"Gosh, I hope not," Jessica whispered warmly in my ear.

The tingling that sentence caused was a pleasant sensation, so I attempted to compound it by sliding an arm about the woman. But my questing hand encountered only a hard square object I could identify as George's ammo pack. In disgust, I put the hand in my pocket where it belonged. Phooey.

Darkness came and went as the flying monster performed a search pattern, plainly seeking what made the loud noise earlier. The hole where the Gate used to be was covered by a lintel overhang, and unless Big Bird landed it would remain hidden. But if the creature did come to earth and discovered the damage, a fight would be imminent and I guess-timated our chances of winning at about fifty/fifty. Father Donaher was the only person not bone weary by this point. One of the minor benefits from a Jump Start.

Suddenly, the sun returned. Scanning the sky, only the ever-present cloud was discernible, but we stayed where we were for a while longer. When satisfied that the creature wasn't trying to trick us out of hiding and had truly gone, the mage lifted the spell and we held a fast console.

"Opinions?" I asked, resting a foot on a cart wheel.

"It was a narrow escape," Richard said, munching on a high energy, organic, snack bar. "I couldn't have maintained that spell for much longer. Just about down to my socks in magic."

Smugly, George waved the matter aside. "No problem. I got a HAFLA here that should take the monster out easy."

"And that is?" Donaher prompted.

"A napalm bazooka," George said, patting a canvas wrapped lump.

Mindy arched an eyebrow. "Good lord, we have such a weapon?"

"Two, actually."

"Great! Let's kick some butt!"

Clapping my hands, I got their attention. I had been afraid of this attitude. "No," I said firmly. "No more explosives, or rifles. Put those silencers on your pistols and keep them there. From here on, we go quiet. Our task is to discover exactly what is happening here and stop it. Not waste time and endanger civilian lives indulging in an unnecessary monster hunt."

Resting his weapon on a shoulder, George grimaced. "And if it attacks?"

"We hide and run away. Halting that cloud before it reaches the mainland has got to be our top priority."

Hesitantly, the group accepted that, but they were less than thrilled by the idea of running. Following my example, rifles were slung and the slim Bureau silencers screwed onto our HK 10mm automatic pistols.

Mindy exchanged the explosive arrow in her bow for a simple barbed razor tip and Richard struggled to load a crossbow.

Rummaging through the supplies, Father Donaher pulled on a cloth cap and asked what our next move was.

"Let's take the road," George offered, gesturing with his head. "It appears to lead straight into the heart of the island. As good a place to start our hunt for the owners as any."

I agreed. Mindy was given point duty again and we started pushing our heavily laden carts down the old road, the rubber wheels bumping along with a kind of natural rhythm. There was little to see and nothing to hear, but a faint whispery wind. It was an unnatural silence. No birds, no insects, no people, no nothing. Made my skin crawl and I wondered if we were the only people alive on the island.

"Very probably," Jessica said in her unnerving manner.

"What?" Richard asked, joining the conversation in the middle.

The telepath gave a shiver. "This island is deserted. Can't you feel the years pressing down on us? The countless ages, the oppressing silence of undisturbed, eons old death?"

JUDGMENT NIGHT

"No," the mage replied.

"And what about Big Bird?" I asked.

"The jabberwocky? Oh, there are lots of animals here," Jess recanted. "Just no people."

A minute passed in silence.

"Yet," she added in a small voice. An explanation of that cryptic remark was not forthcoming.

Approaching, Father Donaher tapped his hip flask of Tullamore Dew whiskey, 90 proof, $35 a bottle and worth every penny. "Sounds if you need a dose of neural inhibitor."

Wanly, Jessica smiled. "Later. At dinner, perhaps."

Two kilometers, down the road, Mindy returned. The martial artist was dusty from head to toe, frowning and her sword was drawn. That told me she didn't have good news.

"Found a body," Mindy reported bluntly.

"Old?"

"Brand new. Satan Department."

That brought the group to a halt and weapons clicked in swift orchestration.

"How did he die?" Donaher asked, checking the clip in his pistol.

"Unknown," the woman said. "Got to see this one for yourself."

"They got inside," George said, through clenched teeth, a hand going for the stock of the Masterson Cannon.

Grimly, I pulled my own handgun. "Some of them, at least. Okay, get hard people. Leave the stuff, pattern four, double time."

Without comment, the team scattered and following Mindy's directions, we converged on the body from different directions.

Naked, he was laying spread-eagled in plain sight in the

middle of a small clearing. At first I thought the man was simply fantastically obese. But upon closer inspection, no amount of overeating could do this to a human. The body was horribly distended, the skin stretched to the burst point. Face, hands, belly, everything swollen to the absolute limit of tissue endurance.

With my magnifying glass, I started at the feet and worked my way to the head, closely studying every inch, but touching nothing. It was weird beyond words. Every orifice was sealed shut with a sort of clear secretion. On his neck were two tiny puncture marks about an inch apart, closed with tabs of scarred flesh. Finished, I gave a brief summary.

George whistled. "Vampires?"

"Who put blood in?" I said, stressing the last word. "No, this is something perverse and terribly new."

As Rich and Donaher performed a few tests on the corpse, Mindy went through his backpack, and found the usual assortment of weapons and supplies. The only oddity was a set of four batteries in the shape of an ammunition clip for a pistol. Obviously, the *Machlokta d' Sitna* agents must have some sort of energy weapon. A laser most likely, or microwave beamer. We had the room, so I confiscated them.

Glancing at my mission watch, I frowned. Great, in roughly 20 hours the cloud will reach the East Coast and start killing people and now it was a race with Satan Department. The crazed bastards probably wanted to cut a deal with these island guys.

"Maybe they already have," Jessica whispered.

A chilling thought. "Time's wasting. Let's move."

"Wait a minute," George said, lifting a fat curved object into view. "I want to leave our friends a present."

Mindy smiled. "How thoughtful of you! Here, let me help with the fuse."

JUDGMENT NIGHT

Pulling on gloves, we shifted the bloated corpse and George slid an anti-personnel Claymore mine underneath.

"There," he said, stepping back and wiping his hands with a cloth. "When whoever returns for lunch, they will soon embark on a fast journey to the moon in many small pieces."

"The cloud is in the way," Richard reminded.

George grinned. "That will only slow 'em down."

Mindy and I took double point this time and we kept in constant radio communication. Nothing of interest was found, until a few miles later when the road ended at a small pavilion. We approached with caution and checked for traps, but it was clean.

The supporting pillars of blue marble still stood, but the tiled roof was gone, only shattered fragments laying on the ground spoke of its presence. A flecked marble pedestal centered the pavilion and on it were numerous small structures made on colored glass in exquisite detail.

"Eureka! A model of the island!" Jessica cried happily.

"Photographs," I ordered. Cameras clicked and George started sketching on a pocket note pad.

"Apparently it is laid out in concentric circles," Father Donaher said, crouching low to peer in owlishly from the side. "Here is the cliff and the forest. This appears to be a garden, and lastly, the city proper."

"A walled city," George muttered, indicating a ringed miniature with a pencil. "How odd. Why a defensive wall with no offensive turrets?"

But there were defenses and I searched for the home of Big Bird, the jabberwocky. The tall mountain was located outside the town, on the far side of the island. Fine.

"What could this be," Richard asked, fingering a small area off to the side. "Storage facilities? Homes?"

"A cemetery," Jessica decided.

"Now why would they consider a cemetery important enough to place on the map?"

"Reverence for the dead?"

"These guys?" I snorted. "No way."

A finger pointed. "Look here, in the center of town is a sort of arena, or coliseum," Father Donaher noted. "Observe those columns and archways! Definite Roman influence."

"Unless, ancient Rome was influenced by these people."

Richard scowled at me. "Geez, Ed, just how old do you think this place is?"

"Pre-historic."

"Dinosaurs built it?" Donaher asked sounding amused.

Mindy gave him a smack on the arm. "Don't be a dope. He means it was built before recorded history. And I agree with him and Jess. This place is seriously old."

"Why?"

"Because with the abilities so casually displayed here, these people could have, would have, ruled the world. Yet we never heard of them. Thus, they must have risen and fallen so far in the past that no records or legends still exist."

"That's prejudicial," Richard said, fighting a yawn. "This may be the equivalent of a nuclear missile silo for a peaceful nation and we have only encountered the automatic defenses."

While this was very interesting, the light was beginning to fade and yawns were becoming prevalent. Consulting my watch, it was seven at night. Twilight.

"This conversation can be continued later," I decided. "How about we establish a base of operations before it gets impossible to see."

They agreed wholeheartedly. As I said earlier, a smart group. We pitched camp a few meters off the road in a small

JUDGMENT NIGHT

clearing surrounded by coupes of trees. While Mindy and Jess erected the tents, I prepared the food, Donaher dug a fire pit and George rigged an outer alarm of jingle string. It was simple twine lined with tiny silver bells, all painted a dull black. It was damn near impossible to see in the dark, but the small bells were remarkably loud.

Busy with a hand axe, Richard chopped thorny bushes into small pieces then sprinkled them about our site. After making totally sure that everybody was within the circle, he cast a growth spell and the thorns sprouted into a towering wall of thickets completely encircling our camp. Not only did this give a modicum of protection, but also helped hide the fact we were here. Trespassers are seldom welcome anywhere. George finished it off by draping camouflage netting over the camp, hiding us from any aerial view.

The island was pitch black by the time we ate dinner, with no stars in the sky to brighten the stygian darkness. As a precaution, we used a smokeless cooker to heat the vacuum-packed stew in the MRE packs and turned our lanterns to their lowest settings. No sense advertising what the thicket masked.

We ate dinner, washed and established sentries. But before retiring, Father Donaher held a brief mass for the dead and blessed the campsite. Afterwards, the team held our ritual toast to fallen friends and went to sleep. We spread out so that the group could not be captured in one shot. But also paired up, so we could cover each other in case of attack. Rich with Mindy, Mike with George, Jess with me. The sleeping bags had been destroyed in our journey through the cloud, but there were plenty of blankets. Unfortunately, we did not share.

During the night, I was awakened several times by something very heavy walking past our camp, the ground shuddering at every step. But either the thorn fence deterred intrusion, or else it had had pressing business elsewhere, for the colossus never tried for an entry. Eventually, it moved off into the night and did not return.

TEN

Dawn came as swift as the night. After utilizing the stand of trees decreed the lavatory, I started to brew coffee when Richard stumbled from his tent, yawning and stretching in the dim light.

For a scant moment he stood before the fire, his shadow dancing on the side of a canvas tent. Knowing that our lives depended on fast action, I moved as never before. Drawing my automatic pistol, I pumped fifteen rounds into the chest of Richard Anderson, tracking the body as it fell to the ground. In spite of that, he tried to rise, so I slapped in a fresh clip and let him have another fifteen.

With a jerk, the pistol was gone from my hands, both arms locked behind my back and a stinging pain formed along the front of my neck. I felt a drop of moisture flow into my shirt, somehow I knew it wasn't sweat.

"Talk fast or die," Mindy said softly in my ear.

"Check the body," I croaked, afraid to use my neck muscles. Never having experienced her sword from this position before, I now could truly appreciate its surgical sharpness.

By this time, the rest of the team was sprinting towards us, some fully clothed, one in his underclothes, but all carrying weapons. Donaher and Jess paused for a moment at the body, but Richard was plainly dead, so they continued on to me.

Maintaining a firm grip on his boxer shorts, George leveled his mammoth assault cannon at my belly. "What happened?" he demanded coldly.

"Ed killed Richard," Mindy said succinctly, her grip on

my throat tightening with anger. "Don't know why yet."

"Isn't Richard," I managed to squeak.

"Explain fast," Father Donaher growled.

Gamely, I pointed. The still form laying beside the cook fire was beginning to blur. Ripples of light played over the body and now sprawled on the dirt was a simplified skeleton with exposed muscle tendons and no skin. The insect eyes were fragmented and the gash of a mouth filled with needle sharp teeth.

Mindy released me and I gingerly touched my throat, fingertips coming away red.

"Sorry, Ed," she said, sheathing the sword.

"No prob," I coughed raggedly.

Walking close, Jessica prodded the thing with her M16. "How did you know?" she asked puzzled.

Finding a medical pack, I started rummaging. "Saw its shadow. Not human."

"An illusion," Donaher said, scowling at the monstrosity.

"Yep." I found the ointment and sterile gaze, and started wrapping my throat. Most assuredly, I did not want an infection, and I knew where that sword had been. Many times.

George gave me an impressed look. "Good thing you're a trained observer. Mandatory for a PI, I guess."

"But what about Richard?" Mindy asked worried.

Touching her forehead, Jessica slowly rotated. "I do not sense him anywhere. He's either gone, dead or deeply asleep."

"Let's hope for the best," I said, tying the bandage around my wound. "Okay, spread out. Check under the bushes, in the tree and be careful where you step, he may be buried."

It took awhile, but we did find him. Richard was alive, just unconscious and hidden under a bush with a lump on his head the size of an orange. Smelling salts roused our mage and

Richard told us how he had gone to use the latrine only to awake spitting dirt out of his mouth. A quick review showed the thickets had not been breached, so the thing must have been already hiding in the camp when we erected the barrier. Just plain bad luck. What the hell, happens to the best of people.

For the sake of expediency, we buried the copycat in the same hole. Somehow that seemed fitting, almost ironic. Although, Mindy did cut off the creature's head and buried it on the other side of the camp. I couldn't blame her. Since we did not know what the thing was, even with thirty, hollow-point, steel-jacketed rounds through it, better safe than sorry.

The sun was fully up by the time we finished making sure the camp was secure. Preparing for a long day, we had a hearty breakfast and got ready to move. Using her rainbow sword, Mindy cut us a hole in the thorn bushes, keeping the disturbance to a minimum. Exiting first, I noticed the grass was thicker and greener today, the trees full of brown leaves. Didn't take a genius to realize this island was coming back to life. And faster with every passing hour. Another reason for haste in our actions.

Before departing, we assembled several packs to take along with us, including; medical supplies, food, ammunition, a couple of LAW rockets and a satchel charge. I gave a brief sigh in mourning over the loss of my briefcase.

As we departed, the team filled the hole in the thicket with a trimmed thorn bush, laced into place with concertina wire, courtesy of Mr. Renault. Meanwhile I did a quick sweep about the encampment, but couldn't find any evidence of last night's behemoth. When something which sounded heavy as an elephant did not leave any tracks in soft soil, that made me very, very, nervous.

Tying a few tree branches together, we swept the ground in our wake to hide our footprints. Reaching the pavilion, we undid the branches and positioned them on the berm in what we hoped were natural positions. There were 18 hours before the killer cloud reached the mainland and we might need our hiding hole again.

As the team gathered round the island map, I was not surprised to find the pavilion in better shape today, with more color in the marble and large chunks of its roof back in position.

"Okay, where do we start first?" George asked, shifting his bulky ammo pack to a more comfortable position.

"The town," Jessica stated, as if that was obvious.

Adjusting the cap on his bald head, Donaher agreed. "Definitely. That blank area can have no possible importance or else it would be more detailed, and the mountain is probably just the observation nest of Big Bird."

I was amused. My pet name for the thing seemed to have stuck.

"The town it is," Richard agreed, polishing his staff. In pirate fashion, a red bandana was tied about his head, covering the white gauze pad over his lump. It had proved superficial and the swelling was already starting to go down. Wizards are fast healers.

Reviewing the suggestion, I thumbed a thermite round into my grenade launcher. That was the problem with single shot weapons, you were forever loading the things. "Okay, George on point, I'll take rear guard. Five meter spread, slow walk. Let's not exhaust ourselves early in the recon."

Assuming formation, the group moved out. Incredible as it sounds, in spite of the thick cloud cover, the land beyond the pavilion was bathed in the bright morning sunlight.

JUDGMENT NIGHT

Plainly, it was a tremendous garden, hectares large. Although long dead, ranks of tiny green sprouts were now forcing their way through the cracked soil and multiple rows of trellises adorned with twisting vines were starting to blossom. I wondered why the island was coming alive before the inhabitants? Did the people draw their life from the land and so it must heal first, or was there some agency hindering the return of the Cloud People? Of course, the resurrection may simply have been going up the evolutionary line: plants, insects, animals, monsters, people.

On George's recommendation, we secreted the emergency supplies next to a prominent flower arbor and marked the location with a radio beacon and an anti-personnel mine. As momma always said, when in doubt, use explosives.

Working our way among the brambles and dry weeds, I began to notice the faint outline of a road beneath the ever-present dust. A wide four lane expressway, with a rusty metallic rail running along the median. Mass transit for commuters? I was discussing this possibility with Father Donaher, when we broke through the vanguard of trees rimming the garden and saw the city.

"Trouble," the priest sighed, pushing back his cap.

"Big trouble," I heartily agreed.

Metropolis would not have been an inappropriate word to describe the awe-inspiring expanse of towers and skyscrapers visible. But even worse than raw size, the place was domed by a glass clear hemisphere of something that shone like polished crystal.

Even at this distance, we could tell the lower part of the structure was similar in appearance to the cliff on the beach, a smooth tan stone. But at forty feet, the material became transparent and curved inward to completely encase the city. Following the line of the road, led us to a blank wall with no alcove and keyboard this time. The engineering involved was damn impressive and damn annoying. How could we gain entrance?

I waved Richard closer. "Didn't you used to be in the construction trade?"

Using his staff as a walking stick, the slim man ambled over. "Yep, I was a class C stonemason before I discovered what Fort Knox really guards and accidentally became a wizard for the Bureau."

"What could this dome be made of? Armorlite? Plexiglas? Transparent steel?"

"Ed, not even diamond sheets or compressed carbon filaments would suffice," Richard commented wryly. "There is no known substance that could make a dome this size. The support beams would be crushed under their own weight. It would take something out of a science fiction novel to build . . ." He gestured expansively. "This!"

"Or magic," Donaher added practically.

Richard admitted the point.

A detailed examination of the tan wall yielded a plate of glass, or plastic, embedded at shoulder height alongside the decrepit roadway. The smooth material was in the shape of a hand. We were familiar with these. Pressing your mitt against the glass would activate an internal scanner to read the fingerprints and match them against a master file. Authorized personnel gained entrance, unauthorized personnel would get enough voltage shot through them to vaporize a Buick.

With a pocket EM transmitter, I attempted to electronically jam the scanner and got nowhere. Richard tried to cycle open the doorway with magic, but the portal was sealed even

JUDGMENT NIGHT

tighter than the cliff. He could barely detect that there was an entrance.

Jessica attempted a mindprobe to no result. This left us with three options: failure, Mindy, or George.

"Let me try," George urged, patting the satchel charge slung at his side.

Hesitantly, I agreed and he set our last C4 charge against the wall.

"Rich?" I asked.

The wizard nodded. "No problem. Oh, George? If anything goes wrong and you damage my staff like you did back in Wisconsin, this time I will not turn you into a toad."

"Huh? Well, that's damn nice of you," George acknowledged hesitantly.

Stepping closer, Richard towered over the small soldier. "I will only turn parts of you into a toad."

The soldier gulped. "Fair enough."

Lifting the top flap, the timing pencils were set and we retreated to safety. Richard waved his staff about and after thirty seconds, the satchel disappeared in a violent expansion of light and gushing smoke. It was weird. I felt a gust of wind rush by and ducked under the rain of dirt that followed, but didn't hear a single sound.

Remarkably, the titanic blast got results. As the smoke cleared, we could see that the wall was broken with a thousand gaping cracks. We got a glimpse of buildings inside the structure before the damage started to promptly close as if it was a wound in living flesh.

"So much for brute force," Mindy said, giving her quiver and bow to Donaher. The sword she kept. Her will stipulated that she was to be buried with it in hand. Or else.

The priest slung the quiver over a shoulder. "Ready?"

"Nothing to it, but to do it." Raising her bracelet, she muttered a word and faded from view in the manner of a departing ghost. Dimly, we could perceive the vague outline of her body step round the blast crater and phase into the wall.

A slow minute passed, and a transparent Mindy lurched out and fell to the ground gasping for breath.

We rushed to her and I cradled the solidifying woman in my arms. "Geez, what happened, kid?"

"The wall resisted me," Mindy panted, color flowing back into her face. "Waves of pressure crashing against me. I dug in my heels and kept going, but the pounding constantly increased until I was pushed out."

George popped a stick of gum from a MRE pack into his mouth. "What now, fearless leader?" he chewed.

Scowling, I sighed. "We need a hand."

The rest looked at me blankly, but Richard got the idea.

"A hand from an inhabitant of the island," he explained. "We warm it to body temperature and place it against the scanner. With any luck, we're in."

"Check."

Jessica made a face. "Grisly, but effective."

"It's worked before."

Bending over, Father Donaher helped Mindy to her feet. "What are we supposed to do, circle about looking for another way in, or go search for a graveyard?" he asked, restoring the quiver and bow to their owner. The martial artist tightly held the items as if drawing strength from the weapons.

A graveyard was a swell idea, but since we didn't know for sure where one was, the choice was easy. On a coin flip, we went to the right. The featureless wall moved by with monotonous regularity and an hour later, we reached the rear of the city and paydirt. Only a short distance from the wall was a

JUDGMENT NIGHT

dense row of trees, behind which was an open area all too familiar to this crew.

"Graveyard!" Mindy cried out in triumphant. "Yahoo!"

Promptly, George stuffed a cookie into her mouth. A master of stealth Ms. Jennings was not. She took the indignity with grace, and chewed before swallowing.

Peeking through the bushes, I was delighted to find the graveyard was not domed or even encircled, but just sat there easily accessible. Only a low stone wall, barely a meter high, ringed the place and the front gate was missing.

Using binoculars, I scanned inside the fence. Filling the middle area were endless rows of simple tombstones, all exactly identical, and in each corner of the cemetery was an ornate stone building, no windows, one door. Mausoleums, without a doubt.

However, off to the right of the place was a huge earthen pile dotted with the remnants of busted wooden wheels, broken glass, rusty wire, strips of cloth and general assorted lumps. A garbage dump? They buried their dead alongside a garbage dump?

Either these people had a strange sense of propriety, or else just didn't care where they were buried. It also indicated a rich civilization. Poor societies do not have garbage. Can't afford the waste. Poverty is what truly invented recycling.

Spreading out, the group used what natural cover there was as we advanced upon the place. Once inside, the team spread out along the gravel paths, habit making us avoid treading on the graves themselves. Ya never know, ya know? Hardly any dust was present here, if that signified anything. In front of us, the mountain range lifted to the cloud, the sheer bulk of it hiding the cliff that rimmed this weird island. Rising like a knife thrust from the center was the main, snow capped peak, towering above the others as a king. Was it tall enough for snow?

Calling a halt, I stooped and tried reading the inscription on a tombstone. But the ancient writing, if it existed, was beyond deciphering. "Rich, try talking to one of these, will you?"

Fingering a complex gesture, the mage rapped the tombstone with his staff making it ring softly like a bell. "Awake," he ordered in a Voice Of Command. "Speak to me of this place." A faint growling sounded from the marker that quickly faded away.

"Blast. Sorry, Ed," he apologized. "This rock is too old. Poor thing is senile."

The rock was senile? I just hate it when he says things like that. Always makes my head hurt.

Just then, a sharp whistle called for our attention and leaving the stone dead, we hurried over to where Donaher and Jessica stood waiting impatiently for us.

Reaching the middle of the graveyard, I noted the graves ended a bare circle, some fifty meters diameter. Scattered about on the hard ground were dozens, hundreds, of wooden crosses. Not small grave markers, but human-sized gallows, the beams scarred with numerous nail holes and the wood stained dark by some dripping fluid.

"Dear gods," Richard breathed.

"My feelings in the singular," Father Donaher said, removing the tiny silver crucifix that dangled from his belt and placing it around his neck.

In the hub of this hellish wheel was a glazed pit in whose charred center lay four blackened chains, the thick links ending with heavy cuffs. A crematorium was the first thing that came to mind, but one where you had to chain the corpse down?

JUDGMENT NIGHT

"Alive," Mindy said, her hand twisting on the braided handle of her sheathed sword. "The bastards burned them alive."

"Could have been executing criminals," George offered, rubbing his unshaven chin to the sound of sandpaper.

"Jess?" I asked.

Hugging herself, Jessica could only shake her head no. Poor kid was probably near sensory overload from the amassed negative vibrations of the people who died on this spot. I decided to keep a close watch on our telepath.

Brushing a loose strand of hair under my cap, I saw my wristwatch. "Come on, time's wasting and we need a hand."

George flipped out an entrenching tool. "Dig we must."

"Anybody buried in the ground is long destroyed by worms," Father Donaher stated. "The only hope is a mausoleum."

"Okay. Which?" Mindy asked.

"Does it matter?"

"Yes," Richard said, his gaze shifting back and forth across the landscape. "I can feel that it does."

We waited. Silently, Jess reached out to point a finger at a building apparently no different from any other. That was the one we headed for.

The door to the mausoleum was similar to a beach bum, bronze and simple. I could have picked the lock in my sleep. Cracking the portal, the air that gushed out tasted stale and a bit musty, but without any of the telltale bitter traces of archeology's arch-enemy, methane. This close to a dump, that could be a real danger.

Standing in the rectangle of sunlight, I could see a nearby iron wall bracket for holding torches, sans any torches. Oh well. Twisting the lens on my flashlight to its widest aperture, the bright beam illuminated the vast expanse of the dim room; floor, walls and ceiling made of seamless flecked stone. Seamless. Wonder how they did that trick?

"Clear," I announced.

In brisk order, the rest of the team followed inside. The last to enter, George put an unbreakable Bureau pocket comb in the jamb and let the door close partially.

Except for us, the place was empty, the only thing of interest was the rear wall neatly lined with metal plates. Coffin niche covers. Four by twenty five, an even hundred. The place more resembled a morgue than a mausoleum. We turned our attention to the niches. Donaher took guard by the door. Desecrating graves was a bit beyond the call of duty for a priest.

Getting in was easier than expected. The wall plates were held in place by four bolts, easily removable. The coffin in the niche slid out on grease caked rollers. But it took three of us, each using a small crowbar, to remove the lid. Centuries underwater had sealed the coffin tight. Success came with the sound of splintering wood and the lid crashed to the floor.

Laying inside was a human skeleton, its broken fingers embedded in the wooded lid, stained shavings hanging in mute testimony of the occupants last frantic struggle. Underneath the poor unfortunate was the cracked bones of who-knows how many others. Why the casket had been so easy to breach was now explained. Somebody used it over and over again. This wasn't a graveyard, or a place of execution, but a torture chamber. PIs are by nature peaceful fellows, but I was beginning to think a brisk radioactive bath was just what this stinking rat hole needed. Being buried alive. It was my secret nightmare.

"Father!" I called.

JUDGMENT NIGHT

At once, Donaher was nearby, his shotgun searching for danger. "Trouble?" he asked.

"Yes and no. Can you lay an entire building full of dead folks to rest?"

He blinked. "At the same time?"

I nodded.

"Certainly. But why?"

We explained and as he glanced into the coffin, his face took on an expression of such unbridled fury that I nearly felt pity for the people who did this abomination. Nearly.

As the only other Catholic in the group, I got to play altar boy for the ceremony. Donning the purple sash of his church, Donaher read a brief ecumenical ceremony from his pocket bible, the words sounding large and important in the gloomy still. When he finished, we chorused amen. Instantly, a thumping could be heard, a banging within the mausoleum walls. Oh crap.

Rapidly, the pounding built until the building shook and we fought to stay erect. The bolts holding on the wall plates rattled free and rained to the floor. Then the plates dropped and beams of blinding light erupted from within the coffins. There was no time to head for the door. I only hoped what we had accidentally unleashed was benign, or killable. An explosion of wind roared from the niches to batter us backwards and whip our clothes with stinging force. But not Donaher. He alone stood calm and unruffled in a hurricane of screaming wind. Violently, the door to the outside slammed open, and the tempest of force and noise faded into the distance.

In the ensuing still, the bronze door slowly closed.

"What the hell was that?" I asked, my voice sounding incredibly loud in the sudden silence.

"Ghosts," George said in a tone that made me pivot in a fighting crouch.

Floating above the coffin was a young woman. A vision in white, the lovely apparition was only a glowing torso, the long folds of her flowing gown fluttering where her legs should be, the atmosphere now scented with the honey sweet smell of fresh ectoplasm.

Nobody was frightened. A ghost was no big deal. We had one in the cellar of our apartment building that regularly stole the sports section out of the newspaper and ordered out for pizza.

"Beware" she spoke in a hushed whisper, the words echoing slightly.

In my opinion, a warning was a bad way to start a conversation. Of course, we could understand her, despite that fact she had died eons before English was developed. Ghost are strange that way. Anybody they talk to hears them in the listener's native tongue. I always got mine in Spanish and George in French, even though he barely spoke the language. Born in Paris, when he was two years old his folks moved to Ohio. Drove him crazy. He spent two months learning French so he could speak to the dead. Welcome to the Bureau.

"Beware of what, my child?" Father Donaher asked gently.

She drifted closer to him, the tendrils of her flowing garment moving without hindrance through the coffin. "The masters . . ."

We had already deduced a slave culture here, so this was hardly news.

"Free lady," I said oozing charm. "What transpired here?"

Either she didn't hear me, or didn't want to tell me, so Donaher repeated the question.

She gave a ghostly sigh. "One dark night . . . while they slept . . . we stole their magic," she spoke, her gaze lost in memory. "And ordered the sky to sink the land...we succeeded...and yet failed...for our masters are not dead, only sleeping...even now they struggle to waken...to once more taint the world...with their reign of blood and pain..."

Basked in the unearthly illumination, Father Donaher asked, "Child, what must we do?"

A transparent hand caressed his unflinching cheek. "Stop them if you can," the spirit whispered. "Stop the island from rising . . ."

"How?" I asked impatiently. Damn long-winded ghosts never get to the point.

"How?" Donaher repeated.

But she was starting to fade, her time on earth finished. ". . . to the north is a tunnel . . . look for the broken statue . . ."

"The broken statue of what?"

As if to implore us, the vanishing woman raised her hands. "Find the new magic . . . steal it . . . destroy it . . . An Lan-dus must not rise . . . !"

Then in a flicker of light, the room darkened and the ghostly image was gone.

ELEVEN

It was an odd pronunciation, but we still knew what she meant.

"Ann Landis?" George asked, scratching his head. "Wasn't she a movie actress in the '60s?"

I turned to Mindy. "You're closer, you hit him."

Smack!

"She meant Atlantis, knucklehead," Father Donaher explained, removing the purple sash from his neck, neatly rolling it and placing the religious accouterment into his pack.

"Oh," George said. "I thought the island-state was supposed to be in the Mediterranean Sea, over by Greece."

"So it moved," Mindy snorted rudely. "Big deal."

Richard snapped his fingers. "Hey, didn't that guy on the beach have a Greek dictionary?"

Without a word, Father Donaher produced the volume from his jacket pocket. Thumbing through the volume showed it was not modern day Greek, but in Hellenic. Ancient Greek.

"How did they know?" Donaher mused.

The reason hit me like a punch in the spleen. "They're the new source of magic!"

After so many years of trying, Satan Department had finally found a way to conqueror the world and destroy the Bureau. The details could be worked out later, at the moment all that mattered was we made damn sure they failed. Unfortunately, everybody in the place was bare bones, no hands to borrow. Our only course of action was to try this mysterious tunnel.

JUDGMENT NIGHT

I dug a compass from my equipment belt. North was towards the garbage dump. Best place for a broken statue.

"Double time," I snapped. "Five meter spread. I'm on point, Richard take the rear."

Leaving the cemetery, we moved through the line of trees to the far side of the dump. There we found something else not shown on the map in the pavilion, a sort of military encampment.

A stainless steel picket fence some thirty meters tall surrounded the place, the top of the barrier strung with wire supported by glassy knobs. Electrified wire, without a doubt. An ornate double gate, slightly ajar, fronted the fence. Plus, the gateway was bracketed by a pair of giant purple crabs resting on marble stands, their claws raised as if to do battle. The team exchanged puzzled looks. Purple crabs the size of a school bus? These folks either had strange taste in decorations, or some really bizarre sea life around here.

Using binoculars, I gave the place a fast once over. Filling the encampment were row upon row of iron bar cages, some large, some small, a few on stilts, others in sunken pits. Hmm. There was easily a hundred cages little more than piles of rust and quite a few of the standing cages had broken doors, the metal framework hanging loosely from twisted hinges.

"It's a freaking zoo," I declared, lowering the binoculars.

Mindy pocketed her own field glasses. "Agreed. Well, this certainly explains the weird monsters."

"Why a monster zoo?" George asked, around a fresh stick of gum. "Doesn't make any sense."

"Zoos never make any sense," Jessica retorted angrily.

Glumly, Richard shook his head. "No, George has a good point. What was its purpose? This island is hardly designed for the tourist trade."

"Maybe it was a sanctuary for endangered species," I offered. "Or a kind of wildcard defense against invaders." But both ideas sounded pretty lame.

"It could have been a quarantine pen for pets," Mindy added.

George jerked a thumb. "Pets that required those kind of restraints?"

"Okay, maybe not," she relented.

"Excuse me," Father Donaher hesitantly spoke. "But wasn't there a coliseum sort of building inside the town?"

I scowled. That raised a few chilling possibilities. The old Christian-and-lions routine had occurred in the decadent period of ancient Rome just prior to the collapse of the empire. Maybe the same scenario was played here, with some magical Nero fiddling away while the island sank into the ocean? Sure fit the psychological profile of "The Masters."

Thoughtfully, Richard munched on a thumbnail. "If it is for the coliseum, then there might be an underground transport system for moving the animals that we can use to gain entrance to the city."

That's my wizard. Always thinking.

"Must be what the ghost was talking about," I said. "Let's go."

Thoughtfully, Donaher ran a hand over his endless forehead. "Okay, how do we get in?"

"Something wrong with the front gate?" I asked.

"What about the Cancer twins?" Mindy said, fingering the hilt of her sword. "With explosives banned, how are we supposed to take them out? Drown them in our blood?"

"Bah, I'll use a medium grade sleep spell," Richard said, twirling his staff like a majorette's baton.

"Nonsense, a dose of BZ gas will do the trick," George said confidently, tapping a military gas canister. "That'll have them so confused they may start dancing with each other, or order out for Chinese." Good ol' BZ gas was the unofficial party favor of the US Army.

"There are no detectable organic components," Jess said, scrunching her forehead. "They must be either statues, or robots."

That stopped conversation for a second.

"Either could be the broken statue," Mindy whispered, notching an arrow to the bow.

"Interesting," Donaher said. "But if robots, programmed to do what, I wonder? Greet guests, or repel invaders?"

Jacking the cover on his mammoth assault rifle, George checked the indicators. Even from a meter away, I could see the digital display said 14,000 rounds remaining in the mammoth weapon.

"Who cares?" George announced confidently, sliding the cover to the former position. "We can take them easy."

"Barbarian," Richard admonished. "Why not just walk past the things first and if that fails, try talking?"

None of us could really find a flaw in that plan.

"Well, Ed?" Donaher asked, extending a palm ahead of the group.

I shrugged. "A short life, but a merry one." Experimentally, I rustled a bush to see what would happen. Nothing did. In attack formation, we exited the shrubbery and slowly approached the zoo, our boots silent on the fresh green grass. Keeping a careful watch on the crabs, our weapons at the ready, we came abreast and then passed beneath the towering crustaceans. At one point, I could have sworn that I heard a metallic creak, but neither seemed to have moved, so maybe it was only my imagination. Hope, hope, hope.

Moving through the dusty paths of the zoo, we gave the

timeworn cages a cursory inspection. The place was spartan to the point of being crude. This was definitely no entertainment complex. Reminded me more of a prison. Chains and locks were everywhere, more than seemed necessary. The bars of the cages were barbed on the inside and the sanitary facilities were painfully obvious. The things in the cages were mostly skeletons covered with stripes of fur or bits of scale. However, a few were fully composed, merely desiccated corpses and a couple whole and alive.

Nasty hairy things, with a jointed proboscis and stiff wings, sort of like a cross between a bat and a vacuum cleaner. Strange that the animals were reviving, but no people yet. Slaves, or masters. Where were the damn inhabitants?

"Yuck," Richard said, curling a lip. "Mosquitoes."

I blinked. By gad, he was correct. A hairy black mosquito. Warily, I stepped closer and that was when I noticed something odd on the floor of the cage. Took me a second to identify it, and when I did, the world became very quiet.

"Something wrong?" Mindy asked stepping close, her sword drawn.

"Let's kill all of these things before they finish healing and do a mass escape," I said, checking the clip in my pistol.

"What? Why?" demanded Jessica confused.

Using the barrel of my weapon, I pointed. Laying scattered in the dirty rubbish of the cage were numerous bones, the top most clearly a human leg bone. Aside from the skull, the femur was the most easily identifiable piece of our skeleton.

The telepath gasped and I nodded.

"Bureau regulation #43," Father Donaher quoted, working the slide on his shotgun. "If any non-sentient creature has consumed human flesh it is regarded as too dangerous to let live and must be exterminated."

JUDGMENT NIGHT

As a priest, Michael had very definite opinions on such matters. He never used his weapon on a live human. That would be murder. But blowing away monsters and hellspawn, Donaher considered a holy chore, and one he performed with relish.

"How do you know they're non-sentient?" Jess demanded.

It was a valid question that George answered by rattling the cage door. "These locks would stop a 400 pound gorilla, but not a twelve year old child."

"Agreed," Richard said, the tip of his staff already starting to glow with power. "That thing this morning was only an animal. The sole reason it got the drop on me was . . . um . . ."

"It caught you with your pants down," Mindy supplied.

He almost smiled. "Literally."

Trying to cover every possibility, I exchanged the clip in my gun, for another in the belt ammo pouch. "A silver bullet in the head apiece should do the job."

"Want me to gather some wood and hammer a stake through their hearts?" George offered, pausing to blow a bubble.

"Too time consuming. We're on a tight schedule. But as a fillip, lets wire the front gate with Willy Peter just in case something survives."

Willy Peter, aka, white phosphorus, wasn't as hot as thermite, but it spread better and could fry anything this side of a cyborg whale. Now those babies are hard to kill.

"A Crispy Critter special, coming up," George smiled, pulling wire and things from his shoulder pouch.

Mindy assumed a guard position while the man got to work. "The smoke will draw attention," she reminded.

"Pressure switch," George said connecting a wire to a battery. "Won't detonate unless the gate is moved."

"How long?" I asked.

"Take me five minutes."

"Check."

While the soldier prepared to rig the incendiary charge, the rest of us started moving systematically along the cages, our pistols coughing silver slugs into anything that resembled a head. Sometimes it took three or four shots to make sure we got the braincase.

The team separated to expedite things. There was little danger, we could easily see each other through the assembly of bars. Moving steadily along, I turned into an alleyway boasting a cage large enough to hold a flying elephant. In fact, I was actually wondering if it did, when the ground crumbled at my feet and I started to fall. Dropping my rifle, I made a desperate leap for the iron bars, but failed miserably.

Darkness swallowed me whole.

TWELVE

Plummeting out of control, I yelled. Who wouldn't have? Shouting and cursing has never slowed me down a bit and I guess it never will, yet still I try.

Attempting to angle myself vertical in case I could grab something, my weighty backpack pulled me over and I fell facing the dark top of the earthen shaft. As there was little else to do, I forced my muscles to go limp. Mindy taught it helped saved bones when you hit ground.

But it was a net of some kind that caught me, the strands stretching deep with the force of my drop. As the snare contracted, I tried to ride the forthcoming recoil upwards and land on my feet, but the net came with me and for a while I simply bounced up and down until the undulations ceased and I was still.

A dim luminescence pervaded the dark and faintly I could see that I was sprawled on a giant spider's web. Hoo boy, in spades.

With icy calm, I struggled to free myself, but nothing moved except my left arm, from the elbow down. Every finger of my right hand stuck to the web and no matter how hard I pulled the skin would not come loose from the resinous strands.

Craning my neck, which painfully pulled some hair free, I could see my rifle was dangling about ten feet away. Damn.

Waitaminute, my bracelet! What did I have? Flame Blast? Force Blade? Ah, no. I had Invisibility. Swell. Guess it had sounded like a good idea at the time. Unfortunately, it wouldn't do spit against a spider. They saw in the ultra-violet spectrum. It would spot me in a hot second.

Using my left hand, I searched my body and took inventory. My pistol was holstered on my right hip, totally out of the question. But I could reach my front pants pocket, my medical kit and the ammo pouch for the M16. My combat knife in its reverse shoulder rig was just out of reach. What could I do with it anyway? Fight some two ton monster with a eight inch knife and my left arm down free from the elbow. Right. Afterwards I'd invent a cure for cancer and fly to the moon.

Horribly loud, my wristwatch began to beep. It was the gang trying for contact. Shaking my wrist, I turned the thing off. It would only disrupt my concentration and the noise might attract unwelcome attention sooner than necessary. Besides, I couldn't reach the transmit switch and tell them where I was, so it was useless.

Quickly, I reviewed my situation and options. Of the top six possible courses of action, I took the most daring. Think big, be big, and I planned on living.

Being damn careful not to touch any of the strands with my left hand, I dug about in my pants pocket for my cigarette lighter. I didn't smoke, but the silly things had a thousand uses; burning through ropes, lighting fuses, emergency light source, etc. Plus, this was a Bureau lighter, turn the top and four seconds after you depressed the lever the lighter would blow your hand off. Very useful for distracting enemies, opening locks and getting rid of unwanted seasonal house guests.

It was part of what the Bureau called a city kit. Went along with things like a video camera inside a soda can, gas mask handkerchiefs and our lovely collection of pens. They squirted acid, launched tiny flares, were telescope/microscopes, gave a two minute supply of air, you name it. However, all that cool James Bond stuff was in New York. Seemed silly to haul along an exploding pen, when we were armed with bazookas and grenades.

Yet the lighter gave me comfort. If things got really bad, I could always use its special function and take the Bug Boy with me into the abyss. Beats being eaten alive. Or so I have been told.

omewhere in the dark, I heard a scuttling noise and tried my best to ignore it. If I panicked now, it was the big boom. Keeping a firm grip, I turned the flame control wheel to maximum and thumbed the lighter on. Craning my hand, I aimed the four inch flame at my arm, and started burning the khaki fabric of my military jumpsuit. My goal was the cuff button. The twilled cloth resisted my efforts, but the button thread flamed nicely and in a couple of seconds the charred button fell away. The ventilation slit on the forearm gaped wide and I could now reach my knife. God, did I need that knife.

Pocketing the lighter, I released my combat knife and started to slit the fabric on my shoulder. Razor sharp, the knife did a good job, but my clumsy slices made me damn thankful I was wearing body armor.

Reducing the jacket to strips gave me more freedom of movement, but not enough, so I also cut the straps that supported my backpack. Caught in the web, it wasn't going anyplace.

That did it. Wiggling out of my jacket, I sat up with a heartfelt sigh. My clothing had been stuck to the spiderweb, not much of me. Using the lighter, I burned away the strands on my right hand. It hurt, but I could do repairs later. Drawing my pistol, I gave it a kiss and briskly unscrewed the silencer. No time for quiet now. Besides, the silencer retarded the muzzle velocity of the weapon and I might need every ounce of punch my 10mm could deliver.

Removing the half spent clip, I inserted a full one, a deadly mix of soft-lead dum-dums, armor piercing steel slugs and mercury tipped explosive rounds. Up yours, Mr. Spider.

I almost lost my sunglasses getting them out of my jacket pocket, but made a last ditch save below the web. Whew. Through them, the pit was even darker and nothing showed. I put them in my T-shirt pocket for safety. Okay, no magic, fine. Physical monsters I could handle by the dozen.

Twisting about, I began burning the strands holding my pants. My plan was to get out of here before the spider came home. Escape should be a cinch. My backpack held rope and a grappling hook shell for the grenade launcher. All I had to do was find secure footing and unless the top of the pit was out of range, I would be gone in a few minutes.

Without warning, the web vibrated. I looked everywhere and found the spider coming at me from the west. Its fat body was round and furry with tiger stripes. The head was an ugly collection of faceted eyes and snapping mandibles. I almost laughed. All this worry and the stupid thing was not much larger than a dog. No more than four feet tall.

Contemptuously, I leveled the pistol and let the beastie have it. The heavy slugs from the banging automatic hit the insect like sledgehammer blows, the plump body jerking with each impact. But no blood showed and as I stopped, the spider began to scuttle forward again, apparently undamaged. Dropping the clip, I reloaded and gave it some more to the same result.

Activating my wristwatch, I beeped the emergency signal, waited and then beeped again. Nothing. Yet my transmission had to be getting out, because their message got in. Suddenly, I had other considerations as the spider spat a long stream of a milky fluid towards me from its mouth. I ducked and the filaments shot overhead. From its mouth? That was not where spiders normally emit strands. Then as I watched, the eyes enlarged into glistening jeweled pools and it haltingly spoke in a foreign language. Shit. Magical. The damn thing must have been hiding, or possessed an aura so black I couldn't even see it in the dark.

In the back of my mind, I made a mental note to laugh at the remark once I got out of here. Correction, if, I got out of here.

Answering the spider in English, I tried to sound puzzled, arrogant and then commanding. Make it think I was a Master. The insect paused and then asked a question. Haughtily, I snorted in disdain. Obviously, not the proper response because the spider promptly charged.

The chugging 10mm automatic pistol forced it away, but each time the creature was getting closer. I might end fighting with the knife, for grenades were useless. Unless I timed a throw perfectly, the canister would fall through the web and explode below the bug doing no damage, or worse, kill me too.

No, wait. That was wrong. Shoving the pistol between my legs, I squeezed my thighs tight to keep it in place. Then with both hands I yanked off my shirt and tied a sleeve around the middle of an incendiary grenade. When life gives you lemons, make lemonade. Or as the Bureau always says in their training films: make your problems work for you.

I dodged another stream of spider spit and pumped a full clip of bullets into the thing. Before it could recover, I twirled the shirt above my head and it let fly. The throw went true, the grenade arcing beautifully, my shirt spreading behind like a camouflage cape. As expected, the canister dropped through a gap in the web, but the shirt caught on the sticky strands. With a jerk, the grenade came to a halt and hung there only a foot below the web.

Curious, the spider paused for a precious moment to stare at the dangling bomb, so I cried out in pain and went limp.

Instincts are hard to fight. Eagerly, the insect raced towards the clearly helpless prey and the Willy Peter grenade detonated into flame. The shock wave knocked me back and my right arm hit the web again.

Covered with white phosphorous, the flaming spider screamed in a high pitched shriek and raced straight at me. Switching the pistol to my left hand, I gave it the clip. But the burning bug dashed right by and slammed into the wall with a sickening crunch. Its eight legs weakly clawing at the dirt, the terrible torch limply slid down to hit the floor—which from the light of the fire I could see was about ten feet away. Oh brother.

The web was burning, so I had to make haste. Holstering the pistol, I used the lighter to cut the major strands supporting me and I fell to land on my feet. Yes! In a circle of flame, the heavy assault rifle above ripped loose. Moving fast, I made the catch. Then using the lighter, I cleared off what few pieces of web were still attached. It was gummy, and hot to the touch, but in working condition.

Over by the wall, the spider was still feebly moving, so I thumbed a HE shell into the grenade launcher and blew the stubborn corpse to bits. Bouncing off the wall of the pit, the burning head rolled to my feet and took a snip at my boot. Oh give me a break. I stitched the head with a burst from the machine gun and then stomped on it with my Army boot for good measure.

JUDGMENT NIGHT

Satisfied that super-bug was finally deceased, I located my backpack and started uncoiling the rope for the climb to the surface.

* * *

Struggling out of the hole, I elbowed my way onto the dusty ground and rolled over to safety. Whew. Getting to my feet, I brushed the dirt from my T-shirt and looked about. Nobody was in sight. Something important must have taken them elsewhere. I tried my radio. Again, nothing.

Holding the cut straps of my pack in one hand, I keep my rifle ready and walked out of the dead end scanning the cages. Moving to the front gate I found a spent gas canister laying on the ground. Not our brand. Empty shells and brass casings were scattered everywhere. A blast crater spoke of explosives, and a charred zigzag indicated a lightning bolt. Amid the wreckage were strips of bloody cloth and Mindy's supposedly indestructible sword, broken into bits.

The sight chilled my bones. To do that would take major magic and contemporary firearms. Only a single answer for that combo.

"Satan Department," I cursed, through grit teeth.

THIRTEEN

Furious, I could have kicked myself for speaking aloud. Moving fast, I retreated into the shadows of a nearby broken cage and waited for retaliation. But everything remained quiet. Using my sunglasses, I tried scanning the zoo, but the aura of the dire cloud above overpowered any local emanations. I switched to binoculars. Nothing was moving. Good, my mistake had not been fatal.

Taking a moment to think, I reviewed the situation. There were no departing footprints in the dirt, so they had probably flown. The blood stains had partially dried, so this happened awhile ago. The chances of finding my friends by tracking were pretty slim. Deductive logic was the answer.

Satan Department would not have hauled dead bodies along with them, so my friends were still alive. For now. Where they had been taken was fairly obvious. The Arabs must be somewhere bivouacked in the city. If our theory was correct and the mad scum had helped raise the island, then they would have a way in. Maybe even the front door.

Okay, it was a good hour walk to where we had hidden the emergency supplies, even further to the camp. I decided not to go back. Timing might mean everything in saving my friends.

Besides, I was relatively well armed. Two clips for the pistol and three for the machine gun, one of them silver. The combat knife, two grenades, a smoke canister, one 40mm HE round, a dozen garrotes, the derringer, a switchblade, a cross, Holy Water, garlic, salt, wolfbane and the Invisibility bracelet. Not too shabby. But first off, I had to locate that tunnel.

JUDGMENT NIGHT

A double-granny knot tied a pair of socks to the straps of my backpack making it functional once more. I hid the switchblade in my underwear, hung the cross around my neck, took a bite of garlic and tucked a grenade into the backpack. The Bureau special derringer was already in my right boot. Returning to the gate, I took the pieces of the broken sword with me. It was a token act of faith. I would find my friends!

Starting at the front, I worked an overlapping pattern, trying not to miss anything of importance as I searched the zoo for that statue. Cages, cages, fence. Cages, cages, fence. Cages, cages, fence. Fence, fence, gate. Frustrated, I was getting ready to start checking the purple crabs and then hit the garbage dump when for the Nth time, I went by a dry fountain in the middle of a prominent intersection. But on this pass I noticed the pedestal crowning the rising set of tiers was topped by a jagged lump. Going closer, I saw it was a cloven hoof broken off at the ankle. The orange metal was deeply eaten with green rust and must have been like this long before the island sank. Bingo.

Climbing into the empty water basin, I felt incredibly vulnerable standing there, running my fingers over the main support block. I half-expected a bullet to hit me at any moment, but it was the sole piece of the fountain large enough to hide a secret door. If only the fountain was running, I would be safely out of sight under an umbrella of water. Probing a cornice, I found a small piece of loose marble that could be pressed, so I did. With a click, the entire corner of the block swung aside just above the water line, exposing a narrow passage leading downward. Pegged wooden planks lined the walls and a moldy wooden ladder offered questionable access. With no choice, I crouched low and entered.

Standing precariously on the slimy wooden rungs, I found

a chain hanging from the underside of the fountain, near the water pipes and gave it a pull. The cornice grated close, as expected and once more I was in the dark. Twisting the generator handle on my flashlight to charge the battery to max, I hooked it to my belt and started my descent.

It was a long, uneventful, climb.

Reaching bottom, I fanned the brilliant white beam around. There was only a single exit. A small tunnel about a meter in diameter on ground level. In front of it was a human skeleton entangled with the linked-bones of a two-headed snake with wings. The fight had been a tie.

My compass said the tunnel headed due south, towards the graveyard. But who would dig an escape tunnel that led directly to the exit point? It must twist about to reach the city if the lady ghost didn't lie to us. I was betting a great deal on that assumption.

Removing my pack, I laid it on the ground. Velcro belts strapped the flashlight to the barrel of my rifle, which I then laid atop the bundle. Pushing it in, I followed and began crawling along the tunnel, the flashlight beam bobbing ahead.

The passageway was gritty, the soil fused, or glued, into a crude sort of cement. Buckled ridges every three meters supported the roof. The air was dank, rich with the smell of the sea.

George would have hated this place. The main reason he weighed so much was little tunnels. Years ago when he was a skinny private in the Army, he had done a tour of duty in Viet Nam and because of his slim size, George had been designated a tunnel rat. The Viet Cong loved to dig tunnels and go hide in them. When the US military found one, they couldn't use gas because the Cong had masks and they couldn't use explosives, because the warrens were so complex the entire thing would

JUDGMENT NIGHT

not be destroyed. So some poor putz had to boldly go in there and flush the enemy out. It was usually the newest, thinnest, recruit who got the dirty job because the death toll was horrendous. The underground passages were lined with deathtraps; crushing weights, nests of poison snakes, roofs that would cave in, buried Cong who would let you crawl over them and then stab you in the belly. After a few of these hellish tasks, George spent every spare minute eating, stuffing his face to become as fat as possible until he simply couldn't do the job anymore. Really couldn't blame him. Might have done the same thing myself.

Years later, after destroying a platoon of zombie KGB agents with a truck load of salt pork, he departed the service to join the Bureau, but maintained his portly shape. I only hoped my buddy was still alive.

Eventually, my beam showed a side chamber with another ladder, going up this time. As I was making good time, I decided to check it out. Might be important.

Leaving my pack and rifle in the tunnel, I screwed the silencer onto my pistol and started climbing. A rung broke on my journey to the top, but no harm done. Reaching the end of the ladder, I pushed a hinged panel out of the way. Total blackness. Twisting the lens of my flashlight on its lowest setting, I shielded the weak beam with my hand and swept the light around. Dimly, I could see the burned ruin of a house. Only the barest outline of crumbled motor on the ground marked the boundaries of the building. Not one single stone was atop another.

Extending the beam, I could vaguely discern sprawling ruins that stretched into the darkness, far beyond the limits of my flashlight. But what could this be? An underground city? Why? Maybe this huge cavern was where the Masters kept the Slaves.

Certainly would have retarded escapes and explain the tunnel I was standing in. But why was the place destroyed? This did not look like the work of the cloud. Even if it could have gotten in down here.

A soft glow in the distance caught my attention, and I trained the binoculars in that direction. Things were a bit fuzzy at first. Focusing, I found a forest of multi-colored sticks, standing upright as if the ends were shoved into the ground. Punching for computer augmentation, I traced a straight line joining another to form a point. Star? No, a pentagram. A pentagram formed of painted sticks.

My blood went cold. I had found the answer to my question. Those were not sticks, but wands. Magician wands. Wood, copper, bronze, iron and silver. Hundreds, maybe thousands of them, in a galaxy of lengths. I even located several gold staffs as long and resplendent as Richard's wand. Enough stored power to . . . sink an island?

But this was impossible. How could anybody steal the staff of a mage? Might as well just stick your head in a microwave oven. The result would be the same. Unless, of course, that didn't matter.

Suddenly I realized that this was where the slaves had performed the ceremony to destroy the island. Who knew how many of them died just to bring the staffs down here, and how many more perished forming the pentagram when every touch meant death. Poised in the center, were three shriveled figures, two men and a woman. Their desiccated remains still standing on their feet, hands raised as if in the middle of a gesture. Brave souls who must have died casting the spell that sank the island. They never even knew if it worked.

I had to do something, so foolish as it sounds, I threw a salute. This was the most heroic act I had ever encountered, ever

JUDGMENT NIGHT

heard of. Alone in the dark, I made a solemn vow never to refer to these people as slaves anymore, but partisans, resistance guerrilla fighters.

Inquisitively, I scanned the underground cavern as best I could. But there was nothing more to see, the destruction of the sla . . . of the partisan city was complete. Must have been a nasty side effect of the illegal conjure. Magic had laws and breaking even a minor one was a dangerous act. Feeling ill at ease, I descended the ladder, gathered my pack and moved. But in the back of my mind, I wondered—if I had my briefcase, could I do the same thing? Kill myself to destroy the island? In painful honesty, I didn't know for sure. Just did not know.

Returning to the tunnel, for an hour I crawled, lost in thought, when I encountered a small cave-in. The ceiling was smashed, the collapsed soil completely blocking the tunnel. Swell. The ground was sandy in texture and the broken pieces of the tunnel sides appeared fresh. Getting a hunch, I used my compass and did some quick calculations. Yep. It was our work. The satchel charge we used had more effect then we supposed. It also meant I was almost under the wall.

Another hour passed as I dug with my hands, shoving the sandy soil behind and kicking it further down the tunnel. My gloves gave some protection, but I would have happily traded my pension for a shovel, or even an entrenching tool. Drip

Too tired to escape, I lay there and waited for the rest of the tunnel to fall, but the ceiling thankfully held. After a while, I took a grenade and buried it in the loose soil. A pistol would have been better, but I couldn't spare mine. As a fast exit was impossible, if something chased me down this passageway, I wanted a bit of insurance. Plan for disaster, reap success, Ben Franklin. Or was that Doc Savage? Damn, I always get those two guys confused.

Fifteen more minutes of crawling and I reached the end of the tunnel. In the chamber at the bottom of the ladder, I gratefully stood and stretched listening to my joints creak. Some water from the canteen and candy bar later, I was feeling fit for duty again.

Removing the flashlight from the barrel of my rifle, I shouldered the backpack and started climbing. At the top, a simple hinged panel offered an exit. For a change, the hatch was bolted closed from this side. How nice. I gave the bolt a drop of oil just to be safe, and eased it back slowly. Didn't make a sound, god love it. Carefully opening the hatch, exposed a split canvas curtain. Exiting warily, I parted the flap with my rifle barrel and stepped into a small empty tent, about the size of a summer cottage. A metal pole supported the umbrella top, the cloth walls were lined with wooden shelves and the open front bisected at waist level with a flat-topped counter. Reminded me of a carnival booth. Across the way, I saw a line of similar booths, the side of a tall brick building behind them. Maybe this was an alley market.

Keeping circumspect, I moved to the counter and looked about. Nobody was in sight. The ground was paved with asphalt, and remarkably free of the ever-present dust like outside. Shouldering my pack, I hopped over the counter, and worked my way stealthily to the front of the alley.

What confronted me was a major intersection, with sidewalks and the streets filled with a motionless traffic jam of weird three-wheel vehicles. There were street lights and traffic signs. Garbage cans and billboards. Glass and steel skyscrapers towered above me. It was bizarre. The place could have been any modern metropolis; London, Berlin, Miami. Yes, at last, I was in the city proper, and in very big trouble.

FOURTEEN

The streets were packed solid with life-size statues of people, thousands, zillions of people. Men and women, young and old. In full color and exquisite detail, all with shockingly similar features: small noses, large jaws, blonde hair, black eyes and skin the color of honey. This was no race I knew. Mostly they were wearing short white togas and knee length flowing capes, but a few were in everything from full body black leather jumpsuits to something that resembled chainmail lingerie.

As if frozen in time, the stationary throng went off in all four directions of the intersection and into the distance. It was as if the entire population of the city had piled into the street and been zapped into mannequins. But what really caught my attention, was that each held a wizard's wand or staff pointed at the dome overhead. A nation of mages. Zounds. No wonder Satan Department rose these guys from their millennium old watery grave. They could conquer the world before lunch. No problem.

Almost imperceptibly, the people near me began to turn their eyes in my direction. Jumping Jesus! They weren't frozen in time, only tremendously slowed and still conscious. Quickly, I moved away. Yet wherever I went, if I stood still for more than a minute, they started to notice me and turn. Had to keep moving and find a place to think.

Dashing round a corner, I inadvertently bumped into an old woman sporting a leering grin and holding a long silver staff.

In extreme slow motion, she started to fall to the ground.

Turning, I snatched a cape off a nearby man and placed it under her to cushion the impact, when I saw a necklace of polished human finger bones about her scrawny neck. Little bones, like those of a child. With a curse, I kicked the cape into the street. Let the bitch drop.

Good thing George wasn't here, or else he would have simply mowed down the entire population with that assault cannon. Which might not be such a bad idea, except that we simply didn't bring enough ammunition to do the job properly.

Stepping out of sight into an alley, I tried to decide what to do. Okay, I was in the city. What next? I could search the city to locate and destroy whatever was raising the island. Should be pretty easy to identify. The thing must be enormous. Or I could try and find my team. That would give me much needed personnel and equipment. Their captors would surely knew where the machine was, what the machine was and how to reverse the process.

Sounded good, but time was against me. Unfortunately, my friends could be anywhere. This was a complex metropolis and totally confusing. I glanced at my watch. Only four hours till the killer cloud got too close to America and the Pentagon would launch the nuclear missiles. I decided to allot one hour to search for the team, before turning my attention elsewhere.

Then it occurred to me that with this many wizards, magical items should be abundant. I tried my sunglasses and was delighted to find that the dome blocked the majority of interference from the cloud and they could now function properly. Cool. Maybe I could steal something that would help in the search.

Moving briskly through the crowd, I spotted hundreds of personal items that registered magical; shoes, hats pins, rings,

JUDGMENT NIGHT

spiked ben wa balls, whips, dildos, nearly every damn one with an aura as black as their owner. Not born stupid, I wasn't touching any of that stuff. Along the way, I encountered a possible solution to my problem, the aura of the item was green, laced with black. Neutral, leaning towards evil, but not pure evil like the rest. Still, I decided against it. Too dangerous. The only way to survive in this business was calculated risks, not wild gambles.

Since I had to dig my way in, I assumed the Satan gang used the front door. So I started my search at a mammoth edifice near the gate, but that proved to be only a tavern. A mirrored bar lined one wall and plush velvet seats curved in tiers to face a pit in which lay a big dartboard that had the outline of a human in the center. Feeling ill, I departed posthaste.

Taking a chance, I went directly to the tallest skyscraper, an impressive glass monolith in the center of the city. But there were no stairs and, of course, the elevators didn't work. Or, maybe they did, but even slower than usual. Disgruntled, I moved on.

An elegant white sandstone building looked important, but proved to only be a gymnasium. I was surprised at the advanced design of the exercise machines. Guess there were only so many ways to get buff.

In the main room was a pool large enough to land our seaplane, and it was filled with a group of buxom mermaids frozen in their struggle to operate a lock on a grilled gate that lead to a run-off canal. Their long cascading hair was the loveliest shade of green, while their large breasts were firm and high, with two nipples each. Most likely they were only concubines or harlots, I reasoned. Stark naked except for a few pieces of jewelry, it was blatantly obvious that the mermaids were true females, because they only sported scales and fins from the knees down. But more importantly, the shapely backsides were scarred by whip strokes and broken chains dangled from their necks. Trying for a mass escape, eh ladies?

Glad to help, I put a water-proof map of New York in the hand of one emerald haired lovely, gave another my switchblade and shot the lock to bits. An enemy of my enemy is my friend. Ever so slowly, they started to move their eyes towards me. I smiled politely, bowed and moved onward. Then I returned to my search.

Cannibal restaurant, kindergarten brothel, hospital-from-hell, obscene museum, tacky shopping mall, miniature golf course, my fruitless search continued until the buzzer on my watch sounded. Enough. This was impossible. They could be anywhere within the cubic kilometers of this huge megalopolis. A needle in a haystack was a cinch compared to this. You could always sit on the haystack, or set it on fire and sift through the ashes. I debated setting off a grenade and letting Satan Department find me, but couldn't take the risk. If they managed to capture the whole group, what chance did I have fighting them alone?

Stupidly, I had been depending upon running across a clue leading to their whereabouts: the sound of gunfire, screams, drops of fresh blood, a disruption in the jammed streets, even a trail of cookie crumbs. It had been a foolish hope, and now I had to accept the fact that I was alone.

Quickly, I checked my watch. Two hours remaining. Time was running out and without Jessica or Richard to pry the information I needed from these living corpses my options were dwindling to a precious few. Perhaps, I was now ready for a desperate gamble.

Retracing my way to an earlier corner, I explored the torpid crowd until I located the petite woman with a puckered acid scar. In the standard toga, minus cape, she was intent upon holding her iron wand at the dome. Hanging tantalizingly from her belt was my new goal. According to the rules of magic, lacking permission, the old owner had to be dead before I could take possession. As I stood there working up my nerve, her hostile gaze started to lower towards me. Fast, I shot the iron wand out of her hand as it turned my way. Tumbling through the air, it hit the chest of an outrageously fat man dressed in tiny pink bikini briefs. The wand clung to the sagging rolls of spotted flesh and crackling ethereal discharges slowly crawled over his corpulent body. In spurts, steam began to hiss from his ears as his brains began to boil.

Blood had yet to flow from the ruined hand of my target, but her face showed the pain and shock. Despite the foul nature of her people, I really hated to do this. Felt too much like kicking a cripple, but I was committed to the plan by now and couldn't stop. Besides, it was my world or hers. Plus... oh hell. Pumping two rounds into her face, I put another two into her chest aiming for the heart. With any luck, death would be instantaneous.

As her body began its leisurely journey backwards, I holstered the pistol and slashed at her belt with my combat knife. Sluggishly, the cloth strands separated, the ends casually drooping. Inch by agonizing inch, the magic lamp started to slid off her belt. Made of tarnished brass, the enclosed reservoir of the oil lamp was the size of a shoe, with a looped handle on one end, a short up-curved spout at the other and the words "rub me" on the side. Such an innocent object. Only my Bureau glasses told the truth. It had an aura powerful enough to sink a battleship.

As it cleared the end of the belt, the lamp dropped in normal speed to clunk on the sidewalk. Snatching my prize, I took off at a run, jockeying through the crowd like a fullback dribbling the puck towards the hoop with bases loaded. Or however that goes, I'm not much of a sports fan.

Three corners later, I saw a shop with an open doorway and dashed inside. The establishment proved to be a leather goods store, with mostly whips and underwear on display. The proprietor, or rather the person I believed to be the proprietor, was a muscular man with beard and moustache. He was in the process of tripping over a chair as he headed for the street. I side-stepped the airborne fellow and went to the rear room. As hoped for, it was his workshop, shelves filled with tanning supplies, delicate knives and stretching racks. Pulling up a chair, I sat and got ready to do my battle of wits.

Considering the age of the island, roughly 5,000 years, this was a genie before the reign of King Solomon, Master of the Gjinn. Thus it would not have to follow his rules on three wishes. One might be all I would get. So it had to be correct the first time. Wording would be very important. According to the Bureau manual, a wish with the word "and" was considered two wishes.

If you asked a good genie for immortal life and untold riches, it might give you both. A neutral genie would only give you the first, or nothing. Improper wording voids the wish. An evil genie would happily give the immortality part and then, as a lark, also make you blind, deaf and paralyzed, so you could suitably enjoy forever. Yes, genies were swell folk. Tons of fun at parties.

According to my glasses, this gjinn was neutral, slightly favoring evil. Not quite as dangerous as playing jump rope in a mine field, but pretty darn close. My sole hope was that five thousand years in the lamp would seriously slow him down.

Male, or female, the gjinn had to be a bit stir crazy after being confined for that long a period.

I rubbed the lamp.

There was the mandatory puff of smoke from the spout, a clap of thunder and the genie appeared. A male. Big, bold and bare chested, wearing balloon pants, embroidered silk belt, a gold earring in his ear and his bald head topped by a huge white turban with a big red jewel in the center. Reminded me of Mr. Clean. I expected him to salaam, but instead the gjinn clutched his head and reeled backwards as if in pain.

"Holy freaking spit!" he cried in colloquial English. "Alexander, the Roman Empire, the Dark Ages, the Renaissance, the Industrial Revolution, two World Wars, nuclear weapons, the Sexual Revolution, laser beams, home computers, video games, VCRs, landing on the moon, MTV, cloning, internet porn!"

Breathing deep, the genie wiped a film of sweat from his brow. "Wow. Things have really changed since I've been gone."

Nervously, I wet my lips. So much for being out of circulation. I'd never seen anybody catch up on current events so fast.

Hoisting a leg up on the tanning table, the gjinn was now dressed in snakeskin cowboy boots, blue jeans, red flannel shirt, a full head of hair and a ten gallon hat.

"Yes, it is a toupee," he admitted. "Okay, pardner, shoot. I have a hot date waiting for me in Tulsa. What is your wish?"

Here we go. "My wish is for you to tell me, in a language that I can easily understand, precisely everything I need to know to successfully complete what I consider my current assigned mission, in regard to this island as a threat to my accepted contemporary civilization."

There was a pause as the gjinn chewed that over. "Pretty good," he grudgingly admitted. "Short, succinct, gets right to the point, plus you didn't use the word 'and.' Not bad at all for a mortal. How do you know so much about genies?"

"I'm a big Barbara Eden fan."

He smiled. "Plus, a Bureau 13 agent."

Hoo boy.

Smiling wider, the gjinn clapped his hands together and then rubbed them hard. "Ah, done. That was easy. Okay, listen close. The independent nation of Atlantis would never consider a treaty with non-magical scum like your kind and they will attempt to conqueror the planet again as soon as they are free." He winked. "So what you want to destroy is at the top of Mount Lympus, you folks call it Olympus, its the biggest mountain on the island. The entrance to the mountain is in the temple that you incorrectly thought to be a coliseum. The city armory is to the left, down the main street nine blocks. Your team is on the nineteenth floor of the pyramid skyscraper to the south of us. They are being tortured. One is dead. One is being violated even as we speak."

Violated? My heart leap to my throat, but I refrained from speaking. He paused as if waiting for me to interrupt, then went on. Bastard seemed to be enjoying himself.

"Yes, I am. Oh, your Bureau scientists were wrong, the cloud will reach New York, in 80 minutes, not three hours. At which point your government will immediately launch a salvo of exothermic Proton missiles. Boy, even I don't want to be here when those babies go off. Presently, the National Guard is trying to evacuate Manhattan and let me tell you, it is not a pleasant sight."

He was telling me more than I asked for, more than I needed, or even wanted, to know. I sensed a trap and heroically kept mum.

"Say, you are smart!" the genie chuckled. "Anyway, in

JUDGMENT NIGHT

summation, always remember that defeat lead to victory."

Startled, I looked up from resetting the timer on my watch. What did he just say?

Doffing his hat, the gjinn fanned himself. "Ye-haw! I haven't been witness to this much excitement since Zeus and Ra duked it out for hand of Kali. Well, good luck, sport. You're going to need it!" In a puff of smoke, he and the lamp were gone.

Pulling out my note pad, I quickly jotted down the pertinent points. It appeared to be exactly what I wanted. Yet why would he mention the armory? I was well armed. Unless, what I had wasn't enough. Damn. Grimly, I set my watch to sound every ten minutes. Still remaining was the question of getting my friends, but with . . . 75 minutes to go, I did not have the time to arm myself and attempt to free them. One, or the other, not both. The world or my friends. Sadly, there was no choice.

". . . one is being violated even as we speak . . ."

Forcing my mind closed to that, I headed for the armory.

* * *

The directions took me to a vacant lot. Surrounded by tall skyscrapers, this flat expanse reeked of importance. Only one small building on the block was evident. A squat, brutish construct of unfinished concrete with narrow slits in the walls as windows. A pillbox. No guards were evident.

The sidewalk about the block was edged with a neatly trimmed hedge, quite green and alive. Beyond, was a glass lined moat some four meters wide, two meters deep and awash with a boiling vicious liquid that looked as friendly as a rabid tax collector.

The approach was easy enough to find, a single break in the hedge offered access, however I could see no way to get across the moat. On the street, an old man was poised mid-step running from the direction of the armory. I gave him a quick inspection, but even with my sunglasses, saw nothing on him to assist me in gaining entrance. Just his wand. Did they fly over?

My watch beeped. Seventy minutes remaining. Okay, fly it is. Slinging my rifle over my neck and shoulder so it couldn't drop, I pulled out my combat knife, retreated to give myself plenty of room, charged and jumped.

The breath was knocked out of me as I hit the other side, my feet dangling dangerously over the edge. Plunging the knife into the grass, I managed to lever myself out of the moat and rolled away until safe. Standing erect, I now noticed a sprinkle of loose soil floating across the moat to the street. Suspicious, I kicked a bit more out there. It scattered and most fell, or rather the dirt in front of me disappeared with a hiss in the moat. The soil to the left stayed up. Gently prodding with my knife, I discovered the truth. An invisible bridge, set just off to one side. Coming in, you simply stepped to the left, crossed the moat, then stepped to the right. Pretty crafty. Anybody not paying attention would go straight to their death.

Freeing my rifle, I judiciously began walking towards the pillbox. Suddenly, the air shimmered briefly as I passed an illusionary shield and the real armory appeared before me. Lord Almighty, these people didn't trust anybody. A stygian fortress completely filled the block, its outer walls constructed of stones bigger than a truck and lined with a good dozen turrets. Each roof was an indented parapet, in the style of a castle and between the square notches I could see siege arbalists, racks of gunpowder rockets and what appeared to be a Gatling Gun style rotating cannon. It was as if somebody had taken the old fashioned, muzzle loading, cannons from 14th century pirate ships and strapped eight of them together. The weapon must

JUDGMENT NIGHT

have easily weighed ten tons and yet it had a hand crank. Wow. I did not wish to see it in action. Or the operator.

Entry to the fort was easy. The portcullis was raised a crack, and the riveted metal gates ajar. Maybe they were still in the act of closing behind the old man in the street. The courtyard was deserted of people, yet dotted with triwheel vehicles and on both side were penned herds of gargoyles, their stone wings clipped to prevent flight. Weakly, the skinny beasts growled menacingly. In a cavalier manner, I flipped 'em the bird.

Unexpectedly, the squat pillbox I saw earlier was still there, its recessed door closed, but unlocked. Inside, I found a bonanza of weapons; tall cabinets full of glass tipped spears—the hollow heads containing a fluid similar to the stuff in the bubbling moat, chests of transparent shields bearing the inverted triangle symbol, frames holding stainless steel body armor, a rack of chainsaw swords, a mound of black powder kegs and boxes of petards. The place was a treasure trove of deathdealers!

An oddity was a tiny crossbow on a pistol frame. The weapon rested alone on a rack to hold ten of the things. It wasn't loaded, so experimentally I released the safety and pulled the trigger. There was a sharp twang and a miniature arrow shot from the end of the stock. Instantly, the feathered bolt expanded to normal size, double normal, triple! It became a baseball bat, a fence post . . .

In a crash of mortar, the telephone pole arrow slammed through the pillbox wall, leaving a jagged hole gaping wide in its tumultuous wake. As a fine mist of dust rained from the concrete ceiling, I respectfully set the safety and place the gun in my backpack. Oh yes, this I kept.

Not withstanding their lethal design, none of the other devices were really useful to me, armor was too small, except possibly for the black powder petards and I couldn't trust the quality. After a geological age, the powder might have lost its ginger and be about as explosive as coffee grinds. I had no wish to be hoisted on my own, as the saying goes. But was this crossbow what the genie sent me here to get?

Thoroughly, I ransacked the place and behind a curtain on the rear wall found a quite modern style vault, with combination lock and everything. Cackling gleefully, I dug into my pack, located my stethoscope and merrily whirled the dial. This was child's play for a Chicago dick. Four clicks later, the vault unlocked and I pulled the massive portal open. Patiently waiting on the other side, was an enormous purple dragon, the splayed dorsal fins glowing red-hot in anticipation. Yikes! I tried to throw the vault door closed and failed.

Spreading its huge jaws, the leviathan vomited a boiling gout of orange flame towards me. Frantic, I kissed the floor as the fiery plasma blast washed overhead. Aw, nuts! I had wolfbane with me, but no dragonbane. Unlimbering my rifle, I launched my last 40mm round at the stomach of the beast probing for a weak spot, followed by a burst of the M16. There was a tiny squeal amid the war-noise and the big dragon vanished.

Eh? Hesitantly, I rose to my knees. Laying dead in the vault was a tiny lizard, chained in place next to a bowl of gnawed sticks and a nest of rags. It didn't make any sense until I realized there had not been any heat from the flame, nor was there the usual smell of brimstone. So the little guy had been an illusion dragon. Mighty dangerous those. It could have made me see anything it wanted to: a writhing Medusa, charging manticore, oncoming freight train, anything at all. If I believed what I saw, the illusion would kill me. I wondered how

JUDGMENT NIGHT

many died using dragonbane against a lizard to whom the herb would be only tasty shrubbery. Thank goodness for area-effect weapons.

Then I almost hurt myself with a grin. If the mages of Atlantis had this deadly an animal guarding the vault, what incredibly valuable goodies must be on deposit?

The vault chamber was merely a plain cube, the rear wall covered with an empty pegboard slotted for different size magic wands. I knew where those were. Scratch marks on the floor showed where something big and heavy had been dragged away and a couple of topless barrels smelled strongly of blood. Yuck. In a stout wooden case, I found a melon sized crystal ball with a short fuse dangling from the top. This I placed in my shoulder pouch for easy access. I wondered who powerful the bomb was? It might even replace my lost nuke.

A pair of plain swords in cheap leather scabbards hung of opposite sides of the vault and their Kirlian auras told why. One was solid white, the other solid black. As there was nothing else of interest in the place, I took down the white sword for inspection.

"Is there evil to be vanquished?" a booming voice asked in my mind.

After a moment, I said yes and inquired as to its name.

"Justice," the sword spoke in a stentorian bass. *"When fighting for a worthwhile cause your skill will increase tenfold, no poison can harm, no spell bewitch. I shield my holder against heat or cold and any lethal conjuration will be returned to the enemy caster twofold."*

Replacing the sword to its peg on the wall, I crossed the chamber and, using a fingertip, fleetingly touched the handle of the black sword.

"Are you my new master?" a soft voice asked in my mind.

This time prepared, I avoid the question and asked for a name.

"*Revenge,*" the voice said. "*Anger and hatred fuel my magic. In any battle, I will guide your arm to kill swiftly. No matter the wounds, you will fight to the end. I eat the souls of the defeated, none but my master may wield me and survive, and I will come to your grasp when called, no matter the distance.*"

Saying I heard somebody call my name, I placed it on the peg and stepped away. Whew. These were some serious swords. Each possessed unheard of abilities. Hmm, Justice, or Revenge? What the hey, with both I could defeat an army!

Taking the black sword, I started to walk across the vault, when in the middle of the chamber I found myself treading floor. No matter how hard I exerted, my boots slid frictionless on the textured metal, as if I was doing the classic mime routine "walking in a strong wind." Suspecting the reason why, I laid the black sword atop a barrel and discovered I could advance again. Claiming the white sword, the same happened. They refused to get within ten feet of the other.

In a weird way this made sense. Justice and Revenge were not likely to be pals. I had to choose. Maybe I could drag one on a rope behind me? No, dumb idea. I could see it catching on doorways and getting entangled in bushes at awkward moments. Well, if I was limited to only a single sword, I knew which.

Returning the Sword of Justice to the wall, I appropriated the Revenge and strapped it around my waist cattycorner to my pistol. Normally, I would have nothing to do with a solid black weapon. I had passed by dozens in the street. But this was an emergency and the sword offered a straight enough deal, the use of its magic for a soul-feast. I just had to keep careful watch that it didn't go after mine. Besides, I honestly did not know if my mission was a worthy or just cause, but it damn sure was based on hatred. I was out to commit genocide on the island folk and Justice might fink out on me would I needed it the most because my motives were not pure enough. Revenge would revel in the bloodshed.

"*Are you my new master?*" it asked softly in my mind.

"Yep," I replied.

"*Then taste of the power. Draw me.*"

I did, and suddenly all of my doubts fled like ghosts from the sun. What was there to worry about? With my training and weapons, I didn't need my team. Bunch of pansies, anyway.

Striding from the vault, I headed for the street, my steely gaze boldly daring somebody to cause trouble.

"*Master, are we soon to do battle?*"

"Yes. Within mere minutes."

There was a telepathic sigh. "*At last.*"

Once more, my wristwatch sounded its warning. Fifty minutes till the missiles flew. I sidestepped across the moat and at nigh Olympic speed I sprinted through the crowded city. Destination: the coliseum.

FIFTEEN

My boots pounded a savage disco beat on the pavement and the city flew by in a blur. Of course, I made it to the temple in record time. How else?

The place resembled your typical coliseum. An endless series of gray stone columns about a hundred feet tall supported an elaborately carved colonnade. Only a single doorway was apparent, at the top of a broad expanse of white marble stairs wide enough to march in the Mormon Tabernacle Choir sideways.

Bounding up the stairs, I jumped a turnstile, and proceeded along a mosaic tile corridor, past a lavatory and a snack bar with a flashing neon beer sign. Okay, maybe these island guys weren't totally evil. Briefly, I checked both doors. Nothing special about either. Where was the entrance to the mountain top?

At the end of the corridor was a huge, brass double door, the surface adorned with mystic symbols, and blocking the entrance, was a guard twice my size. He was dressed in a suit of polished red armor, the style a wild mixture of a dozen cultures, its every attribute seeming to be offensive. Held before him, the point resting in the light gray floor, was a long sword some two meters in length. The blade a shiny black material, its edges feathered with rippled wafers that glinted as prisms in the fluorescent light.

"Hold!" the dire sentry commanded.

Without missing a step, I shot Armor Boy once through the tiny mouth slit and cut off his head with a backhand

JUDGMENT NIGHT

swing, eating the soul before the body pieces hit the floor. Battle, yes! We loved to fight! Lived to fight!

I didn't bother to check and see if the door was locked. Just blew her open with a grenade to announce my presence with authority. But there was no mountain, just the inside of the coliseum.

Sheathing the blade, I marched forward. The whole interior was one vast room, to be measured in acres, not meters. Truncated walls became the ceiling, leaving the stupendous central span free of obstructing support columns. And the cool expanse of the marble abyss was totally bare, except for a lone chair and a man.

At the far end of the palatial room, dominating the entire scene, was a true giant, sprawled asleep on a mammoth throne of metal bound stone. A humanoid dinosaur, the being must have been fifty, sixty feet tall, totally defying the Inverse Square Law of biology. Only primordial magic of the most puissant kind could support this voluminous a life form.

His smooth skin was dark purple and totally hairless. Great club hands rested on oddly formed knees, with hooked claws tipping each blunt, powerful, finger. His head was cleft, almost split in two, the pig-like nostrils separated and the bulbous closed eyes seeming to point in different directions. There were no ears. A jagged crown of gold encircled his head. He was stark naked and blatantly male. It would take an army of rabbi's armed with chainsaws to make this guy Jewish.

So this was the king of Atlantis. I was not impressed, having seen similar giants before, although not on such a grand scale. The grotesque physical mutations were a permanent side-effect of using far too many Growth potions, mixed with Strength and Anti-Aging. Everybody wants to be an immortal superman, but are always too damn dumb to realize that there will be a price.

Promptly, I dubbed him "Fred," after a schoolyard bully I once beat the living snot out of for bothering my kid sister. Ugly and big don't make them tough. I was tough.

Completely unafraid, I advanced and drew my sword. Or rather, I tried to draw the black sword, but it was stuck in the sheath. Hey, why had I sheathed it in the first place?

"Him, Master? You want to fight . . . Him? Lord O'Don?"

Odin, shmoe-din. I pulled harder. "Yes!"

"The being that created me? Forging my blade from lifeless metal, bathed in the fire of his own soul?"

"That's the guy! Come on, let's take him!"

"Fare thee well."

. . . and the madness departed, flowing from my body like sewage down a drain. When my mind cleared of the sword's influence, I stared at it in horror. Holy Hannah, what the fuck was this thing? The Amazing Blade of Stupidity? I unbuckled the belt, let the scabbard drop to the floor and kicked it away. Goodbye, so long, farewell.

However, the blade had gotten me this far. Steadfast, I donned my Bureau sunglasses and got the second greatest shock of my life. The big guy's aura was orange and purple. Orange and purple? Impossible. What the hell did those colors mean? Just how far had this clown mutated?

Sluggishly, huge eyelids began to flutter as Odin started to come awake. Was this caused by me blowing the door, or was something else rousting Fearsome Fred from his much needed beauty sleep? In response, my watch beeped. Forty minutes till the missiles fell. Damnation, where was that door?

"Who are you?" the titanic goyim loudly rumbled, the rafters of the building shaking.

JUDGMENT NIGHT

The words did not match the motions of his mouth. Must be another built-in translator like the Gate. Okay, think fast, Alvarez.

Removing my cap, I bowed. "A humble worshipper, Lord Odin."

Shit, wrong pronunciation, but he didn't seem to notice.

An arm thicker than a Greyhound Bus rose and pointed in my general direction. "And what is that before you?"

I gave the sword a little nudge with my boot. "A meager offering, Mighty King. A magic sword." Well, sort of.

The rubbery lips parted in a double smile. "Ah yes, I recognize the offering. It is the toy I built in my youth "

Toy? He considered this sword a toy? Cowardly, yes, but it was no child's plaything. Or maybe it was to him. Gulp.

"I was unaware that it has been missing," the grotesque monstrosity continued. "How long have I been asleep?"

Tactfully, I tried to change the course of the conversation. "Many years, your highness, but that is unimportant. There is trouble on the mountain and-"

"Nothing I do is unimportant!" Odin bellowed, nearly deafening me. Then he blinked. "What happened to my door?"

Yes! The door! No, the idiot meant the exploded front door. I wanted to shout at him to stop meandering. Fred was obviously not a morning person.

"An accident, sire," somebody said behind me. "We'll have the slaves clean it away immediately."

My heart stopped. That voice! Twirling about, I could only wordlessly stare with unabashed joy as the gang came walking towards me, Donaher picking his way carefully through the steaming ruin of the bronze door. Alive! They were alive! Jess, Mindy, George, every blessed one of them! Wearing battle helmets and loaded down with all of our weapons. Including the stuff from the plane and even my briefcase! Yowsa, back in business!

How the hell had they gotten that stuff? Briefly, I checked them out with my glasses to make sure they weren't zombies, or under mind control. Nope, auras read clean.

"Who are these beings?" Odin said frowning, sniffing the air suspiciously.

Damn. Momentarily, I'd forgotten The Amazing Colossal Nudist. The team needed to talk and fast. This called for emergency measures. I whispered, "Jess, love, do you feel able to do a Conference?"

She smiled. "No problem." Taking a deep breath, the telepath joined our six minds into mass communication.

* * *

There was disorientation, and as the throne room disappeared I found my team standing on a cloudy plane. After heartfelt greetings were exchanged, I briefed them on what had been happening with me.

Typical, Ed, thought Donaher in summation. *Run around blowing up things.*

Thanks, I said mentally. *What happened at the zoo?*

Satan Department agents swooped out of the sky on a flying carpet dropping gas bombs, sent Richard. *A nasty new type of neuro-anesthesia. Our gas masks were useless. It worked by skin contact. We woke chained to a wall in a high rise building downtown. Things were getting ugly when George saved us.*

How?

George broadcast a grin. *They took every visible weapon and thoroughly searched us, but never considered untying our boots and looking inside.*

Before I could respond he continued. *Oh, they found the Bureau derringer tucked in the boot,* I said inside. *Under my sock.*

Not surprising. In spite of their many positive features, Army boots take five minutes to get off. Any weapon hidden in there would be useless in the short term. And George's socks would dissuade even the most ardent examination.

That's why I put it there, he agreed.

Put what where?

Arching an eyebrow, George looked at me as if I was retarded. *My magic bracelet.*

Ah. Guess I was out of sync today. The bracelet only required contact. You could swallow it and the bracelet would still work.

Yep, thought Mindy. *When our captors were busy. entertaining themselves, George waited until they were in a cluster and then hit the bastards with a flamelance. Fried most of them where they stood. The two that survived, Jessica mindblasted.*

Entertaining? I asked. My heart was pounding in my chest and I wasn't sure I could handle hearing the details.

Richard answered. *Apparently, Big Bird had brought them the plane and Hassan's body. They were furious over a fellow Arab working against them and decided to . . . punish the traitor.*

I could sense their repulsion and got the picture. Feh.

They mostly did it just to psychologically soften us, noted George pragmatically. *Old interrogation trick.*

Disgusting.

But effective.

A brutal thought swirled from Mindy. *Before the chief agent died of his burns, I made him eat it.*

Eat what? I asked.

Mindy gave me a hard stare. I made a fast mental note to never, ever, piss this lady off. *So how did you find me?*

Richard talked to the spirit of a dead Satan Department agent and we discovered we had to get to the coliseum, pronto. So we climbed to the observation platform above the city library and had to get rid of a reverse vampire.

Reverse . . . its what killed that water-balloon guy in the forest.

Bingo. The monster injected blood into you, liked sunlight, garlic had no effect and was fatally attracted to the good Father. But once we hammered the stake out of its heart, he died quick enough.

Hammered the stake out?

A telepathic nod. *When we tried to use the optical telescope mounted in the observatory, we found the creature's nest inside, with another blood bloated Satan Department agent laying in the straw. The dolt had a drained laser pistol in his pudgy hand.*

Fool.

Richard agreed. *A concentrated light beam weapon would only heal, not hurt, a reverse vampire.*

Did you take the weapon? I asked eagerly.

Yes. I take all useable weapons. Why?

I have the spare power magazine from the guy in the forest! Jess, take us back!

* * *

In a melting dissolve, we were back in the temple. As the team scooped out the place, a sudden thought came to me. One dead, one violated, said the genie. But both were Hassan. The gjinn had been having a bit o' fun at my expense. I hoped a horse stomped on his foot at the rodeo. Wonder if anything else he said could have alternate meanings?

"Yes!" Jessica said aloud. "He told you 'defeat lead to victory,' not, 'defeat leads to victory.'"

I arched an eyebrow. "What possible difference is there?"

In response, she pointed. There between the gargantuan, three toed, feet of the gray giant, was a little tiny man-size door. Defeat . . . da feet. I hate genies.

"His goodbye joke," the telepath said aloud.

JUDGMENT NIGHT

"For the last time, who are you strangers?"

Almost forgotten about our mutant host there. He didn't sound particularly angry, but then our conversation had taken only a second, as it was conducted at the speed of thought.

Clearing my throat to speak, my watch sounded. Thirty minutes to go. No time to waste chatting. I had my team and the location of the door. Time to boogey.

Subserviently, I smiled. "Excuse us, King Odin," I said calmly walking towards the door underneath him. "But there is trouble on the mountain and we must take our leave."

A double-scowl distorted his faces. Rudely, the big guy didn't even say, "None may use that door, foolish mortals!" He just launched a lightning bolt from his foreheads. The crackling discharge hit the marble floor in a blinding explosion and as the smoke cleared, there stood a dozen crystal humanoids, their flat plane skin as transparent as glass.

The hollow interior of the first was filled with a swirling white powder. The insides of the second crawling with buzzing hornets. The third was topped off with a red-white liquid that resembled molten steel. Others held: worms with snapping teeth, a blood skeleton, a fire demon, a storm cloud with eyes, boiling oil, winged piranha fish, cobras, tarantulas, scorpions and a big one appeared to be empty. Yeah, right.

George raised his assault cannon, then lowered it. Shooting these guys would be an incredibly bad idea.

"Abraham Lincoln!" I shouted, knowing it was our only hope.

Turning their attention to killing-the-leader in the chair, Richard began to chant the word "tunafish" nonstop. Drawing the Veri pistol, Father Donaher boomed a Navy flare directly into Odin's face, the sizzling impact almost lost in the giant's scream of rage and pain. George stitched him with caseless high explosives. Mindy shot him in the throat with a poisoned arrow, and I pumped my last 40mm grenade into his exposed groin. I don't fight dirty, I fight to win.

Purple hands clawing at his ruined face, Odin howled and lightning randomly crashed everywhere, forming crystal warriors on the roof, the walls, atop his own knee. There were hundreds of them, maybe a thousand, and they all started marching straight towards us.

"Siagon Bug-out!" I cried.

Retreating for the door, the team dodged lightning bolts as best we could, dashing between the waddling crystal warriors. Richard waved his staff in a complex pattern and a heavy braided net fell over six of the things, binding them together. Jessica grabbed her forehead and stared. Nothing. Donaher shot a group with Holy Water. They got wet. George started throwing canisters of tear gas, vomit gas, stun gas, and BZ hallucinogenic. Bastards seemed to like the stuff. Mindy tried a Kung-Fu nerve pinch on the neck of one filled with army ants. It took a swing and almost busted her jaw.

More lightning. More crystal warriors.

Fumbling with the mechanism, I paused to launch the last LAW at Lord Odin, but he had a magical shield erected and the streaking rocket vanished in mid-air without a trace.

As we reached the door, Odin the Odious began to swing a foot in our way, so Mindy shot the floor with an incendiary arrow. Flame erupted and the foot jerked away from the wave of heat. Up close, we could now see that a prominent lock on the marble door barred our exit. A short burst from George's assault cannon blew that to smithereens. With a creak, the bedraggled door swung aside. At top speed, we charged through the flames and into the blackness beyond.

SIXTEEN

... and we stepped onto a stone ledge high on the side of Mt. Lympus. Raw stone was to our right, and on the left was a parapet.

Over the stone railing we could see the domed city far below spreading out like a museum exhibit, with the rest of the island lost in the distance. We must have been transported a hundred miles in a split second. As the team spread out in a standard defense pattern, a cold sea wind ruffled our hair and my skin began to prickle at our nearness to the gray cloud. Whew, smelled like Jersey in the summer.

I moved away from the door to try and get a better look around when from the other side of the parapet a hideous iron gorgon hopped into view. Its skin was a uniform dull gray, with fiery red light beaming from its mouth and misshapen eyes.

"Halt!" the monster commanded. "To pass me, you must first answer a riddle!"

"Come again?" Mindy gasped in shock.

"Yes, a riddle! A mighty tree, small in size, digs and digs, for a tasty prize." The metallic beast leered expectantly. "Answer or perish. What am I?"

"Dead meat," Donaher said stroking the shotgun and firing. The storm of double-ought buck blew the gorgon off its perch and it tumbled over the edge with a very surprised expression.

Mindy patted the priest on the shoulder in congratulations. This wasn't a frigging game, we were here on business.

Glancing over the edge, I watched the creature bounce off several rocky ledges, losing an arm here, a leg there. It was flapping its iron wings like crazy, but still quickly dwindled into the distance becoming a tiny speck hurtling towards what was certainly going to be a most uncomfortable meeting the dome over the city.

Rejoining the crew, I noted that the ledge we stood on was part of an impossibly long flight of stairs that disappeared into the mists below, and extended to the distant snowy peak of the huge mountain. Slinky heaven. Zigzagging across the steep slope, each level of the stairway was adorned with a towering statue of a rampart griffin made of bluish ice. More guards, had to be. This Odin was going to give paranoids a bad name.

Why can't we ever get an easy assignment? Like that time when a mad wizard at Stonehenge cast a spell to bring down the moon to destroy the world. We arrived just as he was finishing the conjure so I chanced a hip shot with my Magnum from 200 meters. The bullet got him directly between the eyes and as he slumped over, the massive release of ethereal power stored within him exploded into the nighttime air, a burning lance of hellish destruction that radiated away harmlessly to have absolutely no effect on anything. It was a freak occurrence, but we sure remember it fondly.

"Wonder what the answer was?" George said, hitching his bulky weapon to a more comfortable position, while he surveyed the area for more dangers. At the moment, we were in the clear.

Leaning heavily on his wizard staff, Richard curled a lip. "Toothpick."

"Sounds right. How did you know?" Jessica asked.

"Stupidest answer I could think of. Riddles are for morons."

JUDGMENT NIGHT

"No argument there."

A martial arts cry sounded and I turned to see Mindy flip a crystal warrior back through the magic portal. Crap! I had hoped they would lose interest once we were out of the throne room. Gesturing frantically, Richard shouted something and a brick wall sealed the entrance. Then he added a cinderblock wall, and a rickety picket fence.

"That should hold them for awhile," Donaher stated, thumbing fresh rounds into his weapon.

"Bloody well hope so," Richard panted. "I'm nearly drained. Don't think I could levitate a balloon."

Suddenly, a savage pounding sounded from the barrier and the fence quivered.

"Double time, harch!" I shouted.

We took off at a sprint, and actually made it halfway to the top before I called a halt. Thinking about the crystal warriors had given me a brilliant idea. I only hoped it worked.

"Michael," I said. "Get the briefcase." From below I could still hear a muffled pounding on the sealed door. Determined little things. Must get paid by the hour.

"What ever you're doing, make it fast," George warned, pointing the Masterson Assault Cannon down the stairs at the barrier. "Cause those bastards will be here in a New York minute!"

"Minute is all I need." Dropping his haversack, Father Donaher passed over the case and I whipped off my bandana. "Mindy, cut me!"

Her knife flashed and blood welled from a shallow gash on my forearm. Gritting my teeth, I soaked the cloth in the blood, then tied it firmly about the handle trigger till I heard the telltale click. "Richard, turn the cloth into glass." I ordered.

"Why?" he asked, looking askance.

"Just do it, mister!"

"But I'm so weak . . . ah, that's why the blood sacrifice." A visible nimbus of light formed around the mage as he summoned the last dregs of power. Then Richard thumped his staff on the bloody rag and it ever-so-slowly turned into a band of glass. Wasting no time, I punched the activation code into the combination lock and hurled the case off the side of the mountain. It sailed through the air like an imported leather frisbee and went neatly over the edge of the cliff.

"This is for Raul!" I shouted, shaking a fist at the unseen city of mages. "Choke on it!"

Her eyes going wide in disbelief, Jessica stared at me. *Ed, you didn't just—*

"Better believe it, babe," I answered grimly. "Move with a purpose, people! Ten seconds and counting!"

Immediately, the team started racing up the broad staircase. The higher we went, the colder the air got and the slippery the icy steps became, yet we never fell. This is exactly the kind of scenario that US Army boots were designed to handle. Well, okay, maybe not the exact situation. Then again, who invented these things? Could have been one of us, in the future, traveling into the past, to help save the present. I've seen it happen before. That's how we got free cable.

Bounding along effortlessly, Mindy asked, "Hey chief, why the rigmarole with the handle?"

"The Snoopy is a suicide weapon," George explained panting, his unshaven face red with the exertion of hauling the heavy backpack of ammo. Caseless or not, a couple of thousand rounds of anything slowed you down. "The atomic device detonates when you release the handle. Very 1960's Cold War sort of thing."

JUDGMENT NIGHT

Stroking an upper lip where his magnificent moustache used to be Father Donaher muttered something about the Pentagon and the seventh level of Hell. Wasn't that the one reserved for idiots?

Mindy merely grunted. "So when the briefcase hits the dome and the glass breaks-"

Blinding light erupted from below the cliff as if a million flashbulbs went off, and seconds later a thundering hurricane rushed upward carrying a barrage of shrapnel that heralded the goddamn loudest boom I ever heard. The whole island shook. Loose stones rolled down the mountain, and the stone stairway cracked apart into a million pieces, entire sections breaking away to start slipping down the slope. An avalanche of snow rushed past us, and I turned about to see the newly exposed summit of the mountain. Now in plain sight was an undersea diving bell positioned on top on the rocky peak. A 20th century diving bell covered with Arabic writing.

Even as we fell to the vibrating steps, I cheered in victory. If that wasn't our goal, the source of new magic from Satan Department, then it would do until we found the real one.

Frantically crawling together, Richard joined hands with Donaher and Jessica. The three began to hum tunelessly and the air around us filled with a sparkling rainbow of colors as the lethal wave of gamma radiation wave was neutralized. The gesture was appreciated, but dying of cancer was not our most pressing problem at the moment.

The mountain was still trembling when the radiation finally faded away and we struggled to our feet. The team looked haggard, but there was no time for a rest. If we won, the team could relax later. Heck, I'd buy them a deluxe week in Euro-Disney. Nice short lines for all the rides. But if we lost, there would be an infinity of profound sleep in the pine box motel.

"A briefcase nuclear charge," Donaher growled, straightening his cap. "I suppose it was necessary."

"Abso-freaking-lutely," I replied grimly,

"So much for Odin," Mindy agreed. "Even a small nuke will just ruin your day."

"Then its over?" Jessica asked hopefully, lowering the barrel of her M16. "We've won?"

I started to answer when I spotted the ice griffins bounding down the stairs towards us, their icy fangs bared for battle. Right behind them was an army of snowmen rising from the pristine white blanket covering the ground, hundreds of ice spears and glittering axes in their pudgy mittens. Checking the other direction, I saw the crystal warriors swarming out of the magic portal, the brick and cinder block wall smashed into rubble.

"Don't break out the champagne quite yet, babe," I said, spinning around and triggering a short burst from the M16 at the diving bell. But the deadly wreath of perfectly imbalanced tumblers merely chewed up some of the fat snowmen blocking the way. Damnation, they must know why we were here, and were acting as a living shield. We had to get closer. A lot closer.

Father Donaher gasped and I turned around again fast, my weapon at the ready. Then I gasped, too.

Rising into view from below was the dark top of a mushroom-shaped cloud. Even as we watched, the fierce thermal currents from the expanding dust shroud pushed away the magical cloud cover and clean pure sunlight came streaming through the widening hole. Ah, sweetness. Then my watch beeped with the ten minute warning. Never rains, but it pours.

"Hold off the attack!" Jessica shouted into her wristwatch, fiddling with the controls. "Bureau, do you copy? Hold off the missiles!"

JUDGMENT NIGHT

There was no answer, only static. The hole gave us a brief window to the outside world, but this close to a nuke storm we might as well yodel for all the good a radio would do. But wasting precious seconds, we each tried our watches anyway, just in case, and got zero results.

Now what?

"Cheech and Chong!" I ordered, and my team raced toward the diving bell. That was the key.

Pausing for only a split second, Father Donaher let the rest of us pass by while he whispered a short prayer in Latin to bless a satchel charge and then laid it reverently on the stairs. Then the big priest took off like a Wiccan leaving Texas. We were three levels away when the C4 charge cut loose, the strident blast only a pop compared to the nuke, but the detonation shattered an entire section of steps.

Slapping in a fresh clip, I fired a few rounds at the trapped crystal warriors as they gathered on the other side of the smoking hole and made rude gestures. A few tried to go around and immediately slipped on the icy slope, sliding out of control straight down the mountain and sailing majestically over the cliff into the heart of the mushroom cloud.

"Your mother was an ashtray!" Mindy shouted.

Good one. Just then a shadow engulfed us from above, and I spun around already firing. I had expected this. Big Bird had arrived. The misshapen form of the jabberwocky was bristling with claws, beaks, tentacles, horns, stingers, wings, heads, jaws, teeth, fangs, tusks, and every orifice dripped saliva, green ooze and some really icky stuff, too. The team cut loose with their weapons, sending a hellstorm of lead and silver at the winged wonder. Hissing, barking and screaming all at the same time, the jabberwocky soared away from us bleeding from a dozen minor wounds. After reloading, we quickly started running up the stairs once more. Yards counted now, maybe it was time to switch tactics.

Without pausing, I tossed Richard the crossbow pistol, but kept the laser gun. Flipping the safety with the tip of my knife, I easily broke off the poisoned needle that popped out to stab my finger. Ah, Satan Department was so predictable. The tiny digital meter on the handle displayed the Arabic symbols for nine and eight. Was that 98%, or 89% charged? Actually, either way was okay.

Minutes later, we reached the second level from the top and we were confronted by a line of snarling ice griffins. They were big, but slow, and we blew 'em apart. But as I slammed my last clip into the hot breech of the M16, our pal Big Bird came silently arching around the mountain only yards off the snowy ground. Trying to attack us from behind eh?

"George!" I shouted firing a short burst that way. "Incoming! Ten o'clock low!"

Spinning about, the plump soldier cut loose with the Masterson. In a steady yammering, the 10mm caseless rounds of HE stitched across the chest of the beast in a series of sharp explosions, scales and feathers spraying outward in bloody geysers. Then a telephone pole size arrow took the thing in one of its many mouths, splitting the snake head apart. Jess and Mindy hosed it with silver bullets while Donaher held off the army of approaching snowmen. Damn. They were coming at us from every direction!

Taking careful aim, I turned the stolen laser pistol on the living nightmare. The scintillating beam snipped off three of its barbed tails and cut a bloody furrow in the burning fur of its belly. Oh, that had to hurt. But despite the wounds, the flying monster came at us again and again, each time only to be repelled at the very last moment by sheer firepower. This thing

JUDGMENT NIGHT

was harder to get rid of than a Jehovah's Witness!

As the jabberwocky wheeled away into the sky once more, I snapped off a shot at the diving bell, but only managed to vaporize one of the many snowmen standing protectively in front. That settled the matter for me. If they wanted the sphere intact, we just had to blow that sucker to Hell. However, the power gauge on my futuristic weapon was now reading 24%. We were rapidly running out of ammo, options, time and luck.

"How you guys doing?" Donaher shouted, his shotgun booming in counterpoint to the steady chatter of Jessica's machine gun. The spent brass hit the stone stairs to musically bounce away.

"Not good," Richard grunted, launching another telephone pole. There was a touch of gray at his temples, and even for a wizard he seemed pale.

"Wish we had a second nuke," George snarled riding his bucking weapon into a tighter pattern. Wings and things were steadily being blown off the flying abomination, but Big Bird seemed to have an endless supply of both limbs and hostility.

"Hot damn, we do!" I cried, slapping my forehead. Still firing, I awkwardly dug about in my shoulder pouch and lifted out the crystal ball bomb from the armory. "This ought to blow it into hamburger!"

"Great!" Mindy cried, releasing an arrow towards the last ice griffin hobbling our way. The blast blew it apart into twinkling shards, and she turned her attention to the snowmen. But one of her quivers was completely empty, and the other was dangerously low. Soon this fight would go hand-to-hand, and that was when we'd start dying.

Lowering the crossbow pistol, Richard seemed to have trouble speaking as he stared at the orb. "Where did you . . . how . . . You want to throw *that* at the jabberwocky?" he gagged.

"Are you insane? *Gimme!*"

Grabbing the sphere from my hand, Richard quickly tucked the crossbow into his belt, and awkwardly flicked his pocket lighter. The tiny butane flame danced about wildly in the wind, but the fuse finally caught with a sharp hiss.

"Throw it!" George yelled impatiently, firing the Masterson in short bursts to conserve ammunition.

"No way," Richard replied smugly, and just stood there happily watching the fuse rapidly shrink. It was already down only inches away from the bomb.

With surprising speed, Father Donaher charged at the wizard to grab the sphere when there was a blinding flash of light from the thing. Bracing myself for death, instead my vision fluttered as if the entire universe was switching through a hundred television channels, no, a hundred realities, in a split second. It was dizzying, but oddly pleasant, then the bizarre effect ceased fast as it began.

Searching my body for any damage, I was seemed to be fine and then realized that all of us were now completely healed. Every scratch and bruise was gone without a trace. Our khaki jumpsuits were whole, clean and pressed with nice creases in the legs. Even our combat boots were polished to a mirror shine the envy of any Marine recruit. Each of us was freshly washed and shaved, and I felt totally revived, brimming with vim and vigor. Yowsa. The laser pistol in my manicured hand registered 100%, my ammo pouch was heavy with clips and new grenades festooned my chest. Even Richard seemed to be recharged, his silver staff pulsating with ripples of fairy energy.

"Sun Bomb," the wizard explained happily. "It ate a year of our lives, but I don't think anybody would really mind, considering the circumstances."

JUDGMENT NIGHT

So that was what I was supposed to find in the armory! God, I love genies. What swell folk they are. Then a ripping sound came from my haversack and Mindy's intact sword fell out. Springing forward, she caught it an inch from the ground.

"Baby," she cooed in delight, stroking the razor sharp blade. "Didums miss me?"

"Oh no," Father Donaher whispered from behind his bristling red moustache. "No, it can't be . . ."

"Richard, you incredible nincompoop!" Jessica shouted, sending the sentence both vocal and mentally.

Glancing around to see what could possibly be that bad, I damn near had a coronary. The smashed flight of stairs were completely repaired, the crystal warriors charging upwards in waves. The ice griffins were intact again, the snowmen were whiter than white, and now a tremendous igloo bristling with icy needles covered the diving bell. But more importantly, the jabberwocky looked twice as large than before with more wings, more fangs and an expression that could make battleships faint. Hoo boy.

"Sorry," Richard said sheepishly. "Didn't know it would do them, also."

Her hair neatly coiled in a dainty coiffure, Mindy turned and kicked the wizard soundly in the butt. "Sorry?" she screamed. "I'll make you sorry, manna-for-brains!"

"Incoming!" George shouted, over the fiery stuttering of the Masterson "High noon!"

Whooping like the ultimate car alarm, the jabberwocky dove straight for us this time, vomiting streams of bluish liquid from its myriad of mouths. Gesturing wildly, Richard erected an ethereal shield that barely managed to deflect the fluid. Shooting off at an angle, the watery substance hit an outcropping of granite which vaporized into wisps of steam.

"How come it didn't do that before?" Jessica demanded dropping a spent clip from the M16 and slamming in a fresh magazine. But pulling the trigger nothing happened. Angrily, she dropped the clip, smacked it against the stock to prime the first round, then shoved it back in and started wildly shooting.

"Must have been weakened from the destruction of the temple," Richard suggested, launching another telephone pole arrow at the winged wonder, while lightning crackling from the tip of his glowing staff to sweep across the amassed snowmen. Big Bird successfully dodged, the snowmen didn't and exploded like popsicles in a microwave.

"Joseph and Mary! Don't tell me the freaking temple is also repaired?" Father Donaher demanded, firing his shotgun in every direction.

"Hell, I don't know."

"Lord save us!"

"Amen!" we chorused purely out of reflex.

Diving close, the jabberwocky hissed, screamed, and spit out a barrage of ice spears. The silver slivers impacted everywhere in a saturation bombing. Jessica took a spear in the chest and was knocked off her feet, a bone audibly breaking despite her body armor. I caught an ice shard in the hip and a spear went by my head so close I felt the breeze of its passage and momentarily saw my own distorted reflection.

Frozen shrapnel hit us hard as the rest shattered on the stairway. George got a shiny splinter rammed into his arm, Mindy leapt and twisted through the onslaught undamaged, Donaher was grazed in neck and head, while Richard transformed the deadly debris coming his way into snow and only received a powdery dusting.

Dropping the shotgun, Donaher tore his backpack apart and took a stance with a HAFLA napalm launcher in each hand. Shaking the blood from his face, the good father triggered the weapons simultaneously. On twin columns of flame, the rockets streaked away. The first missed the beast completely, arcing harmlessly off into the distance. But the second hit the monster smack in the gut with grisly results. Every head screamed at the same time as a writhing clump of burning tentacles fell off its mutilated body to expose a bleeding hole of raw flesh. George concentrated his weapon on the open wound, blood spraying as the armor-piercing rounds chewed deep inside the beast.

"Ed, cover me," Richard ordered, kneeling on the ground. Hastily, he began brushing away the snow and ice to clear some space.

"Cover you?" I snarled spraying the griffins with my laser. Their icy bodies exploding into steam at the touch. Spinning about, I started carving chunks of the staircase away. The crystal warriors tried to dive into the beam, so I stopped double-quick. Too damn many kamikazes around here to suit me. "When I get the chance, I'm going to kill you!"

"Twice!" George added with a snarl, the left arm of his uniform dark with blood.

But Richard did not respond, his nose buried in a book of spells. Pulling out chalk and string he began hastily drawing a pentagram on the cold stone. He was preparing to cast a major spell in the middle of battle? That was insane. But following the angle of his staff, I soon saw the reason why he was frantically at work. White lines were crawling across the azure sky. Moving too fast to see with the naked eye, I could only trace the position of the incoming projectiles by the contrails they left behind. The missiles were early.

Desperate, I raised my wristwatch and then lowered my arm. There was nothing anybody could do now. Without conscious thought, I took Jessica by the hand and she squeezed hard in return as we watched the arrival of the end of our lives.

Like the arrows of Hercules, down came the ICBMs in a precise military cluster. Protectively, the gray cloud moved in trying to block the way, but the missiles punched right through without hindrance.

As the ICBMs cleared the protective layer of clouds, Richard stood and screamed a magic spell, the words of power visible in the air for a shining second before fading away. Instantly, the missiles detonated into a stupendous fireball that became encased in a glowing green globe of magic. For one astonishing moment, the multiple explosions stayed there, suspended in the air. Nobody spoke. Even the rocks seemed to be holding their breath in anticipation.

Then from the bottom of the ethereal globe, there erupted a twisting cone of radioactive flame that spiraled earthward, the very atmosphere annihilated by the passage of the pyrotechnic deathbeam forged from the raw detonation of ten thermonuclear warheads.

The quasi-solid rod of destruction went straight through the jabberwocky, its resilient body exploding into allotropic vapors. Unstoppable, the incredible ray stabbed into the island below, in blinding radiance the repaired ruins of Atlantis were reduced to superheated steam, both the adamantine Dome and magical shields meaning less than vacuum to the starkly indescribable fury of the mauling power ray.

As it winked out, we gasped in relief at the return of normal sight, and the lambent atmosphere closed the horrible rend with a thunderclap that nearly knocked us off the mountain. After a few minutes, we could see again and from this angle there was no sign of the domed city below, or of the jabberwocky, only some luminescent ash floating about in the tortured sky. But then the incinerated particles began coalescing back into a crude animal shape.

Blinking twice, George swallowed his gum. "Its regenerating after that?" he squeaked.

"Richard, honey-sweetie-baby, do something!" I cried, backing away from the terrible sight. "Finish off that mother!"

Resting heavily on his wooden staff, the gray haired mage tried to raise his crossbow pistol and failed. Age lines were deeply etched into his leathery face, the carnation in his lapel reduced to a brown, wilted lump, and as Richard opened his mouth to speak, all of his corn-yellow teeth fell out.

"Rest, buddy, we'll handle this," I said, drawing the laser and 10mm pistol. "Okay, we're going with the original plan of the slaves . . . ah, partisans, and sink this stinking island once and for all. Head for the igloo!"

Sensing our intentions, the horde of snowmen formed a line and locked arms. Oh swell, frozen Ghandis. In spite of our renewed firepower, it would forever to blow a path through those arctic assholes. Time we did not have.

"Toss me your bracelets!" Mindy ordered brusquely.

We hastily complied. Not bothering to put them on, the woman simply stuffed the copper bands into her T-shirt, then lifted off the stairs and vanished.

As we watched, a whirlwind of destruction moved through the snowmen, frosty arms and legs falling off as something hacked them apart like an invisible flying lawnmower. And you know what a bitch those are. In a matter of seconds, the snowmen were gone and there was a clear path to the igloo nestled between a boulder and a flat-top ridge of granite.

"Follow me!" the empty air called.

Ignoring the pain from our assorted wounds, we shambled up the stairway as best we could. The footing was treacherous, but at least all this ice would help reduce the swelling.

Oh hush.

As we reached the dome several hidden snowmen jump into view and we blew them away without pausing our stride. However, the dome was a smooth expanse, sans door or even the standard entrance tunnel. Throwing caution to the wind, I drained the laser and carved off a large chunk of the dome so we could simply walk inside.

Under the snowy shell was the diving bell, its burnished steel hull covered with mystic symbols and lots of Arabic writing. Undogging the water-tight hatch, we swung the portal aside and braced for an attack. But there were no boobytraps or assassins waiting inside, only mounds of sensory equipment. Positioned in the center of the machine maze, covered by a dome of bulletproof Armorlite, was a diorama; a tiny, but exact reproduction of the underground slave city, including the pentagram of wands. Surrounding the model, mounted on a universal support, was a glowing red ceramic circle crossed by a bar bisecting it on an angle. The circle and bar were the international NO symbol. The red aura indicated anti-magic. I now had every answer to the puzzle.

"What is that place?" Donaher asked curiously, brushing back his wild crop of thick curly hair.

I frowned. "Questions can wait for later. First we must cancel the spell, and pronto."

"Can't. I'm drained," Richard said smacking his toothless gums. Leaning against the open hatch, the wizard was breathing hard and looked as if he had been dead for a week. Make that two.

"Red," Jessica murmured, arms wrapped about her chest. "That's anti-magic. It cancels magic, which is why the island has risen."

JUDGMENT NIGHT

Standing guard outside, George angrily shouted. "So zap the anti-magic!"

"With what?" Father Donaher demanded. "Magic and anti-magic will have no effect on anti-magic."

"How about using some anti-anti-magic-magic?"

Ah, now there's the military mind for you. "Won't work," I answered.

"Okay, let's try shooting it," Mindy suggested.

Finally, a good idea. "But from a distance," I directed, favoring my aching hip. "Let's go!"

Scrambling for distance, we assisted each other down the stairs, shooting any snowman stupid enough to rise from the snowbanks. Hovering above the island, Big Bird was partially reconstructed. Reaching the top landing where we had some combat room, George hosed the diving bell with caseless rounds from the Masterson, blowing the armor off the sphere in ragged chunks and pieces.

Then a javelin thudded into the stone between his boots, as an army of blue skeletons climbed into view over the horizon. The undead soldiers were astride crystal warrior lions and holding the entire contents of the city armory, including the Sword of Revenge. The hellspawn army must have been safe inside the doorway leading to the mountain when the city was destroyed. Aw, crap. The remaining ice griffins took this opportunity to start circling us, and a horde of snowmen rose on every side to move in for the kill.

Plumber. I should have become a plumber.

"Fire!" I shouted and we hit the diving bell with every working weapon and spell we had.

The armor vanished under our barrage, the machinery ripped apart into sparkling trash, the Armorlite dome shattered, the city was obliterated, and the red of the anti-magic symbol winked out. Instantly, a miniature mushroom cloud formed where the diving bell had been and the entire island shuddered all the down to its foundation. The crystal warriors went motionless, the snowmen crumbled apart, the griffins fainted and I got a feeling in my stomach usually only received in high-speed express elevators.

"We're going down," Jessica croaked.

There was a squawk and the coalescing jabberwocky polymorphed into a tiny seagull. Probably the poor innocent creature the horrid monster had been altered from in the first place. Whispering a prayer of forgiveness, Father Donaher then blew it apart with the shotgun just to make sure.

"Okay, now we've won," I stated, dropping the exhausted laser.

All around us the rumbling and shaking got steadily more powerful. Standing on the highest point of the island, we were getting a grand view of the demise of Atlantis. The ocean washing over the outer cliff and sloshing across the garden plains to pour into the rad blasted ruin of the once mighty city. The water erupting into hissing steam at the touch of the molten stone. Higher and higher rushed the tide, the foamy brine rising over the broken Dome and rocky foothills as the devil island returned to its stygian grave. There was nothing else we could do, so we just stood there watching the Atlantic reclaim is dark prize. Would have traded my soul for an inflatable rubber dingy.

Dropping his weapon, George turned to Donaher and extended a hand. "Goodbye, Mike. Been grand knowing you, buddy." They solemnly shook hands.

Ed, I've always loved you, Jess mentally sent.

"Later, babe!" I snapped. "Come on, anybody got an escape plan?"

JUDGMENT NIGHT

"Nope," Richard said, smacking his toothless gums.

"Negative, chief."

"Uh-uh."

"Of course," Mindy said with a smug expression. "I saved this for just such an occasion." She brandished a muscular arm adorned with a copper bracelet. "Took it from the boss Satan Department agent. It holds a Portal spell."

My muscles relaxed at the sight of salvation. "Well, use the thing already!" I ordered, over the growing noise of the sinking island.

Calmly, the woman gestured and a golden lattice pattern formed in the air. As the center cleared, we saw a strange sort of control room with dozens of armed men wearing turbans and swords walking about doing things. Turning in our direction, one of the soldiers pointed and shouted something. Must have been a warning, as the rest started rushing forward their automatic weapons steadily firing.

"Holy Mother, its their headquarters!" Donaher shouted, as a hot bullet zinged by parting his hair.

"Oops," Mindy whispered.

Quickly I tossed in a grenade and the martial artist threw the bracelet away as the foaming ocean washed over us in a crashing wave. We clung together, trying to fight the undertow and stay afloat, but it was no good. The brutal currents were like anchors on our limbs. Dumping our weapons and equipment seemed to make no difference. Down we went.

Swirling helplessly, my team was pulled lower and lower into the murky depths of the Atlantic Ocean. I fought for the surface until my straining lungs became exhausted and I lost consciousness. My last frantic thoughts were of my beloved Jessica and how much I always wanted to learn to play the accordion. Such are the convoluted thoughts of a dying man.

EPILOGUE

We woke up in the military hospital of Fort Dix, New Jersey, with Horace Gordon himself sitting on a stool waiting for us.

Apparently, the group of escaping mermaids had found us in the tow of the island and rescued us, hauling our unconscious bodies to a Navy submarine patrolling outside the deathcloud. We thanked them profusely for saving our lives. But I have always considered it highly suspicious that all of the men arrived feeling remarkably relaxed and with the strong desire for a cigarette, including, the good father. But what the hey, it had been a long time for them. Even longer for some of us.

Gordon immediately recruited the aquatic beings as Bureau 13 Waves, our new underwater division. The mermaids seemed to be more interested in battling pollution than criminals, but that was no problem. The Bureau had always been ecologically inclined.

Happily, the ladies desired no salary, because for the next couple of years the Bureau was going to be on a very tight budget. All of our surplus funds going to purchase a million metric tons of underwater setting concrete to pour over the ruins of Atlantis, making damn sure that even if the pentagram was disturbed, the island would not, could not, ever rise again. Case closed.

From our sick beds, we applauded the splendid idea.

The next day, a portable teletype disguised as a bedpan brought us the news of a mysterious tidal wave had erupted from the Elburz Mountains in Africa, the run-off water ending a nasty drought for thousands of starving farmers. Elburz had been the secret HQ of Satan Department and we did not expect to ever hear from them again. And with the elimination of the enemy organization, the attacks on Bureau personnel dwindled down to the usual level of a vampire here, a UFO there. Nothing we could not handle.

To the world, the entire incident of Atlantis was disguised as an attempted terrorist coupe, complete with poison gas attack and a submarine battle. The story was not totally believed until a production company in Hollywood bought the movie rights and tried to cast Tom Cruise.

Of course, the President requested the true, full, detailed report of the incident, so as the team leader, it was my duty to comply. I sent him a one page telegram reading: "Dear sir. We won. Signed, Team Tunafish." I hear he has it framed and mounted on the wall of the Oval Office. Nice.

In retrospect, Strategy & Tactics chastised me for not taking the two magic swords from the armory. Stabbing Lord Odin, or the jabberwocky, with both at the same time would have caused a bipolar ether flow, capable of destroying any living organism. In no uncertain terms, I told Strategy & Tactics where to stick both of the swords at the same time.

Unfortunately, in spite the vast magical and technological resources of our organization, there was nothing that could be done for Richard Anderson. We had Anti-Aging drugs, but nothing could restore his lost vigor. His spell to contain multiple nuclear explosions had drained him dry of all magic and aged him permanently. No Re-Charge, Sun Bomb or Jump Start could change that. He was 96 years old. Period. End of discussion.

Sadly, the Bureau gave the vaunted mage his walking papers, a gold watch and an astounding lump sum of cash for his retirement. What with the irregular nature of field agents reaching tenure, the pension fund was overflowing with excess capital.

His goodbye party in our Chicago apartment was quiet and dignified. But afterwards, Richard departed immediately for Miami to gather an expeditionary force of sexagenarian soldiers to start on a hunt for the Fountain of Youth. Upon my request, his Personnel File was removed from Retired and placed in the Non-Active List. If humanly possible, Richard Anderson would return.

After leaving the hospital, Jessica propositioned me. Shocked at the brazen hussy, I proposed in retaliation and she accepted. Ha! That'll teach her who is the boss around here.

But of course, dear.

Our wedding was held in Madison Square Garden with the whole Bureau watched the ceremonies over a special scrambled television broadcast, relayed via a UN communications satellite commandeered just for the occasion. Even several of our sister organizations tuned in to watch the wedding: The Farm in England, Operation: Sunshine in Israel, The Sons of Van Helsing in Germany, Fantasmique in France, H.E.K. in Japan, The Alliance in Chile, and Wally's Spook Club in Australia. They also all sent in gifts. How nice.

During the procession, there was a minor scuffle involving some carnivorous plants from another dimension, but it was handled quietly. On the other hand, my bachelor party leveled a small town in my home state of Wyoming, but it wasn't really our fault. How were we supposed to know that NORAD headquarters would be so easy to take over?

Father Donaher performed the ceremony, Mindy was maid of honor, George best man. Afterwards, in uncharacteristic generosity, Horace Gordon offered us a two month honeymoon. But we turned it down, having had quite enough vacation excitement. We both wanted something dull for a change and so went to work in the Bureau file room, organizing the secret annals of our covert organization.

After submitting his regular monthly coded report to the Vatican, Father Donaher was delighted to receive special dispensation from the Pope to use healing spells. Mindy took a week off to go Italy and have a short talk with her *sensei da tutti sensei* about her supposedly "indestructible" sword, and George started having an affair with the cab driver who gave him a lift back in Manhattan. She was a lovely lady who kept boasting that it sure was not flab wrapped around George's manly waist. Personally, I had no wish to hear the sweaty details.

Incredibly, Raul Horta and Amigo the wonder lizard, returned to our group. Apparently, a renegade Bureau team had kidnapped the mage to assist them in traveling to a parallel universe to try and halt the evil clone of Horace Gordon from stopping the creation of Bureau 13. They succeeded. Well, sort of.

But that story is still classified.

THE END

Printed in the United States
28286LVS00001B/270